Milne Rae

Morag

A tale of the highlands of Scotland

Milne Rae

Morag
A tale of the highlands of Scotland

ISBN/EAN: 9783743345492

Manufactured in Europe, USA, Canada, Australia, Japa

Cover: Foto ©Andreas Hilbeck / pixelio.de

Manufactured and distributed by brebook publishing software (www.brebook.com)

Milne Rae

Morag

MORAG:

A TALE

OF THE

HIGHLANDS OF SCOTLAND.

———•◦•———

NEW YORK:

ROBERT CARTER AND BROTHERS,

530 BROADWAY.

1875.

CONTENTS

CONTENTS.

MORAG

I.

THE FIRST MORNING IN THE GLEN.

DO you know the joyous feeling of opening your eyes on the first morning after your arrival among new scenes, and of seeing the landscape, which has been shrouded by darkness on the previous evening, lying clear and calm in the bright morning sunlight?

This was Blanche Clifford's experience as she stood at an eastward window, with an eager face, straining her eye across miles of moorland, which undulated far away, like purple seas lying in the golden light. Away, and up and on stretched the heather, till it seemed to rear itself into great waves of rock, which stood out clear and distinct, with the sunlight glinting into the gray, waterworn fissures, lighting them up like a smile on a wrinkled face. And beyond, in the dim distance, hills on hills are huddled, rearing themselves in dark lowering masses against the blue sky, like the shoulders of mighty monsters in a struggle for the nearest place to the clouds. For many weeks Blanche had been dreaming dreams and seeing visions of this scene, as she sat in her London schoolroom. "And this is Glen Eagle!" she murmured, with a satisfied sigh, when at last she turned her eyes from the more distant landscape, and climbing into the embrasured window of the quaint old room in which she awoke that morning, leant out to try and discover what sort of a building this new home might be. A perpendicular, gaunt wall, so lichen-spotted that it seemed as if the stones had taken to growing, was all that she could see; and under it there stretched a smooth grassy slope, belted by a grove of ancient ash-trees. A pleasant breeze, wafting a delicious scent of heather, came in at the open window, and played among Blanche's curls, reminding her how delightful it would be to go out under the blue sky; so she ran off in search of her papa, that she might begin her explorations at once.

Mr. Clifford, Blanche's father, was very fond of sport, and generally spent the autumn months on the moors, either in Ireland or Scotland. Hitherto his little motherless daughter had not accompanied him on any of his journeys, but had been left to wander among trim English lanes, or to patrol the parade of fashionable watering-places, under the guardianship of her governess, Miss Prosser. This year, however, Blanche had been so earnest in her entreaties to be taken among the hills, that her father had at last yielded; and it was arranged that she should accompany him to Glen Eagle, where he had taken shootings. Miss Prosser looked on the projected journey to the Highlands of Scotland as rather a wild scheme for herself and her little charge, having no special partiality for mountain scenery, and a dislike to change the old routine. But to Blanche, the prospect was full of the most delicious possibilities; the unknown mountain country was to her imagination an enchanted land of peril and adventure, where she could herself become the heroine of a new tale of romance. The "History of Scotland" suddenly became the most interesting of books, and the records of its heroic days were studied with an interest which they had never before excited. In the daily walks in Kensington Park, on hot July afternoons, Blanche Clifford wove many a fancy concerning these autumn days to be ; but in the midst of all her imaginings, as she peopled the hills and valleys of Stratheagle with followers of the Wallace and the Bruce lurking among the heather, with waving tartans and glancing claymores, she did not guess what a lowly object of human interest was to be the centre of all her thoughts.

On the evening of the 9th of August Blanche stood with her governess on the platform of the Euston Station, ready to start by the crowded Scotch mail. Mr. Clifford having seen to the travelling welfare of his dogs, proceeded to arrange his little party for the night. The shrill whistle sounded at last, and they were soon whirling through the darkness on their northern way. The long railway journey was broken by a night's rest at a hotel, which Blanche thought very uninteresting indeed, and begged to be allowed to go on with her papa, who left her there. After the region of railways was left behind, there was a journey in an old mail-coach, which seemed to Blanche to be at last a beginning of the heroic adventures, as she spied a little girl of her own size scaling a ladder to take her place in one of the outside seats, to all appearance delightfully suspended in mid-air. She was about to follow in great glee, when she was pulled back by Miss Prosser, and condemned to a dark corner inside of the coach, where a stout old gentleman entirely obstructed her view. Neither was Blanche a pleasant companion ; she felt very restless and rebellious at her unhappy fate, and every time the coach stopped and she was allowed to put her head out of the window for a few precious minutes, she cast envious glances at the happy family whose legs dangled above.

The coach stopped at last to change horses at a low white inn, and Blanche's delight was great to recognise her father's open carriage waiting to take them to Glen Eagle, which was still many miles distant. The change was delicious, Blanche thought as they were driven swiftly along the white, winding road, round the base of hills higher than she had ever seen, through dark pine forests, which cast solemn shadows across the road, along sea-like expanses of moor, stretching out on either side. Blanche was lost in wonder and delight at those first glimpses of the mountain-land of her dreams. Her geographical inquiries were most searching, and her governess had to acknowledge ignorance when her pupil wished to identify each hill with the mountain-ranges depicted on a map-drawing, which Blanche had made in view of the journey. They were still several miles from their destination, when a heavy white cloud of mist came coiling round the hills, creeping along the lower ridges of rock as if it started to reach the top, like some thinking creature possessed with an evil purpose. At first the mist seemed only to add an additional charm to the wild landscape in Blanche's eyes.

"O Miss Prosser!" she exclaimed, in great glee, "isn't it so pretty? It seems as if the fleecy clouds that live in the sky had come to pay a visit to the moors, and were going to take possession of everything."

"Why, Blanche, how fanciful you are! It is nothing more nor less than that wretched wetting Scotch mist one hears of. Come, child, and get into your furs. How thoughtful of Ellis to have brought them. Commend me to Devonshire and muslins at this season of the year," said Miss Prosser, as she drew the rug more closely around her, and shrugged her shoulders.

The mist was creeping silently over the valley, and coming nearer and nearer, till at last there seemed hardly enough space for the horses to make their way through, and Blanche thought matters looked very threatening indeed. Seating herself by Miss Prosser's side with a shiver, she said, in a frightened tone, "I do wish papa were here. These clouds look as if they meant to carry us right up with them. Don't you begin to feel rather frightened, Miss Prosser?"

When her governess suggested that the carriage should be closed, Blanche felt rather relieved on the whole, and becoming very quiet and meditative, finally fell fast asleep, curled up on one of the seats, from whence she was carried by her father, when the carriage reached its destination. She never thoroughly awoke till the bright morning sun came streaming in at the curtainless, deep mullioned window of the old Highland keep where she found herself.

Attached to the shootings of Glen Eagle was a half-ruinous castle, which Mr. Clifford had put into a sort of repair, fitting up a part of the building for the use of his household, though there was still many an unused room, dim with the dust of years, among the winding passages and cork-screw stairs. In old times it had been a fortified place, and Scottish chieftains had reigned there, and from its grey towers kept watch and ward over the strath, where were scattered the dwellings of the clans-men. It stood in the heart of the glen, rearing itself grim and gaunt and grey, surrounded by a massive wall, which had once been for defence, but was ruinous now, and pleasant turf sloped down from the castle, and flourished along its cope.

Though so long untenanted, there were still some remains of its ancient furnishings, which the Highland lord on whose land it stood left unmolested, in honor of the home of his ancestors. In the large dimly-lighted entrance-hall, there hung many relics of the olden time. Dirks and claymores that had done deadly work long ago, were beautifully arranged in various patterns, on the dark panelled walls; numberless trophies from the glen were ranged round—stately stags' heads with branching horns, and outspread wings of mountain birds; and a fox too, whose glass eyes seemed to leer as cunningly as the original orbs when they cast longing glances at the feathered inhabitants of the farm-yard.

Blanche had descended the broad staircase, and now gazed timidly round at these strange ornaments of the ancient hall. She felt as if she could not endure the leer of the fox one minute longer, and catching a glimpse of the pleasant greensward through the great door, which stood open, she darted out. The mountain breeze had a reassuring effect, and Blanche felt safe and happy again, as she stood gazing on the fair scene, in which the bleak and the beautiful strangely blended.

To the left of the castle, on banks which sloped towards the river, were masses of feathery birk-trees, with their white crooked stems gleaming in the sun, and through the net-work of green Blanche could catch glimpses of the river as it took its winding way through the glen. On a sunny, upland slope, rising from the other side of the river, there were some corn-fields waving, which were only now yellowing for the late harvest.

To the right there stretched a great pine forest, with the dark green spires of fir fringing the horizon; and down in the valley there gleamed a sheet of water, lying like a looking-glass framed among the heather. The mist of the previous evening had all cleared away, and the golden sunlight streamed on hill and glen, showing the tracks of the little winding brooks, making the white stones gleam, and the water that rippled through them sparkle like diamonds, lighting up the bright green patches on the hills, which seemed so alluring in their sun-lighted hues, that Blanche did not guess how treacherous they might sometimes prove for unwary feet, and longed to reach them.

Here and there a little cottage seemed to grow out of the heather, scarcely distinguishable but for the white lime under the brown thatch, and the blue smoke which curled from its tiny chimney.

The little English maiden gazed in ecstacy on·this scene, so new and strange to her. A delicious feeling of adventure and freedom kept singing at her heart, as she scampered off round the grey old keep in search of her papa, for without a companion her happiness was incomplete. She knew well what she meant to do. Into each of these tiny cottages she should like to peep, all the bright green places she wanted to explore, and those gleaming sheep-roads in the heather seemed to have been made expressly for her. Wherever little English feet could tread, her father had promised that she might go, and she felt very sure that her feet would be quite able for anything so pleasant. Her castle-in-the-air was quite outrivalling in proportions the one that towered above her, when she heard a voice which brought her quickly back to real life, with its rules, its proprieties, and its lessons.

"Miss Clifford, this cannot be permitted. Ellis tells me that you have dressed without her assistance, escaped from your room, and no where to be seen; and after hunting through endless stairs and passages, I find you here, without your outdoor things, and with boots that were meant for civilized life. I knew what would happen; no kind of discipline can be kept up in this wild, lawless place."

Blanche was too exuberantly happy at the moment to be damped by any rebuke.

"O dear Miss Prosser! I'm so sorry you've had to look for me. I really couldn't rest in bed. I'm sure it must be quite late, besides; I felt so wide awake. Has papa had breakfast yet, I wonder? I'm in search of him now. He promised to take me to the hills, and I want to begin at once."

"My dear child, what are you talking about? Your papa has been gone for hours. This is the famous 'Twelfth,' you know. He started at sunrise, I believe, with several gentlemen who arrived yesterday. The barking of the dogs awoke me, and as I was unable to close an eye afterwards, I got up, and have been busy helping Ellis to make a schoolroom pleasant and habitable for us."

"Papa gone!—papa not to be back till evening! How could Ellis be so cruel as to let me sleep! I wish I had heard the barking of the dogs," burst forth Blanche, in grief and dismay.

All of a sudden the glen grew dim to her eyes, and the hot tears came raining down. Miss Prosser began to act the part of a comforter, and to make suggestions of breakfast and a pleasant walk in the afternoon when lessons were over. But Blanche would not be comforted; the proposal of a walk seemed a mockery to her, when she remembered the adventurous rambles which she had been planning. She followed her governess with reluctant steps, casting wistful glances at the moorland as she passed into the dark hall, where the old fox seemed to leer more cunningly than ever, as if he were enjoying her disappointment.

"Now, Blanche, dear, haven't I contrived to make our new abode look wonderfully home-like? Ellis and I have had quite a hard morning's work, unpacking and arranging, I assure you."

A knot rose in poor Blanche's throat as she looked blankly round. There, sure enough, she could see, through her tear-dimmed eyes, an exact reproduction of the London school-room, which she hoped she had left far behind. On the wall hung the familiar maps and blackboard, and the table was covered with the well-known physiognomies of the school-books of which she had taken farewell for many a day. Every trace of the glen was effectually excluded; a low window looked out on the green slope, and a rising knoll of grass almost shut out the sky.

"I had such difficulty in selecting a room," said Miss Prosser, with a satisfied glance round her; "but I think I have made a happy choice. Ellis found one at the other side of the castle, which seemed habitable enough, but it looked out on that dreary moorland, so I avoided it."

"How can you call it dreary, Miss Prosser? It is the most glorious, beautiful land I ever saw. Do take a window that looks on it. But I'm sure papa never meant me to have lessons —I shan't; I can't really stay indoors; I shall go out and seek papa;" and Blanche finished with a wild burst of tears, while Miss Prosser sighed over her naughty pupil.

It is very plain to see that Blanche was by no means a perfect little girl; and as we follow her, we shall be obliged to acknowledge that she was wilful and wayward often enough. But we are not going to make a catalogue of Blanche's faults; they will peep out at intervals, and stare out occasionally, as little girls' faults are apt to do, and not theirs only; so that we must quite shut our eyes, if we are not to see them.　We need not do that, but with open eyes—though true and kind as well as open—we shall follow Blanche through these autumn days, and see what they brought to her.

BLANCHE CLIFFORD.

IN one of the southern counties there stood a stately English home, with silent halls and closed gates, awaiting the time when Blanche Clifford should be of age. It had been her birthplace, though she never remembered having seen it. Her young and beautiful mother had died there on the Christmas Eve when Blanche was born, and her father had not cared to revisit it since. Even his baby-daughter had been only a painful reminder of his loss, and he had left her in his great dreary London house, with a retinue of servants to wait upon her, and had gone away for years of travel in many lands.

During Blanche's helpless infant years, she had been carefully nursed by a faithful old soul, who had been her mother's nurse when she was young. Mrs. Paterson, or Patty, as Blanche always called her, was guardian, nurse, friend, and playmate all in one. She romped with her little charge till her old legs ached again; sang songs and ballads to her with unwearied fervor in her old quivering voice, which, though thin, was still true, and Blanche thought it the sweetest voice in all the world.

The old nursery which they inhabited underwent wonderful and various transformations during those early days. Now it was the sea where she bathed, or her dolls sailed, in stately ships of varied manufacture, into their haven on the rug; sometimes it was the Zoological Gardens, and Patty became the bear, receiving Good Friday buns, and every available cupboard contained a ravening animal. And when Blanche got wearied with her romps, she would coil herself on Patty's knee, and the hours till bedtime would pass all too quickly, as she listened to delightful stories, which never grew old, of the time when mamma was a little girl.

But these pleasant old nursery days had passed away as a tale that is told, long before the time when our story begins. Dear old Patty was struck down by painful illness, and had to leave her little lamb in strangers' hands; and now Miss Prosser reigned in her stead. Then lessons had begun. Blanche's governess, being a skilled instructress of youth, was disturbed to find her little pupil sadly backward

in all branches of education; for of actual lessons she had none while under Patty's care.
Her acquirements consisted in being able to
read her favorite story-books, and to repeat
and sing an unlimited number of songs and
ballads, for many of which she had found notes
to suit on the grand piano that stood in the
deserted white-draped drawing-room, where she
and Patty used to resort for their walk on wet
afternoons.

We shall not linger over the years that
elapsed between Miss Prosser's coming and
our introduction to her and her pupil. We
should only have to tell of long days of school-
room routine, when Blanche at last got fairly
into educational harness, and came to know
many things which it was right and proper
that she should know. She could tell a great
deal of the geography of several countries, was
quite at home among the Plantagenets and
various other dynasties, could repeat an unlimited number of French irregular verbs, and
knew something of the elements of more than
one science.

When Mr. Clifford, after years of absence,
at last ventured to return to his deserted home,
it was something of the nature of a surprise to
find an eager, loving little woman's heart await-

ing him, and he rejoiced over his child as over a new-found treasure. And though Blanche never remembered having seen her father, yet he had always been her cherished ideal. Constantly she had dreamt of him by night, and talked of him by day ; and her favorite occupation was to write a letter to papa ever since she had been in the pot-hook stage of that acquirement. His return home was the greatest event of her life, and brought a brightness into it that was unknown before. It is true that she did not see much of him, even when he was at home; for the hope of an hour's play and prattle with him, in the precious after-dinner hour, was often disappointed by the presence of gentlemen friends, who would talk politics, and discuss other dark and uninteresting subjects, till Blanche at last glided away in a disconsolate frame of mind, and went to bed with a disappointed heart. Occasionally, however, she had her papa all to herself, and these were precious, never-to-be-forgotten hours. Sometimes a half-holiday was granted, and she went for a ride in the Park on her pretty little white pony, Neige, and these were always memorable happy occasions. But every light has its shadow. After having known the pleasure of being with her father, Blanche pined for him when he was absent, and looked forward longingly to the time when she should be quite grown-up, and able to be his companion always.

These autumn days in the Highlands, Blanche had hoped to spend entirely with her father. She did not guess how engrossed he would be in sport, nor that her governess thought it wise and well to provide the means for a few hours of lessons, daily. She took her place among her schoolbooks with a smouldering sense of wrong and grief in her little breast, which did not get extinguished by an hour's bending over an open " History of England." Indeed, the prospect of committing the Wars of the Roses to memory, seemed to promise to turn out as lingering a process as the triumph of the White Rose, recorded in English annals. Blanche looked wistfully round, in the hope of finding some pleasant distraction, some trace of the mountain-land which she could not forget that she had actually reached at last, though certainly her present surroundings did not suggest it.

A pleasant breeze that swept in at the open window was the only mountain element that could not be excluded from this schoolroom, which had suddenly followed Blanche

to the Highlands, and held her captive. The
window was on a level with the ground, and
a grassy knoll intercepted the view beyond;
.there was nothing really to do or see anywhere, so at last Blanche gave herself lan-
guidly up to her lesson, thinking she was the
most ill-used little girl in all the world. She
was gazing absently at a map of England
opposite, in a lazy search after Tewkesbury,
when she noticed a shadow flit across the
sunlighted wall, but before she had time to
turn her head, it had vanished, and Blanche
again betook herself to the battle of Tewkesbury, with a strong effort of attention. Suddenly, as she happened to look up from her
book, to fix a fact in her memory, by repeating it aloud, she saw standing at the window,
not a shadow this time, but a real flesh and
blood little girl, gazing intently at her. A
brown little face peeped out from among a
mass of tangled, raven-black, elf-like locks,
and a pair of keen dark eyes rested on
Blanche, with admiration and wonder in their
gaze. The little figure was arrayed in a tartan dress of the briefest dimensions, which
hung in fringes, and displayed brown bare
arms and legs, well-knit and nimble-looking.
After Blanche's first gasp of astonishment

at so strange and unexpected an apparition,
it occurred to her that the image could probably give some account of itself, and she
was wondering what would be the most suitable mode of address, when, as if divining
her idea, off the creature darted, round the
grassy knoll, and out of sight. Blanche
sprung to the window, and looked excitedly
round to see if she could possibly follow.
The window was close to the ground, and
her foot was on the sill, ready to start off
in pursuit, when just at that moment in
walked Miss Prosser.

" Why, Blanche, what are you about? You
look quite excited, child ! "

Blanche's first impulse was to confide to her
the cause of her excitement, but, on second
thoughts, she resolved not to reveal it. To her,
the sudden apparition of the little elfish-looking
maiden was quite a romantic adventure; but
she felt doubtful if it would appear in the same
light to her governess, who frequently objected
to Blanche's friendly advances to the little London flower-girls, and her delicate attentions to
crossing-sweepers. Moreover, Blanche had a
vague terror lest a pursuit of the little unknown
might be set on foot, not of such a friendly character as her's was meant to be, so she resolved

to keep her own counsel. Still the vision of the weird-looking little maiden, whom she had caught devouring her with great soft eyes, like a gentle timid animal of the forest, kept haunt ing her. What did she want? where did she live? she wondered. Perhaps she might not have any home. She looked very ragged, certainly, and very poor she must be, for she wore neither shoes nor stockings, were the reflections that actively coursed through Blanche's brain, as she narrated the Battle of Tewkesbury to her governess, who had just reason to complain of a very absent-minded pupil.

When the hour for the afternoon walk arrived, it did not seem quite so tame and unattractive as it had done to Blanche in the midst of her more ambitious morning plans. She was by no means the broken-hearted, ill-used person which she fancied herself a few hours before, as she tripped gaily down the broad, flat, grass-grown steps of the old court-yard, and stood again on the soft turf, waiting for Miss Prosser. Presently she spied a familiar friend coming towards her, in the shape of a great black retriever. He came wagging a vigorous welcome to his little mistress, whom he was quite overjoyed to see after his long and depressing journey, in company with the pointers and setters.

He had indulged in the most unfriendly feelings towards the whole pack, but being muzzled, he was not able to give them a bit of his mind, as he would fain have done.

"Well, old fellow, and how are you? I believe you've been all over Glen Eagle already, and know every bit. I wish I were you, Chance. You may be glad enough you can't speak, old dog—though you sometimes look as if you would very much like to; for if you could, you would be sure to have lessons, and, instead of scampering about the hills, you would have had to tell Miss Prosser all about the Battle of Tewkesbury," said Blanche, laughingly, as she returned his warm welcome.

Chance was a great friend of Blanche's, and had been presented to her as a compensation for her banished dolls. His upbringing had, however, caused her much more anxiety than that of her flaxen darlings. He had been a terribly troublesome baby, and developed a frightful bump of destructiveness. He took so very long to cut his teeth, and was always helping on the process by using various appliances in the shape of boots, gloves, and muffs. But at length his partiality for these, as articles of consumption, somewhat abated, and he developed instead the useful faculty of carrying them, and restoring them to their owners, generally with much reluctance, but withal in a sound condition. He possessed various other accomplishments, which Blanche had taken pains to teach him, but they were of a more striking than graceful character, it must be allowed. He could shut a door, which feat he performed with his two great paws, with a terrific bang, to the utter detriment of the paint and polish, not to speak of the nerves of the household. His manners were still, even at mature age, sadly wanting in repose, and when he was in society, Blanche never felt quite comfortable as to what he might do next, so very gushing was he to his friends, and quite alarmingly demonstrative in another direction towards strangers. As he stood on the castle steps with his little mistress, he spied a kilted native, at some distance off, and was preparing to pounce upon him, when he was collared by Blanche. Then it occurred to her that she might be able to get some information from this Highlander about the subject which was still uppermost in her mind—the mystery of the little window-visitor; but Miss Prosser just at that moment emerged with finished toilette, all ready for the promised walk.

On returning from the walk, Blanche wandered in among the old ash-trees, and seating herself on a lichen-spotted stone, she resolved to wait there, in order to catch the first glimpse of her father on his way from the moors. The walk along the dusty high road, by Miss Prosser's side, had by no means suited Blanche's adventurous plans for the day. But to-morrow it would be different, she thought, resolving that she should awake very early in the morning, and as soon as the dogs began to bark, she would go out and join her papa, and he would be sure to allow her to go with him.

Presently she heard her father's voice, and saw him coming sauntering along the avenue of birch-trees which led to the castle. Running forward to meet him, she said eagerly, " O papa! you will take me to-morrow, will you not ? I do want so very much to get upon those glorious hills."

Blanche stopped suddenly, for, behind her father, she caught sight of a man, staring intently at her, whom she felt sure she had never seen before. He was a dark, keen-looking man, with iron-grey hair, a smooth face, and heavy eyebrows, which met on the straight ridge of his nose. He was tall and spare and agile-look-looking, dressed in shepherd-tartan, and across his shoulder one or two game-pouches were

slung.   He seemed rather taken by surprise
when Blanche suddenly emerged from among
the ash-trees, and now he stood seemingly absorbed in examining the trophies of the day's
sport, with which a pony by his side was laden;
but he was really surveying the little girl by a
series of keen glances.

"Why what an enterprising little puss it
is, to be sure!" replied Mr. Clifford, laughingly.
"You shall certainly go to the hills, but we
must first try to find a pony, seeing Neige is
not within reach.   Look what a grand day's
sport we have had, Blanchie," and taking her
hand, Mr. Clifford, led her to where the pony
stood, laden with the game.

Blanche gazed horror-struck.   The only
dead creature she had ever seen was a pet
canary, on which a stray cat had designed to
sup, when the delicate morsel was taken from
between the feline teeth, and had received a
burial worthy of the historical Cock Robin.
But here were more birds than she could count,
as beautiful, and perhaps as lovable, as the canary of pathetic memory, killed, not by stray
cats for their suppers, but by her own kind
papa and his friends.   There they hung in
masses, with their bronze feathers shining in
the sun, the speckled wings that flapped so

merrily in the morning, hanging limp and list-less now, the little heads downward, and the tiny beaks and eyes half open, just as they had been fixed in their death agony.

"This is my little daughter, Dingwall," said Mr. Clifford, turning to the man standing alongside, whom Blanche had noticed. "She would give me no rest till I brought her to see your Glen, and now she actually wants to go to shoot with us."

"Oh no, papa! indeed I don't—not now," broke in Blanche, in a tone of distress, and, glancing at the gamekeeper, she saw him still looking at her with a queer smile on his thin lips. Whether it was from his connection with the dead spoil, or from something in his face which repelled her, Blanche made up her mind that she did not like the keeper.

Presently he untied one of the brace of grouse, and lifting a wing under which the cruel death-wound was visible, he held it up, saying, "Maybe the leddy would be likin' to hae a wing for her hat: I've heard o' the gentlefolk wearin' sic things; but 'deed it's but few o' them we hae seen this mony a day."

"Oh no! please not. I should not like to have a wing at all," said Blanche, clasping her hands in a beseeching attitude.

"Why, pussy, what is the matter? Am I not to be forgiven for starting before you were up this morning? Never mind; we shall beg Miss Prosser for a holiday to-morrow, and you shall go to the moors, mounted on a little Shetlander."

"It is not that, papa. I'm afraid I shan't want to go to the moors any more now. I think it must be very dreadful. These poor killed birds! how can you stand and see them all die, papa?"

"Well, I can't say I should like to make a microscopic inspection of their dying moments. After the aim is taken and the shot fired, the fun is over."

"But, papa, how can you shoot those happy birds flying in the air, and not doing any harm?"

"Why, goosey, for the same reason as you knock down your nine-pins—for the sake of sport, to be sure," replied Mr. Clifford laughing at the distressed face of his little daughter.

"Come and shut up this little philosopher, Major," he continued, turning to one of his guests, a kindly-looking old gentleman, who had come sauntering up and joined them. "She is quite shocked at the monstrous cruelty we have been guilty of to-day. I begin to feel quite like the Roman Emperor you were telling me of the other day, Blanche; only flies were his special partiality, were they not?"

"Ah! depend upon it, Blanche has been having a course of Wordsworth," said the Major, as he shook hands. "Is it not he who says—

> ‘Never to blend our pleasure or our pride
> With sorrow to the meanest thing that lives?’

But I shouldn't have thought you had arrived at the Wordsworthian stage yet—eh! Miss Blanchie?" said the kindly old gentleman, as he looked smilingly at the distressed little damsel.

But Blanche was in no mood for joking just then; she glided away towards the castle, and, finding her way to her room, she sat down at the window from which she had got her first glimpse of the glen.

The bright morning light had all vanished now, and the hills looked grey and solemn in the gathering twilight. A great silence seemed to have fallen on the moors. Blanche could hear no bleating of sheep, no cry of the moorfowl, no merry whirring of wings; and, to her fanciful little brain, it seemed as if the valley were mourning for its dead, for the little birds that would never sleep on the heather again, or mount to the sky with the returning sun.

And as Blanche sat thinking in the gathering darkness, she got among those crooked things that cannot be made straight by any theories of ours, those mysteries which we must be content to leave to the wise love of Him who has told us that not a sparrow falls to the ground without the knowledge of that heavenly Father who had watched over this little girl always, counting her of more value than many sparrows.

Blanche was not sorry to have her reveries interrupted by her maid Ellis coming into the room, bringing lights with her. And as she laid out the pretty white frock and blue sash, in which Blanche was to be dressed for the evening, she said, " Well, missie, and how have you enjoyed your first day in the 'Ighlands of Scotland?—more than I've done, I hope? There's cook raging, fit to make one's life a burden about all those birds to pluck. She says it will just be game, game, right on now, till one feels ashamed to meet a bird."

"Oh! hush, Ellis. Please don't speak to me about those birds. I cannot get them out of my head. It does seem so very sad."

"Why, Miss Blanche, you're as bad as cook. For my part, I think they're uncommon good eating."

"It isn't that, Ellis; but only think how happy they all were this morning among those hills, and now—I wonder how papa could do it! It does seem so cruel."

"Come now, missie, that's what I won't stand to hear noways—the master called cruel! A more kinder 'arted gentleman don't step. He wouldn't hurt a fly—that he wouldn't. You'll be a callin' my old father a murderer next, because he's a butcher, I suppose, missie?"

"Oh! that's quite different, Ellis," said Blanche, apologetically. "But, to be sure, what lots of killing there is! It does seer very dreadful, when one thinks of it."

"Well, missie, you don't think it dreadful to eat a mutton-chop when you are hungry, I'll warrant." And this retort seemed quite unanswerable at the moment; so Ellis had the last word, as the last curl was adjusted, and her little mistress descended to join her father and his guests in the drawing-room.

Blanche watched wistfully for an opportunity of a quiet talk with her papa; she had so many things that she wanted to say to him. There was still a secret hankering in the bottom of her heart to go to the moors, for she could not bear to think of another day without

him.　But the time came to say ' Good-night'
before any opportunity for a private talk offered itself, and Blanche went to sleep after
her first day in the Highlands with a disappointed heart.

III

MORAG'S HOME.

ON the rocky ledge of a hill overlooking the Glen, there was perched a little hut, which seemed as if it had huddled itself against the rugged, grey crags for protection, and stood on its morsel of grassy turf trembling at the wild scene around. The mountains, which from the valley looked serene and blue, reared themselves above the tiny white shieling in dark towering masses, and the river seemed like a silver thread as it took its winding way through the strath.

On the same Christmas Eve as Blanche Clifford was born in her sheltered English home, another little girl had come into the world in that rocky eyrie among the mountains; and Morag Dingwall, too, was left motherless from the hour of her birth. Her father was gamekeeper at Glen Eagle; the hut had been built by his grandfather, who, in his day, ruled over the realms of deer and grouse in the glen; and it had once been a better-cared-for home than it was in these later days. Careful fingers had striven to repair the ravages of the wind and rain, for the little shieling was mercilessly exposed to both; the shelter the great gray rocks offered being a treacherous one, and its foundation damp. There had once been an attempt made to delve a *kailyard* out of the unfruitful soil, and the turf in front of the cottage was kept smooth and trim. But the present possessor of the hut did not seem to care to make the most of his barren, rocky home; he merely grumbled about it from time to time to the land-agent, the only representative whom he ever saw of the Highland lord who owned the Glen. But the factor thought that such a great strong fellow as Dingwall might mend his own roof, while the keeper thought that such a great rich fellow as the laird might give him a new roof, and a new house too; so year after year the rain had come drip, drip, through the porous roof on the earthen floor, ever since Morag could remember, till she had got quite used to it, and to a great many things besides.

The keeper was a strange man, and had led a strange life in his early days, the people of the Glen said. When a lad he had suddenly left Glen Eagle one winter, and he appeared only to have returned to take his father's place, when the old man was laid in the little grave-yard on the hillside. And a better gamekeeper could not have been found. He knew every foot of the Glen by heart. He was the best angler in the country side. There was no keener eye and no steadier hand in all Strath-eagle; he could spy the game at incredible distances, and knew every winding path, each short cut, all deceptive bogs. People said that the little Morag was the only human being whom Alaster Dingwall ever really loved. He had reared his baby-daughter with his own hands the kennels had been her nursery, the dogs her playmates. As soon as she was able to toddle, he had taken her to the moors, often strapped on his back, fast asleep. Before Morag was seven years old she had become al-most as hardy a mountaineer as her father, going with him to the hills, carrying his game-bag, trotting by his side, with her little bare feet among the heather. She could handle an oar and cast a rod as well as most people; it was her little deft fingers that *busked* the hooks for the loch, and did a great many useful things besides. Long ago the keeper had entrusted the cares of housekeeping, such as they were, to Morag. It was she who cooked, washed, mended, and kept things going in a kind of way. Occasionally the father and daughter would start on an expedition to the village, which was miles away, to make purchases at the merchant's shop, and lay in a store of provisions before the period of snowing-up came round. These were always red-letter days in little Morag's calendar. Sometimes, though very rarely, there was an attempt made to replace the little tattered tartan frock by a new garment, bought at the general store. If you had happened to look into the hut on a winter evening, you might have seen the father and daughter bending in perplexity over a wooden table, on which were strewn the rough materials for Morag's new frock. Great and many seemed the difficulties in the way, but at last Dingwall would boldly put in the scissors, a big and rusty weapon used for general purposes, and then the various stages of dress-making would be gone through, clumsily enough to be sure; but in process of time, Morag would stand in her finished garment, a more proud and happy little girl than Blanche Clifford, in the latest novelty of her London *modiste*.

They were a very silent pair, this father and daughter. Often they would wander whole

days among the heather together without exchanging words, or sit in the *ingle neuk* by the
fire of peat and pine in dumb silence, while they
cleaned guns or busked hooks, during the long
winter evenings. But notwithstanding his grim
silence, and whatever he might appear to the
outer world, to his little daughter Dingwall he
was always kind, and she loved him with all
the intensity of her still, Celtic nature, and
thought that he was the very best father in all
the world. During her short, solitary life she
had never known anybody else, and had
hardly exchanged words with a living soul, old
or young. Poor little Morag had grown up
utterly untaught. Like the pointers, her playmates, she had grown very clever in some
things—in mountain knowledge, in dexterity
of fingers and agility of limb. But there were
wants in her nature utterly unsupplied, cham-
bers in her heart and soul into which light had
never penetrated. Made in the image of God,
she had never heard His name; redeemed by
Jesus Christ, she knew not that such a One
had lived and died for men. Though she had
grown in the midst of God's glorious works, she
did not guess that He who made the " high hills
as a refuge for the wild goats," who " sent the
springs into the valleys which flow among the

hills," was the loving, pitying Father who had watched her lonely wanderings, and would bring this blind child by a way that she knew not, and make " darkness light before her!"

Most of the children of Scotland learn at least to read and write at the parish school, so Morag Dingwall's case was therefore an exceptional one, and arose partly from her peculiar circumstances. She was an hourly necessity to her father, who, besides, held in scorn other training than that which loch and mountain afforded. The few books which the hut contained led quite a fossil existence; they were stowed away by the careful little Morag in the bottom of a great wooden box, her mother's *kist*, in the depths of which all the valuables were buried to save them from the inroads of the weather, when the pelting rain beat through the broken roof, as it often did. Still, these buried musty books had a great fascination for Morag; often she would peer curiously into them, and long to know what they contained. She often wondered whether her father understood their contents; she thought not; but so great was her under-current of shyness that she had never ventured to ask him. Often on a quiet afternoon, when her work was done, she would slip one of the old books from its hiding-place, and lying down on the soft turf, would ponder over its unknown characters, with an intense longing to understand them. She felt sure that those closely-printed pages must contain much that it would be delightful to know; but they were not for her. With a sigh she would close the book, and gaze up at the fathomless blue sky and the everlasting hills around her; and sitting at the feet of the great, wonderful mother Nature, she learnt from her many things that books could not have taught her.

Morag had a true eye for beauty. It is sometimes said that mountaineers do not appreciate the scenery amid which their lot is cast; and perhaps it is so far true, that when the stern hard necessities of life multiply, they may dull the sense of the wonder and glory of nature in minds which were originally sensitive to it. With our little Morag, however, this deadening process had not begun. She revelled in all the beauties of her mountain home; with a poet's love she gave voices to the brooks and woods, and peopled in her imagination the solemn pine forest, the gloomy ravine, and the breezy mountain top.

The Glen was many miles from the nearest parish, with its church and school. There

were dwellers in Glen Eagle who went to
both, but the keeper Dingwall was not one
of them; and so it happened, strange as it
may seem, that little Morag had never been
within a church, never heard a sweet psalm
sung, nor joined in a prayer to God.

On the still Sunday mornings she would
sometimes watch the straggling dwellers in
the valley wending their way along the white
hilly road to meet in the little village kirk.
Morag often glanced wistfully towards it,
when she went with her father to make their
purchases at the merchant's shop, but then
it was always closed and silent. How much
she wished that she could see it on the day
when the people all gathered there! She
had a vague idea that the little company went
to worship a God who lived far, far away
in the blue sky, where her mother had gone,
somebody told her once, long ago; and since
then she had not cared quite so much to go
to the grave under the shadow of the hill,
but loved more than ever to gaze into the
blue sky, and to watch the sunset glories
before the amber clouds closed upon the many-
colored brightness of the evening sky.

Somehow Morag always felt more lonely on
Sunday than on any other day. In the long

still afternoon, when her father went for a walk with the dogs, she would wander down from the rocky shieling into the pine forest, which was a great haunt of hers—the *fir-wood*, she always called it. Sometimes she took one of the old books with her, and lying down among the brown fir-needles, she would gaze longingly at the unknown characters. She noticed that most of the church-goers carried books with them, which she discovered to be identical with one of the musty collection in the old *kist:* so a halo of mystery grew up round this book, which seemed to belong to everybody; and Morag longed that she could find the key to it as she looked up from the yellow pages of her mother's Bible, and gazed dreamily through the dark aisles of pine at the blue sky.

Happy are we that this Book of Life is an open page to us! But if it is, though an open, a dull listless page, if our hearts do not burn within us as we read its words, then more unhappy are we than this lonely untaught maiden, this seeker after God; for of such He has said, "They that seek me early shall find me!"

Morag had her code of right and wrong, which she held to with much more firmness than some who have the knowledge of a living, present Helper, along with the voice of con-

science.   She did many things every day that
were not always pleasant, because something
within said, " I ought," and avoided some things
because that same voice whispered, " I ought
not."   ·

In the cold, dark winter mornings, the " I
ought" said, " Get up, Morag, and light the fire,
and make breakfast ready for the kennels; if
you lie in bed longer, you won't have time to
do it before making ready your father's breakfast, and you know that the dogs depend on
you ;" and the little girl would jump out of
bed, with her first footsteps on the half-frozen
rain that often lay on the earthen floor, and set
cheerily about her morning's work.

The shooting season was generally the dull-
est time of the year for Morag ; her father being absent at the moors with the sportsmen all
day long, the little shieling was more than usually solitary during those long autumn days.
The shooting-party generally lived in the village inn, so it was a great piece of news for the
keeper and his daughter when they heard that
the new folks were to live in the castle of Glen
Eagle.   It had been uninhabited ever since
Morag co 'd remember; she delighted to wander roune ts grey walls, and to peep in at the
narrow windows, t l had spun many a fancy in

her little brain concerning its ancient uses, and former inhabitants. She watched from afar, with great interest, the preparations for the arrival of the new shooting-party; and on the morning of the " Twelfth " she stood looking wistfully after her father, as he set out for the castle, with the hired keepers and a host of dogs, to meet the gentlemen on their start for the moors.

The shieling seemed very lonely that day to Morag, when her work was done, and she sat watching the shooting-party on the distant hill, where her keen eye could still distinguish them, like dark, moving specks among the heather. At last it occurred to her that she might go to the old castle, and see what transformations the newcomers had wrought. She felt quite safe from the fear of seeing anybody, while the gentlemen were absent: it never struck her that they would not leave their home, as she left her hut, silent and tenantless: so she sauntered down the hill, and wandered among the feathery birch-trees which skirted the road to the castle. She felt rather disappointed to find that everything looked exactly the same, to all appearance, as it used to do; for it would have been difficult to change the exterior of such a grim old keep.

After she had made an exploring tour round, she sat down on a grassy knoll to rest, and then she noticed that the window opposite was opened up, and the sash raised. A feeling of curiosity took possession of her, and she thought surely there could be no harm of peeping in, when all the people were so far away on the hills. She approached cautiously, and looking in, she saw the loveliest little damsel that her eyes had ever beheld, seated amid, what appeared to Morag, a perfect fairyland of delight. Was there not a beautiful table covered with books in bright gay bindings?—and this happy creature was bending over one of them, with her golden curls falling around. For we know that Blanche Clifford was at that moment in the thick of the Battle of Tewkesbury, in a very disconsolate frame of mind. Morag saw that she had been unobserved, and lingered about the grassy knoll, thinking that she might venture to take another glimpse of this wonderful interior; but this time the golden head had been suddenly raised, and a pair of blue, dreamy eyes surveyed her with astonishment. Morag gave a terrified glance round her, and then turned and fled, with a beating heart, never slackening her pace till she got beyond the castle grounds.

By the time she had reached the shieling, Morag began to doubt her own eyes, when the vision of the fair English maiden, with her wondering, blue eyes, rose before her. She waited impatiently for her father's return from the moors, in the hope that he might throw some light on the matter; though when he did come she was much too shy to make any inquiries. Supper was over, and Dingwall had taken his seat at the *ingle neuk* to smoke his pipe, while Morag sat cleaning a gun with her tiny, but strong little fingers, as she silently pondered over the castle scene, and at last came to the conclusion that the bonnie wee leddy must have been one of the ghosts which were said to haunt the old keep. Her father at last broke the silence by saying, between one of the whiffs of his pipe—

"I'm thinkin' we've gotten the richt kin' o' folk this year, Morag. The master's the best-like gentleman I've seen i' the Glen this mony a day. It would be tellin' you and me, lass, gin he were the laird himsel';" and Dingwall glanced grimly at one of the many standing grievances, the porous roof of the hut. Morag's heart went pit-a-pat, for surely it could not be a dream, and what she wanted might be · coming soon; but whiff, whiff went the pipe,

4

and silence reigned for another quarter of an hour, as Dingwall speculated whether Mr. Clifford might not even bring his many suits before " the laird himsel'," and get redress for some of his grievances.

At last he said, as he laid down his pipe, " Eh, Morag! but I havena been tellin' ye aboot the winsome bit leddy he's brocht wi' him. She cam runnin' up til him, and he brocht her to tak' a look o' the birds, and said, ' This is my daughter, Dingwall. She would give me no rest till I brought her to Glen Eagle,'" narrated the keeper, repeating Mr. Clifford's introduction, which had evidently gratified him. " She had been wantin' to go til the moors," he continued, " but the sicht o' the deid birds seemed no to her likin', and she ran off some frichtened like. Ye're no sae saft, lass, I'm thinkin' ; " and Dingwall smiled his grim smile, and relapsed into silence again.

But Morag had heard all that she wanted. It was no vision, then, after all, but a real, live, lovely maiden, of whom possibly she might catch another glimpse if she had only the courage to approach the castle again. She did not venture to tell her father that she, too, had seen the winsome little leddy. Her extreme shyness and reserve always made it an effort to tell anything that required many words, and she put all her thoughts and reveries into the steel of Mr. Clifford's double-barrelled gun.

IV

THE FIR-WOOD.

"WHAT a glorious day it is, Ellis! How I wish I could spend the whole of it out of doors!" exclaimed Blanche, as she lazily stretched herself, before making the supreme effort of getting out of bed. "You've no idea how dreadful it is to be shut up for a whole morning in that horrid schoolroom, with the 'History of England,' and that wearisome geography book. I have got the boundaries of China, and ever so much, for my lesson to-day. I'm sure I don't care to know how China is bounded. I shall certainly never go there, on any account. Do you know, Ellis, the Chinese are so cruel? They shut up women, and pinch their toes, and all kinds of things."

"La! missie; you don't say so?" exclaimed Ellis, getting interested, for she delighted in the sensational.

"Oh, yes; indeed they do. They are such horrid creatures! So ugly, too. I've seen pictures of them. Do you know, Ellis, they actually wear tails?" continued Blanche, gratified to see that her maid was interested in her information.

"Come now, missie, you'll be makin' them out to be regular animals, and that I won't believe, noways," retorted Ellis, as she vigorously brushed Blanche's long curls.

"But, indeed, the Chinese do have tails. It's just the way they do their back hair, you know, Ellis," replied Blanche in an explanatory tone, as she turned to look out at the window. "Oh! what a glorious hill that is, with its blue peak right away in the clouds! I wonder what is the name of it? How nice it would be to know all the boundaries of Glen Eagle, now— to be able to tell the names of every mountain, and to know which was really the highest; for yesterday that dark hill looked much higher than it does to-day. Don't you remember those soldiers we saw in Devonshire, last year, Ellis? They were making a military survey, Miss Prosser told me. How I should like to make a military survey! It would be real work, you know, and I should go out in the morning and come in at night;" and inspired by the grandeur of the idea, Blanche pirouetted round the room, greatly to the disarranging of

Ellis's careful toilette, and finally she ran away down-stairs to join Miss Prosser.

After breakfast, Blanche was moving away, in a disconsolate frame of mind, towards the schoolroom. She looked longingly through the open door, as she crossed the hall, but at length sat down to her books with a resigned sigh. Miss Prosser had followed her, and stood at the table smiling rather mysteriously, as she listened to her pupil's sigh.

. "You need not sit down to your lessons this morning, Blanche, dear, unless indeed you are especially anxious to study. Your papa has expressed a wish that you should have no lessons for a short time. I must say I rather regret it, my dear Blanche; you are so behind; there is so much ground to be gone over."

With the last remark Blanche heartily agreed; but it was moorland, not mental ground, which she was thinking of. She began to put away her schoolbooks in an ecstasy of delight, while Miss Prosser continued—

"I have a slight headache this morning, and shall not be able to go out to walk with you; but I have given Ellis orders to accompany you, as I really cannot expose myself to the sun."

"Oh, please, do let me go out all by myself, only this once? Indeed, I shall not do anything foolish," pleaded Blanche.

Miss Prosser seemed disposed to be yielding, and at length Blanche started, accompanied by her dog Chance. She got strict injunctions not to get into danger of any kind, and on no account to go beyond the castle grounds; but this boundary line being quite undefined in Blanche's mind, it gave ample scope for extensive rambling.

Blanche felt quite in a perplexity of happiness when she found herself under the blue sky, left entirely to the freedom of her will. It was the first time in her life that she had been so trusted, and she thought it felt like what people call "beginning life." She had crossed the bridge that spanned the river below the castle, and now she stood between two divergent roads, each threading their white winding way through different parts of the Glen. So much did Blanche feel the extreme importance of the occasion, that she had difficulty in making up her mind which path to choose, and stood hesitating, till Chance, with a wag of his tail, set out to walk along one of them, looking back at his little mistress, as if he meant to say, " Come along; anything is better than indecision: we're sure to find something pleasant in this direction."

The remembrance of the little window visitor was still uppermost in Blanche's mind; but she had heard her father say that nobody except their own servants lived within miles of the castle; so she concluded the little girl's home must be very far away, and that there was little chance of meeting with her in her rambles of to-day. Then she had seemed so frightened, and ran away so quickly, that it was not likely she would repeat her visit to the schoolroom window; indeed it was to be hoped not, Blanche thought, since Miss Prosser would be the sole occupant that morning. The little damsel, with her elf-locks, had already begun to take her place in Blanche's imagination among the fairies and heroines of her story-books—a pleasant mystery round which to weave a day dream, when there was nothing more attractive within reach. But on this morning were not Chance and she beginning life together, with all kinds of delicious possibilities before them along this white winding road? At every turn she came upon new wonders and treasures, and her frock was being rapidly filled with a miscellaneous collection of wild-flowers, curious mosses, and stray feathers of mountain birds.

The road lay between stretches of moorland, which not many years before had been covered by trees, but now only a gnarled stump, scattered here and there, told of the departed forest. After Blanche had wandered a long way, following the abrupt turnings of the hilly path, she noticed that a shadow fell across the road, and looked up to see great trees all round, thronging as far as her eye could reach, till in the depths of the forest it seemed as dark as night; while in some parts the sunlight strug gled through, and shone, like flames of fire, on the old red trunks of the fir-trees. Blanche, before she knew it, had already penetrated into the forest, and stood awe-struck gazing down the great aisles made by the pillars of pine rearing themselves high and stately with their arching green boughs against the sky. The remembrance of a grand old minster, where her father had taken her to church one Sunday in spring, rose to Blanche's recollection; those wonderful trees seemed strangely like the fretted columns among which she had stood that day. She had heard her father say that there was no church within miles of Glen Eagle, and she wondered why they could not come here to service on Sundays. The choristers' voices would sound so beautiful, and the great floor, covered with brown fir-needles, and the lichen-spotted stones studded over it, would be much nicer than a pew.

Blanche, as was her custom when she felt happy, sang snatches of songs as she wandered on through the forest, stooping every now and then to gather treasures from among the fir-needles. At last she sat down and began to pick up some attractive-looking green cones, which had fallen the last time the storm had swung the great fir-trees. And as she sat there, absorbed in gathering cones, her voice went up clear and musical through the arched boughs, as she sang, almost unconsciously, some verses of a hymn which she once learnt—

> " There is a green hill far away,
>   Without a city wall,
>   Where the dear Lord was crucified,
>   Who died to save us all.
>
> " We may not know, we cannot tell,
>   What pains He had to bear ;
>   But we believe it was for us
>   He hung and suffered there."

The unwonted sound echoed through the silent forest, startling a roe that had strayed from its covert, and making some little birds lurking among the boughs set their tiny heads to one side to listen to the new song in their sanctuary. There was another listener to Blanche's hymn, who felt as startled by the sound as the timid roe; but who had, nevertheless, stood listening eagerly. When Blanche looked up from the fir-needles, wearied with her search for the cones, it was to see the little maiden, whom she had just been consigning to dreamland, leaning against a tree. There she stood, more real than ever, with her little bare feet planted among the soft moss, and her eyes fixed wonderingly on the stooping little girl. Blanche sprang forward, dropping, as she went, her lapful of gatherings.

"Oh, please, little girl, do not run away this time. I was so disappointed that you would not wait when I saw you at the window yesterday. Only, perhaps, it was just as well, for Miss Prosser walked in the minute after," added Blanche, who always took it for granted that there must be a previous acquaintance with those who made up her small world.

The little native did not seem disposed for immediate flight on this occasion, however; she awaited Blanche calmly, as if the fir-wood were her special sanctuary. Blanche was standing near, when Chance, who had been doing some hunting on his own account, finding the search after cones not exciting enough, came running up to see what his young mistress was about. Blanche sprang forward to meet him; knowing well that he was the sworn enemy of all bare-legged personages, she dreaded the result of a hasty interview with her new acquaintance. He bounded past her, however, and running up to the little girl, he began to wag his tail in quite a friendly manner, and received caresses in return.

"Why, you and Chance seem quite friends," exclaimed Blanche, with a feeling of relief, not unmingled with astonishment. "He is generally so very naughty to strangers; he surely must have seen you before?"

"No, leddy, I didna see him afore; but I'm thinkin' he kens fine, Morag likes a' dogs," said the little girl, in a low, timid voice, as she smiled and patted Chance.

"Morag! is that your name? What a nice, funny name! But you must not call me, lady. I'm only a girl about your own age, you see. My name is Blanche—that means white in French, you know, and it suits me nicely, they say, because I'm fair. But that isn't the reason I'm called Blanche. It was my mamma's name," explained the little lady communicatively, while Morag listened eagerly, as if she were drinking in every word.

"Do tell me where you live, Morag? Is it in one of the pretty little houses on the moorland, that you can see from the castle? I'm so glad I've found you again;" and the little fluttering hand was kindly laid on the sunburnt arm. A light came into Morag's still face; she suddenly lifted the white hand and kissed it reverentially. Blanche felt rather embarrassed at so unexpected a movement, though it stirred her little heart; and after a moment's pause, she said impulsively—

"I love you, Morag. I wish you would come and play with me. I'm so dull all alone. What were you playing at, all by yourself here? Aren't you a little afraid to stay in this dark forest all alone?"

"I wasna playin' mysel'. I was only jist buskin' at the hooks, for the loch," replied Morag, glancing towards a flat, lichen-spotted rock, where the materials for her work were lying scattered about. And then, as if reminded that she must be busy, she went and sat down to work. Blanche followed, unwilling to leave her new-found friend, and curious to see what kind of work a little girl, no bigger than herself, could do. There, on the grey stone which served as Morag's work-table, lay, in all stages of manufacture, wonderful imitations of variegated flies, to entrap unwary fishes. Blanche thought them marvels of art, and glanced with respect and admiration at the skilful little fingers which had even now another in process of creation.

"You must be very clever to make such pretty things, Morag. May I sit and watch you at work, for a little? I have got a holiday to-day, you see. Aren't holidays nice?" said Blanche, glowingly; then she remembered that perhaps this little girl might never have any, and she felt sorry she had said that, when no response came from her companion, so she changed the subject immediately.

"Who taught you to make those wonderful hooks, Morag? It must be so difficult," continued Blanche, as she watched the little fingers busy at work.

"Father teached me when I was a wee bit girlie. It's no that difficult to busk the hooks; maybe you would be liken' to try. It hurts the fingers some whiles, though," she added, glancing at Blanche's slender fingers.

"Oh! thank you very much, Morag. I should like so much to try, if you will teach me. My papa is going to fish in the loch one day soon, and it would be so nice if I could really make a hook for him."

Chance, who had been comfortably ensconced at Morag's feet, started as if he heard footsteps, and Blanche looked up to see Ellis hurrying towards them.

"O missie! how could you ever wander so far into this wilderness, and have me searchin' for you like this?" panted the breathless maid, with a look of relief on her face at having found her strayed charge.

"Oh, my! what have we got here, Miss Blanche? You don't mean to say you've ben a sittin' all the morning with that creature?" burst forth the flurried Ellis, as she caught a glimpse of Morag seated on the grey rock.

"A regular tramp, I declare! Miss Prosser would take a fit if she saw you, missie. Come along, this instant," shrieked the excited maid.

Blanche was by her side in a moment, whispering, with a face of distress—

"Hush, Ellis! don't speak so loud. She will hear, and you'll hurt her feelings. Besides, I'm sure she isn't a tramp—if that's anything bad. She's such a dear nice little girl, and so clever. I'll tell you all about her presently," added Blanche, nodding confidentially.

"Well, you've got to come home this instant, missie. There's somebody awaitin' for you," said Ellis, mysteriously.

"Oh! then, it isn't Miss Prosser who thinks I've stayed too long," said Blanche in a relieved tone. "Go on, Ellis, and I'll come after you in a minute. I must first say good-bye to Morag."

Ellis, thus commanded, good-naturedly obeyed, while Blanche went to rejoin her new acquaintance, whom she found still seated silently at work.

"I'm so sorry I must go now, Morag, but I'll come back again to-morrow. I shall find you here, shan't I? Good-bye, Morag; I must really run now, or Ellis will be cross."

She waited for some reply, but none came, only the soft eyes looked up wistfully into her face for a moment, and the little girl went quietly on with her work again.

Blanche was soon at Ellis's side prattling about her morning experiences, and trying to convince her maid of the irreproachable respectability of her new acquaintance. But the smart Ellis shook her head skeptically; she shared Miss Kilmansegg's opinion (of golden-leg fame), that "them as has naught is naughty," and she would continue to insist, in spite of Blanche's eloquent expostulations, that the little bare-legged tattered native must necessarily be a dangerous tramp, the off-shoot from a whole gang lurking near; and Ellis looked fearfully around, as if out of every bracken might spring a gypsy, and felt sure that had it not been for her opportune appearance on the scene, her little mistress would certainly have been kidnapped.

As soon as the strangers were gone a little distance, Morag laid down her work, and gliding up to the old fir-tree where she had stood to listen to Blanche's hymn, she leant against it, and shading her eyes with her hand she gazed wistfully after them as they disappeared among the pillars of pine. "The bonnie wee leddy, she's awa'. They'll no be lettin' her speak wi' the like o' me anither time," soliloquised Morag, who, like most solitary people, had the habit of speaking her thoughts aloud when alone. "That gran' like woman thocht I was a tramp. I'm thinkin' I'll look some like ane," she murmured, looking down with a new feeling of discomfort on her tattered little garment. "I'll men' it up some the nicht, though, and mak' it look a wee bit better afore the morn. She said she would be back again. Who will the Lord be she was singin' aboot,

that died upo' the green hill? I never heard
tell o' Him. It surely canna hae been on oor
ain hills here aboot," continued Morag, as she
gathered up the scattered materials for her hook-
making, and wandered slowly away towards her
home among the crags.

In the meantime Blanche had reached the
castle, and discovered the mysterious "somebody" who awaited her, of whom she could not
persuade Ellis to divulge anything. In the
cool shadow of the grey tower there stood, awaiting her inspection, a lovely little Shetland pony,
one of the blackest, roundest, daintiest of his
breed. Blanche sprang forward with a cry of
delight.

"Oh, what a little darling! You don't
mean to say he is for me?" The little fellow
turned his bright black eyes on her, and shook
his shaggy mane, as if to say, "So you are my
little mistress! Let's have a look at you. I
hope you are inclined to be pleasant!"

Blanche returned his gaze by throwing her
arms round his neck and hugging him heartily,
greatly to the amusement of the Highlander
who had brought him, and was standing by.

"What lovely eyes he has got, hasn't he,
Ellis? Do you know, they remind me of"—
Morag's she was going to say; but she remem-

bered that was a forbidden name. Presently she ran to find Miss Prosser, that she might come and admire the new favorite.

"He looks so perfectly good and quiet, quite like a dog. I'm sure I may sometimes ride him alone, mayn't I, Miss Prosser?"

"I shall never sanction such a step, and I cannot think that your papa will consider it either wise or proper for you to ride alone," replied her governess, shocked by the suggestion.

"What's his name?" asked Blanche, turning to the owner of the pony, anxious to change a subject which she saw had not met with approval.

"Anything my little leddy pleases; she be not got any name to hersel yet;" and turning to Miss Prosser, he said, evidently anxious to establish the character of his late possession, "She's as quiet 's a lamb, leddy, and there isna a foot o' the Glen she doesna know as weel 's mysel'."

But Miss Prosser shook her head incredulously under her sunshade, as she moved away.

"Nonsense, Blanche, you silly child! Don't you know that horse-dealers are proverbial cheats? The animal is probably the greatest vixen under the sun. Those small ponies are most dangerous and tricky always."

But Blanche, nothing daunted by the alleged bad character of her new favorite, set her little brain to work to find a name for him. As Miss Prosser disapproved of any lady's name being bestowed on one of the lower animals, the selection became more limited. After searching through several volumes of history, ancient and modern, and various volumes of lighter literature, with an assiduity worthy of a better cause, her governess remarked, Blanche decided that, after all, no name seemed to suit the little fellow so well as the one which had at first suggested itself, but was set aside as being too commonplace, that of Shag. So off she trotted to inform the little Shetlander that he was no longer nameless, and to see what he was thinking of his new quarters.

The next day, to Blanche's great delight, her papa announced that he was not going to the moors, and meant to take his little daughter out for a ride. The horses had been ordered round at twelve o'clock, and Blanche spent the morning in aimless wanderings round the castle, wishing that the hour for starting would arrive; a ride with her papa was such a rare piece of happiness, that the prospect quite sufficed for her morning's entertainment, without setting anything else on foot.

At last a practical difficulty presented itself, which she had not thought of before, and she ran off to find her maid to remind her that her riding-habit had been left at home, for she remembered hearing Miss Prosser say that there was no need of including it in the Highland wardrobe, since the little Neige was to be left behind in his London stables.

"Well now, missie, did you never think of that till this time of day? A pretty job it would have been for you if everybody else had been so forgetful," said the maid, smiling, as she took from a drawer a pretty new tartan riding-habit, all ready to wear.

"There now, Miss Blanche, that's what has kept me so busy for the last two days. I've just this minute finished runnin' it up. It's a queer color for a habit, I must say, but it's the best thing to be found at the village shop."

"Oh! you dear good Ellis, how kind of you to make it in such a hurry! It is such a beauty, much prettier than my dark blue at home. Don't you think I might put it on now, just to see how it looks?"

So the riding-habit was rather prematurely donned, and Chance with his mistress were waiting in the hall some time before the little

Shag and his stately bay companion appeared in the court-yard. Blanche was already mounted when Mr. Clifford emerged from the library with his budget of letters ready for the post-bag.

"What a regular Highland lassie it is, to be sure!" said he, glancing at Blanche's gay-colored habit as he mounted his horse.

"It is certainly most unsuitable," apologized Miss Prosser, who had come out to see them start. "But it was really the only material procurable in these uncivilized regions."

"It's a first-rate attire—quite in keeping, I assure you, Miss Prosser. Come along, Blanchie; you will quite charm the deer and the moor-fowl by having got yourself up in their native tartan."

On the riders went, soon leaving the shady birch-avenue far behind, and getting among breezy moors. It was a perfect autumn day, the sky was serene and bright, and a pleasant heathery perfume filled the air. Blanche's long fair curls floated in the breeze, and her face glowed with pleasure as she swept on alongside her father, the little Shetlander cantering as fast as it could lay its short legs to the ground, trying to keep pace with the swinging trot of the long-limbed hunter.

"Shag, as you call him, is quite a success, Blanchie," said Mr. Clifford, as he reined his horse in at last. "I'm afraid he will prove even a rival to Neige."

"Oh no, papa; there's no fear of that; my heart is big enough to love a dozen ponies. Shag is a perfect darling, though. He seems so good and quiet, too; don't you think I might ride him alone, papa?"

"Ride quite alone? I am not so sure about that, pussy. Don't you think you'd feel like the damsel all forlorn. I think you must be satisfied with Lucas when I can't come. Poor old fellow! he prefers his carriage-box to his saddle nowadays, he is getting so asthmatic; but I don't think I can trust you with anybody else."

"O papa! please don't send Lucas with me; he's so old and stupid, and wheezes so dreadfully; and he always says so solemnly, 'Take care missie,' when we begin to go fast. I'd much rather wait till you can come, if I mayn't go alone."

As Blanche cantered on by her father's side, she suddenly remembered her promise to meet Morag in the fir-wood, which she had forgotten in the excitement of the morning. She was hesitating whether she should tell her

papa about her new acquaintance, and wondering if he would call her a dangerous gypsy as
Ellis did, when her thoughts were diverted by
coming within sight of a human habitation of
some kind ; the first they had seen since leaving the castle, so Blanche viewed it with some
curiosity. She wondered whether all the cottages that studded the valley looked as neat
and pretty as this one, which stood in its little fenced-in garden, growing out of the bleak
moorland, where flourished gooseberry and
currant bushes, besides drills of cabbage and
potatoes. The late summer flowers were still
gay and sweet, and creeping rose-bushes grew
on the white wall under the brown thatch,
which looked thick and trim, all studded over
with thick, green moss as soft as velvet. The
little windows were bright and shining, and
the tiny muslin curtains looped up behind
them looked spotless and dainty.

"O papa! what a lovely little cottage; it
looks quite like a doll's house!" exclaimed
Blanche.

"It is certainly a wonderful abode to fin l
in such a wild spot," said Mr. Clifford, glancing at the well-kept garden. "The occupants,
whoever they are, have certainly contrived to
make the wilderness blossom."

Behind the cottage, and evidently belonging to it, was a little patch of cornfield, that lay yellow and shining in the sun, quite ripe for harvest; indeed it was partly cut down, though there appeared to be only one reaper in the field. Blanche slackened her pony's rein to look at the old woman who was bending over a sheaf which she had been binding, with no other help than her frail trembling fingers. Attracted by the unusual sound of passers-by, she looked up from her work, and caught a glimpse of the little girl's face, who had lingered behind her papa, and was looking pityingly across the old grey dyke on the lonely reaper at her toilsome afternoon's work. "They'll be the new folk that's come til the castle, I'm thinkin'. She's a richt bonnie bit leddy that, though," soliloquised the old woman, as she shaded her quiet gray eyes with her long thin fingers, and gazed after the riders. "May the Lord himsel' keep her bonnie in His ain e'en, as she's fair til see;" and stooping down, she lifted her hook, and went on with her work again.

Blanche and her father soon left the pretty cottage far behind, as they cantered on in the delicious breeze, which wafted all manner of pleasant odors and thoughts to the little girl,

who rode gaily on in the sunshine; but it did
not waft to her ears the prayer which had
gone up to God for her, that afternoon, from
one of His true servants, the lowly bent woman
on whom the blue eyes of the little maiden had
been so pityingly cast.

who rode gaily on in the sunshine; but it did
not waft to her ears the prayer which had
gone up to God for her, that afternoon, from
one of His true servants, the lowly bent woman
on whom the blue eyes of the little maiden had
been so pityingly cast.

V

A DISCOVERY.

THE day after Blanche's ride was very stormy. The peaceful Glen seemed suddenly thrown into a wild tumult. Now and then a long low rattle of thunder sounded along the mountains, and the great fir-trees creaked and swung, making all manner of weird choruses among the aisles of pine. The rain had fallen in torrents during the night, and there seemed still an inexhaustible supply in the gray sheets of mist that hovered over the nearer hills. The little mountain rills hurried white and foaming to the river, which moaned and raged along the valley, carrying with it on its wild way to the sea more than one wooden bridge which had been wrenched from its frail moorings by the *spate*. It was a true Highland storm, the first Blanche had ever seen, and she stood watching it with mingled feelings of interest and disappointment. She knew well what she meant to do with this holiday, if only the sun had kept its golden promises of last

night.   But this storm had upset all her plans,
and she was filled with remorse at the thought
of the neglected tryst in the fir-wood, and felt
out of sorts with herself and all the world.
Her last hope of any fun that afternoon departed as she stood in the old hall, and watched
her father and his guests get into their water-
proofs and prepare to start on an expedition to
see the swollen river.   She would gladly have
accepted an invitation, laughingly given by the
old Major, that she should join the party, but
Miss Prosser had been quite shocked by the
suggestion.   "It was improper at any time for
a young lady to go out in rain, and in a deluge
like the present, quite out of the question," she
replied, from the side of the school-room fire,
where she sat shivering.   Nothing was to be
seen from the window, except the rain, which
came plash, plash on the soaking turf in a
dreary monotone of dulness, and Blanche contrived to make her escape while Miss Prosser
had fallen into brief, though sound slumbers.
She took refuge in Ellis's society, whom she
found sewing busily in her room.   But here
things did not go to her mind any more than
in the school-room, for Ellis had taken the opportunity of warning her little mistress that if
she were ever found 'addressin' of that tramp'

again, she would feel in duty bound to inform Miss Prosser, nor could any coaxing of
Blanche's persuade her to promise silence.

"No, missie; I'll not hold my tongue for
nobody. My very heart came to my mouth
when I saw you talkin' to that creature, just as
friendly and unsuspectin' as if she'd been your
very sister, and all alone in that dismal wood,
too. Depend upon't there's a whole gang o'
them lurkin' yonder. Have you never heard
of them as kidnaps children, missie? Why,
they'd take you for the sake of your pretty
curls, if for nothing else. A nice endin' that
would be for you, Miss Clifford!" and Ellis
stitched away in high indignation, as she dwelt
on the alarming picture that she had conjured
up, while Blanche called to mind some of the
stories which she had read of gypsies who had
run off with children. It seemed to her, however, that any excitement would be preferable
to a time of dulness like the present; and she
came to the conclusion that the kidnapped
children must have, on the whole, rather a nice
time of it in the greenwood, and feel sorry
when they are recaptured by their anxious relatives, and sent back to their school-rooms.

Ellis went on stitching in dumb silence,
feeling displeased that her warnings seemed to

be treated so lightly, and Blanche, finding these circumstances far from lively, glided away. After roaming through the winding passages and turret stairs, in the hope of finding some variety, she lighted at last on a quaint, little room, which had evidently been unmolested by charwoman or housemaid for many a day. Its dusty desolation, however, quite suited Blanche's present disconsolate frame of mind. She managed to undo the rusty fastenings of the narrow window, and coiling herself into the deep stone embrasure, she looked dreamily out on the moorland. The storm seemed at last to have almost spent itself. Blanche could catch glimpses of the river, which still lashed itself into wild white foam as it hurried along; but the sunlight was shimmering upon it now. The wind had fallen, the great pine-trees creaked and swung no longer, and the gray sheets of mist, which seemed so stagnant a few hours before, were now slowly creeping from the hills, and making way for the clear shining after rain.

Blanche sat watching the changing landscape from her dusty nook, with the pale sunlight glinting in upon her; and as she gazed, all the discontented, restless thoughts seemed to vanish from her heart, disappearing like the gloomy mists which had been shrouding the pleasant hillsides. At last, after she had sat perched in her watch-tower for several hours, she fancied she heard her father's voice in the court-yard below, and she ran to meet him. Mr. Clifford was standing with all his wet wrappings when she reached the hall. "O papa! how very funny you do look! You are just as wet as Chance when he comes out of the water."

"Well, I'm wet enough, to be sure. But you should see what a wonderful little specimen of the aborigines I've fished up, Blanchie. Come along, and I'll tell you the tale while I warm myself."

Blanche followed into the library with some curiosity. She had rather hazy ideas of what the " aborigines" might mean, but she concluded that it must be some sort of trout taken from the river during the storm.

The Major had returned home some time ago, and was comfortably seated in his arm-chair by the library fire, so Blanche had to wait, with as much patience as she could muster, till Mr. Clifford explained what had detained him. The other gentlemen had gone on to see the *Linn,* he said, but as he wanted to have some fishing next day, he thought

it would be well to see the keeper, and ar
range the matter before returning home.

"I had been to the kennels once before,"
continued Mr. Clifford, "and knew that the
keeper lived not far from them. But I had
no end of bother in finding the place, though
there it was suspended above me all the
while. I set out to go down the hill again,
giving up the search in despair, when I noticed that smoke came from a wretched shell
of a hut, perched on the corner of a crag. And
this turned out to be Dingwall's abode. I
really wonder his Grace doesn't house his ten-
ants better."

"But what about the creature you fished
up, papa?" asked Blanche, fearing that the
conversation was going take too abstract a turn.
"You promised to tell me, you know."

"Ah! Blanche, I see you're all eyes and
ears. Well, I'm just coming to that now. I
knocked at the door of this miserable erection,
but no answer came; and, as it was pouring
rain, I did not feel inclined to wait long, so I
lifted the latch and looked in. Dingwall evidently was not at home. Indeed, I should say
he was quite as comfortable among the heather
as at his own fireside, in the circumstances.
The rain was dropping in from the roof in all

directions, and it was evidently its habit to do so, for it seemed to have excavated reservoirs for itself along the earthen floor. The only soul in the hut was a wretched atom of a girl, who, nothing daunted by this damp state of matters, was splashing contentedly through the wet floor with her little bare feet, trying to spoon away the water in the pools. Such a funny little thing it was. You should have seen her, Blanchie, as she stood looking at me, with her great eyes that peeped out from a tangled mass of black locks. But I daresay I looked rather an alarming apparition in my waterproof and umbrella, which I had the prudence to keep over my head. She looked terrified for a moment, but she did not forget to make her rags touch the soaking floor in a low curtsey, and offered in the sweetest voice to run for her father, who was 'watchin' the *spate*,' she said. You should have seen her, Blanchie; it would have quite suited your love for the sensational."

The portrait was photographic; Blanche's heart began to beat, for she felt certain that she had seen her.

"O papa! do tell me, did she really go away to the river to look for her father? Do tell me, please," said Blanche, in eager tones.

"Well, seeing that she didn't seem to mind the weather, and wasn't likely to catch cold, I thought I might as well bring her here for a little, since her father was not at home, and put her under old Worthy's care, to be warmed and fed and generally comforted. I couldn't get her to open her mouth again, but she followed me down the hill on my invitation."

"O papa! you don't mean to say that she is with Mrs. Worthy now?" and without waiting for a reply, off Blanche bounded in search of the housekeeper's room. And there, in front of a bright fire, seated in a comfortable arm-chair, looking serenely happy in the midst of such unwonted comforts, sat Morag.

"It is really you! Of course I knew it was," exclaimed Blanche, rather incoherently, as she sprang forward with a cry of delight.

Morag rose with an eager bewildered look on her face, but she did not speak, while the impulsive little Blanche threw her arms round the tangled locks, and kissed the brown cheek.

"O Morag! I'm so very glad to see you again. I've been so sorry all day that I did not go to meet you in the pine forest yesterday. So, you are the keeper's daughter," and a shadow of vexation stole across Blanche's sunny face, for the remembrance of the dark, sinister-looking man whom she had disliked rose before her, and she felt a pang of regret that he should be connected with Morag.

"I'm so glad papa brought you here, Morag. What a horrid house you must have to live in! Papa, says that it's a great shame of somebody—I forget who. I do wish that the sun might always shine, and then you could sit among those delicious pine-trees, instead of in-doors," and Blanche went on in a silvery torrent of words, while Morag gazed at her, eagerly listening in glad silence.

Mrs. Worthy, who was seated opposite in her arm-chair, reading the newspaper, viewed this scene through her spectacles with unfeigned astonishment.

"Bless my soul, Miss Clifford, you seem quite intimate like already! The like of you for 'aving a warm 'art to all critters, I never did see," said that worthy personage rubbing her spectacles, as if her old eyes had deceived her. She was a kindly woman, and had been delighted to show all hospitality to the poor little drenched vagrant; but to see Miss Clifford on terms of seemingly old and intimate friendship was more than she could comprehend.

"Oh! it's all right, Mrs. Worthy. I know

Morag quite well; we met in the pine forest. But where is Ellis? has she been here?" And Blanche bounded off in triumph to tell her maid that the dangerous little gypsy of the greenwood was seated in the housekeeper's own private sanctum, having tea and buttered toast, by her papa's special invitation too. Ellis did not seem so much impressed by this wonderful piece of news as Blanche expected, and loudly disapproved of the proposal which followed, namely, that one of Blanche's dresses should be given to the little damsel to replace the tattered tartan.

"'Deed, missie, I'll not listen to such a thing for nobody. Your frocks are all much too good for the likes of her, what I've brought here. If you'd told me you were agoin' to clothe all the poor of the parish, I might have brought something from your boxes of old clothes at home."

"I'm sure you might find something, if you only wanted," pleaded Blanche.

At that moment Miss Prosser's voice was heard calling Ellis, and Blanche overheard her governess say to the maid presently, "Oh, by the by, Ellis, the master wants you to find a frock of Miss Clifford's for a little urchin who has been picked up in the Glen somewhere, and appears to be in a very destitute condition, from all accounts. You had better select something suitable. I believe she is in the housekeeper's room now; so you can go and see what she looks like. Have you anything that will suit the creature, I wonder?"

"Yes, ma'am. There's the crimson dress, that will do. Missie will never wear it again."

"Well, I dare say not, though certainly it does seem much too good for a child of the description. Where is Miss Clifford? Have you seen her? I've been looking for her for the last half hour, but I can't find her anywhere."

"She's just going to get dressed for the evening, ma'am," replied Ellis, evasively, not indicating that she was within call, nor hinting at her little mistress' previous knowledge of Mr. Clifford's protegée; and finally Miss Prosser retreated to perform her own toilette. Blanche was hovering about in a great glee, having heard the result of the conversation.

"Oh! you dear good Ellis! So you are going to find a dress for Morag after all? I knew you would. Do let me take it to her."

The crimson garment was at length forthcoming, in the midst of many grumblings on Ellis's part; and Blanche, accompanied by her maid, set out in procession towards the housekeeper's room.   They found Morag alone; she had risen from her seat in the big arm-chair, and was now standing at a small table on which the housekeeper's books lay.   An illustrated edition of the "Pilgrim's Progress" was lying open, and when Blanche walked in, Morag was looking intently at one of the pictures.   She started and closed the book with an almost guilty look, and when she caught a glimpse of Ellis, her little brown cheek flushed all over, for she had not forgotten her loud-spoken suspicions regarding her.   Gliding up to Blanche, she said softly—

"I'll need to be goin' hame, noo, leddy. Father will be back, and his supper maun be ready; and there's a heap to do forby."

"But you don't really mean to say, Morag, that you get supper ready, and do everything? Why ! where's your mother, or the servant ?"

Morag's eyes twinkled, and she laughed her rare merry laugh at Blanche's look of astonishment.

"We havena got no servant.   I'm thinkin' they're no but for gentry.   My mother deid lang syne.   I never min' upo' seein' her.   There's no jist terrible muckle work, except whiles, when the weet comes in, like the nicht."

"I should like so to go and see you, Morag.

Do you think I may some time ?" asked Blanche, filled with admiration at the thought of the usefulness of a little girl smaller than herself.

"The floor is some weet the nicht, I'm thinkin'," replied Morag, glancing doubtfully at Ellis.

"Oh! but I didn't mean to-night. Perhaps one day soon, when the sun shines, and your father is at the moors with papa," added Blanche, for she had not forgotten the dark-looking keeper; and she did not think that she should like to find him at home.

Meanwhile, Ellis had been standing with the dress in her hand, listening to the conversation. Her closer inspection of Morag rather softened her towards the little native, with regard to whom she had been harboring such dark suspicions. She began to make sundry signs, to the effect that her little mistress should now proceed to present the dress. But somehow, at this juncture Blanche seemed suddenly seized with a fit of shyness. Morag certainly appeared to stand greatly in need of a new garment, but still Blanche felt in doubt whether she would care to receive one. She was so unlike any poor person she had ever seen—so useful, so brave, so complete in herself. At last Ellis got tired of waiting for Blanche, and unfolding the dress, she held it up with a flourish and a toss of her head, saying—

"Now, little girl, Miss Clifford is kind enough to give you this beautiful frock. See you say 'Thank you' for it, and take good care of it too. I declare it looks as good as the day it was bought!" added Ellis, casting regretful glances on the garment, as she laid it on the table beside Morag. The little girl stood looking at the gift with extreme astonishment for several minutes, and then, glancing at Blanche, she went slowly up to her, and said in a low tone—

"Thank you kindly, leddy. But I would jist be spoilin' a braw goon like that. It's no for the like o' me."

"Oh! but indeed, Morag, dear, you must wear it. I don't think it a bit too good for you to wear on week-days; but if you like you can keep it for Sunday, you know. It used to be my church-frock, wasn't it, Ellis?"

"Ay, maybe. But it's no for the like o' me. I dinna never gang to the kirk forby,' added Morag, in a low, melancholy tone, as Ellis left the room to discuss with Mrs. Worthy the strange little native who did not seem to care for the grand frock, although she was in such rags.

"I would like richt weel to ken what this bit bonnie picter is," said Morag, as she turned towards the little table, on which the open "Pilgrim's Progress" was still lying, and pointed to one of the illustrations towards the end of the first part. Blanche had not read the "Pilgrim's Progress," and she did not know what the picture meant at the first glance. There was an expanse of dark rippling water, and struggling through it were two men. One of them looked on the point of sinking, while the other seemed to be trying to hold him up, and pointed to a shining city, which was lying far away in the sun. Seeing how eager Morag was to know what it all meant, Blanche began to feel interested; after turning some pages, she said—"Oh! I see now. That town in the light, far off, is heaven, and those men must be trying to get there, I suppose. But I'll ask Mrs. Worthy to lend me this book, and shall try and find out all about it before I come to the pine-forest next time, Morag."

"Ye'll be able to read a' books, I'm thinkin', leddy," said Morag, looking wistfully at Blanche, as she glanced at the pages.

"Oh, yes, of course, I can read any book that I care to read. But, indeed, Morag, I'm not very fond of reading," added Blanche, in a confidential whisper, as if the fact were a very shocking revelation. "To be sure, I do like a few story-books very much, indeed; but then Miss Prosser does not allow me to read many. I've got some delicious story-books at home, in London. I wish I had them here, and I should lend them to you, if you are fond of reading. I don't think I have anything except those lesson-books here. The 'History of England' is rather interesting sometimes, by the by. Perhaps you might like it. There are lots of nice stories here and there. Miss Prosser says I like to read them because they are stories, and not for the sake of the facts and the dates, and I suppose that is very wrong," sighed Blanche, penitently.

Morag stood listening in silent wonder. The conversation had gone far beyond her depth, poor little woman! and she was about to explain that it was so, when Blanche continued—

"What books do you like best, Morag? I like fairy-stories much best—something about dragons, and giants, and all that kind of thing, you know."

Morag's cheek flushed crimson as she replied—

"A' books look richt bonnie to me, leddy, but I'm no fit to read none o' them."

Blanche felt considerable astonishment at this disclosure. But, noticing her companion's embarrassment, she tried to receive it unmoved, and said, rather patronizingly—

"Ah! well, Morag, but you can do so many useful things besides."

Morag smiled. Her quick perceptions detected Blanche's kindly attempt to cover her embarrassment with a compliment. For now that the critical eyes of the smart maid were withdrawn, she began to feel more at ease, and at last ventured to ask a question, to which she had been very anxious to get an answer since that morning when she stood listening to Blanche's warblings among the pines.

"Yon was a richt bonnie sang ye were singin' i' the fir-wood, leddy. Will the Lord that died on the hill be ane o' the chieftains that used to bide lang syne i' the castle?"

"I'm sure I quite forget what song I was singing, I know so many. But I don't think I do know one about a chieftain, though," said Blanche, shaking her curls in perplexity.

"It tellt aboot a good Lord that deed upo' a

green hill, and suffered terrible, I'm thinkin'.
I heard a' the words ye were singin' richt plain
like among the firs."

"Oh! I know now! Why, that isn't a
song, Morag—it's a hymn. It was Jesus
Christ, of course, 'who suffered under Pontius
Pilate, was crucified, dead, and buried,' the
Creed says, you know."

This statement did not seem in any degree
to diminish Morag's perplexity, and presently
she said—

"Maybe ye would jist say ower the bonnie
words til me?" Blanche repeated the hymn
in her clear, silvery tones, and after she had
finished, Morag gave a little sigh as she said—
"It's richt bonnie. I like weel to hear ye
tell't ower. Is't a real true story, leddy?"

"Of course it's true, Morag. Jesus Christ
died on the cross, you know. But it's a very
long time ago, in the Holy Land. You can
find all about it in the Bible. Ah! but I
quite forgot," said Blanche, flushing in her
turn; and then, after a minute, she continued—

"Morag, I have thought of something.
Would you like Miss Prosser to teach you to
read? I think I'll ask her. But she *is* rather
particular about some things," added Blanche,

sighing despondently, as if she began to doubt the pleasantness of that arrangement ; and presently she exclaimed eagerly—"O Morag! I wonder if I could teach you to read? It would be such fun! I would bring all my lesson-books to the pine forest, and we would spread them on the flat grey rock, and I would teach you everything that I know. Wouldn't it be nice?" and Blanche clapped her hands with delight at the thought.

Morag's face glowed with brightness as she listened to this proposal, and she was about to make some reply when Ellis entered the room. She came to say that Miss Prosser was already in the drawing-room, and that she wondered very much what had become of Miss Blanche, and Ellis insisted that she should come and get dressed without a moment's further delay. Mrs. Worthy entered at that moment with a trayful of good things for Morag; and Blanche, after giving strict injunctions to her little friend not to go home till she had seen her again, followed Ellis to get arrayed for the evening.

The storm had quite vanished now, and the evening was bright and calm. All the weird noises were silent, and a delicious breeze came stealing across the moorland balmy with the breath of pine and birch, and all manner of delightful, thymy fragrance.

Mr. Clifford and his guests were sauntering up and down the birch-walk near the castle, talking and smoking their cigars, when Blanche joined them.

"Well, pussy, so I hear you had already made the acquaintance of my protegée? Mrs. Worthy tells me that you gave her quite a gushing reception. How in the world did you foregather? Till this afternoon, I certainly was not well enough versed in Dingwall's family history to know that he had a daughter," said Mr. Clifford.

" Yes, Blanche, dear, where did you meet the creature?" chimed in Miss Prosser, coming, but not to the rescue. " It can only have been on that morning when I allowed you to go out alone. And you know you promised not to get into mischief of any kind. I wonder when you will gain the desirable self-respect which will save you from making friends of the most unsuitable persons, Blanche, dear!" added the governess, looking rather severely at the little girl, who stood pondering whether she should reveal the circumstances of her acquaintance with Morag, but she had a vague fear lest the window-scene might compromise the respectability of her little friend, in some minds, so she resolved to hold her peace. Her father noticed her distressed face, and stroking her curls, said, laughingly—

" Don't be ashamed of your new acquaintance, Blanchie. I assure you, Miss Prosser, she is a most exemplary little savage You should have seen her at work in her hut to-day ! I wonder if she is still in old worthy's keeping. You might run and see, Blanche, and bring her here if she is. I should like you to have a look of the odd little atom, Miss Prosser."

" Is that the urchin you found sticking in the mud-floor, Clifford ? " asked one of the gentlemen, joining them. " She must be quite a natural curiosity—a sort of fungus, I should imagine. Do let's have a look at her."

So Blanche was dispatched, rather unwillingly, to fetch Morag. She was very glad to be allowed to go back to her again, but she could not help feeling that it was rather a doubtful mission on which she had been sent, and she wondered whether it was quite kind to bring the shy little mountain maiden into the presence of so many strangers.

Mr. Clifford and his party were standing together looking at a gorgeous rainbow which

had suddenly spanned the Glen when the children appeared in sight. They came slowly
along, through the feathery birk-trees, which
were all flooded by the delicate rainbow tints.
A pretty picture they made, Mr. Clifford
thought, as he went forward to meet them among
the white stems. The fair, high-born child in
her white shimmering dress, with her graceful
movements, her delicate, finely-cut features,
her calm white brow, and deep dreamy, blue
eyes, and at her side the little dark, keen Celt,
with her black matted locks, her bright dark
eyes, and her short firmly-knit limbs. Blanche's
arm was thrown lovingly around Morag, and
one of her long fair curls rested on the little
brown neck of the mountain maiden, who timidly surveyed the formidable group in front.
Blanche ran to her papa to whisper that Morag
wanted to go home very much now, to make
supper ready for her father, so that she must
not be kept much longer, and might she ask her
to come back to-morrow! Deprived of her
bonnie wee leddy's protecting arm, Morag felt
very forlorn. The whole party were now in
view, and a very terrible array they seemed
to the little mountaineer.

There stood Miss Prosser in gay flowing
attire; and there were the gentlemen whom

she had watched from afar on their way to the moors; but they seemed doubly formidable now in evening dress, as they stood talking and laughing together. Even the bonnie wee leddy, since she has glided to her papa's side, appeared again to have taken her place in an exalted fairy region, and poor Morag felt alone, without prop or stay. She seemed seized by a sudden panic, and, casting a bewildered glance round about her, she turned and darted away at full speed through the gleaming birch stems, and in a moment she was out of sight.

"Bless my soul, what a droll little monkey!" exclaimed the old Major, dropping his eyeglass. "I expect to see her climb a tree directly and take to cracking nuts—eh! Blanche?"

"Poor little Morag! she is so shy and frightened: that's just how she did before. I'll tell you all about it afterwards, papa," whispered Blanche, as she was about to dart off in vain pursuit of her scared friend.

"No, Blanchie, you must not follow her," said Mr. Clifford, calling her back. "She did look very frightened, poor little atom! It's best to let her go home. Take counsel from your sage nursery-rhyme, 'Leave her alone and she'll come back, and bring her tails behind her.' Little Bo-peep must have patience, you know. Besides, it's quite time for you to go indoors, child," he added, as Blanche shivered. "Good night, darling! Don't distress yourself about your little elfish friend; she will doubtless turn up to-morrow."

Morag did not halt in her sudden flight till she had got beyond the castle grounds, and found herself once more on her solitary familiar heath. Then she began to slacken her pace a little; and now that she had time to ponder the matter over, she thought that perhaps, after all, it was very foolish to run away as she had done. These grand ladies and gentlemen did not mean to do her any harm; and surely she might have trusted the bonnie leddy who had been so kind. Perhaps she might be angry now, and would never come to the fir-wood, as she had promised to do, thought Morag, ruefully. Still, she resolved that she would go every morning after her work at the hut was done, and watch by the lichen-spotted rock in the fir-wood, and perhaps one day she might see her coming through the trees again; and though it seemed too good to be true, perhaps she might be carrying some of those beautiful books, of which Morag had caught a glimpse through the school-room window of the old castle.

Blanche's promise that she would teach her to read was the greatest event of that eventful day, and the thought of it had kept singing at Morag's heart; for a long time it had been the dearest wish of her heart that she might understand the hitherto mysterious contents of the musty old collection of books which lay buried in the depths of her mother's big *kist*, and now at last there seemed a chance of that hope being realized if she had not thrown it away by her foolish flight; and the little girl sighed as she thought of the sad possibility.

Morag had been sauntering on, lost in her own meditations, since she felt herself at a safe distance from the castle. She had climbed halfway up the steep hill which led to her home among the crags, when she turned to see if she could discover any trace of her father on his homeward way.

The sky was cold and grey in the direction of the hut where Morag's steps had been bent, but as she turned westward all was bright and glowing, and Morag wondered that she had not thought of looking before, for she loved cloud-land scenes, and had watched many a sunset and sunrise from her home among the crags. It was one of those intensely golden sunsets that come after storms. The clouds were clustering gorgeous in their coloring, and changeful in their hues, and at every moment they seemed to open vistas with brighter colors and intenser lights within. And as Morag sat and watched the sky, she remembered the picture which she had seen in the beautiful book at the castle. The bright expanse round which the gold and crimson clouds were clustering reminded her of the city lying in the light, in the picture. She thought of the dark rippling water, and the two men who were struggling through it, and looked as if they would be drowned. They must have been trying to reach the shining city surely, and Morag hoped they got there all safe, for the water looked dark and cold.

At last the amber clouds slowly closed on the inner sunset glories, like ponderous gates shutting out the dark night from a bright scene, Morag thought, as she rose from the bank, and began to take her solitary way to her rocky home. Presently she heard her father's whistle, and turning round, she saw him climbing the hill behind her. She ran back to meet him, and began eagerly to narrate her chronicle of this eventful afternoon.

The keeper had never heard his daughter so eloquent before, and he listened with his most well-pleased smile to all that she had to tell about her visit to the castle. How the gentleman had come to the hut, and had taken her away; and how he carried a beautiful umbrella, and held a bit of it over her head— the first time in her life she had been under a canopy of the kind. And then the beautiful room she sat in was duly described, and how the bonnie wee leddy had come to her, and been so kind. When she came to that part of her story, in which truth compelled her to tell that she had finished those delightful pro- ceedings by running away when she was brought before the dazzling company, she was relieved to find that her father was not angry, as she feared he would be. He only smiled, and said, " Ye needna hae been sae feert, Morag, my lass. They wouldna be meanin' to tak' a bite o' ye; but maybe they'll no think the waur o' ye for the like o' that;" and glancing round, as they entered the dreary soaking dwelling, the keeper said, smiling grimly, " Ye didna speir if he would tak' a seat, I'm thinkin', lass? What said he aboot the hoose, Morag?" But Morag could not remember that Mr. Clifford had made any remark on that sore subject; and presently father and daughter relapsed into their usual state of dumb silence, as they went about their evening occupations.

At last Morag crept away to bed, and fell asleep, wondering whether she should really see the wee leddy coming to meet her next morning at the grey rock in the fir-wood, where she resolved she would daily keep her tryst. During the night she kept dreaming that she was with the bonnie wee leddy in dark, cold water somewhere, and that her arm was around her, and the beautiful curls were all drenched with wet. She looked for the golden city lying in the sun, but she could not see it anywhere, and she began to feel very frightened in the dark, rippling water, when she awoke to find the bright morning light streaming in at the little blindless window of the hut, lighting up everything, and sending its kind, warm rays on the damp earthen floor.

Morag sprang out of bed, and was soon at her morning's work with a will. She smoothed her tangled locks as well as the well-nigh toothless comb would make them, and after mending a few of the rents in her tattered garment, she looked anxiously down, in the hope that she did not look like a tramp any more. Her father had told her that she

was a foolish lassie to have refused the " gran'
goon" that had been offered to her; but
Morag did not think so, and felt perfectly
satisfied with her own garment, if only the
critical eyes of the smart maid would not stare
at her so minutely again.

The keeper had gone to the moors for
the day, and Morag's morning duties being
over, she began to think of starting to keep
her tryst in the fir-wood, when she saw her
father hurrying up the hill again.

" Eh, Morag, lass! but I hae a gran' bit
o' news for ye. The maister wants ye to go
outby wi' the wee leddy this afternoon; and
whiles, to tak' her by canny roads when she's
ridin' on her sheltie. I'm thinkin' you'll like
that job, my lass. Ye may awa' til the castle
as fast's ye can rin; he said ' The sooner the
better; my daughter is an impatient little
person.' " And, after this quotation from Mr.
Clifford, Dingwall hurried down the hill again,
surrounded by the scrambling pointers and
setters, leaving Morag dumb with astonishment and delight.

KIRSTY MACPHERSON.

ORAG was at length fairly installed as Blanche's companion in her rides, and many a pleasant ramble they had together in the long bright autumn afternoons. The little mountaineer was still very silent and reserved; but her propensity for running away had quite vanished now, and she could laugh at the shy follies of those first days of her acquaintance with the little châtelaine. It must be allowed, however, that the daily intercourse in no degree diminished the deep reverence and admiration with which she regarded the bonnie wee leddy, who had seemed such a fairy princess when she saw her first; rather indeed these early feelings were deepening into that intense, undying devotion which is one of the characteristics of her race, and one which has often made them faithful to death towards unworthy, thankless heroes. Occasionally the little pony

Shag was left behind in his stable, while Blanche, with her big retriever Chance, sallied forth to meet Morag, at the trysting-place in the fir-wood. These afternoons were golden-letter days in little Morag's calendar, for then the books were brought, and as she lay among the soft moss, surrounded by the thronging pillars of pine, with their roof of green, arched boughs, this child of the mountains made her first entrance to that tower of learning, which, after all, is only one of the many gateways to the great temple of knowledge.

Blanche proved a wonderfully patient, though eager teacher, and never was there a more earnest student than Morag. Still, on the whole, these lessons, as yet, only brought disappointment. Her progress in the art of reading was necessarily slow, and could not keep pace in any degree with her desire to know. Her intercourse with the little English girl had quite roused her from her torpid state, and the fragments of ideas which began to dawn, set her mind to work in many wistful questionings.

Blanche would often shake her curls in perplexity at her friend's strange thoughts and queries; sometimes remarking afterwards to Ellis—with whom Morag had now a recognized existence—"She is such a queer little girl, Morag! She has such deep, long thoughts about everything, and it seems to make her quite grave and sad when she can't understand things we read. I'm sure I am always glad enough to skip the difficult things, and hurry over to the nice, easy, pleasant bits of a book."

To our little Blanche, the world seemed as yet like a happy garden, without any enclosure line, where she might enjoy herself as a butterfly would, fluttering from flower to flower. It would be perfect happiness, she thought, if she might wander from day to day without restraint, hearing pleasant words, saying pleasant things, getting all the enjoyment possible, while avoiding everything which seemed hard or disagreeable. And the years to come, when she would be a grown-up lady, having the freedom that she so longed for, lay in the dim distance like the expected hours of a pleasant summer-holiday, with all kinds of delicious possibilities folded in each. The world with all its wonders seemed like a playroom to her, and the marvels of nature interested her, just as playthings had done in the old nursery days. To her, nature had never spoken in faint mysterious whispers of a beauty and glory higher than its own, as it had sometimes done to the lonely little maiden

in her wild mountain home. Nor did Blanche
understand, any more than Morag, that the God
whose voice is in the storm, who shapes the
grass and blanches the snow, is the same God
who came to dwell upon earth ; not that He
might rejoice and revel in the fair world which
He made, but to be its Saviour from the curse
and the stain with which sin had defiled it.

Sometimes Blanche would recount with dim-
med eye and flushing cheek to her mountain
friend stories of noble deeds or patient suffer-
ings of which she had read or heard ; but there
was one story with which Blanche had been familiar from her babyhood, though it had never
stirred her heart nor had any interest for her at
all, and she felt much surprised and somewhat
disappointed when Morag begged that the New
Testament should be her lesson-book. She
seemed to look on Blanche's smartly-bound
volumes with great interest and reverence, but
always brought with her to the fir-wood the big
old Bible with its musty yellow leaves, and its
smell of peat-smoke. After the lesson was over,
which as yet consisted in a recognition of the
letters of the alphabet, or efforts to spell out
the easy words, Morag would beg Blanche to
read a little to her ; and as the silvery voice
flowed pleasantly on, she would listen with an

eager interest which surprised the reader, and in which she did not share.

On Sunday afternoons it was Blanche's task to read a chapter of the Bible with Miss Prosser; and rather a wearisome one she always thought it. The verses seemed to her like a collection of puzzling phrases strung together, and she was glad when the hour was past, and the book restored to its shelf for another week. At church, too, she always looked upon the Lessons as the most wearisome part of the service, and rejoiced to hear the organ peal again, and the choristers' voices ring through the aisles. But Blanche was really anxious to be helpful to Morag, and it vexed her that there were so many things which she could not explain to her little friend, who was so eager to learn and know everything.

One afternoon, when matters were in this state, the girls started with Chance and Shag to have a long ride. Morag never seemed footsore or tired, however far she walked, and nothing would persuade her ever to mount the pony. Blanche renewed her entreaties each day that she would ride for a little sometimes; but Morag would shake her head in a decided manner, as she was wont to do, saying, quietly, "I'll no leave the heather, leddy; my feet's ower weel acquaint wi't to be gettin' tired." Sometimes she would recount in her low tones, as she trotted by Shag's side, holding a tuft of his mane, walking exploits which seemed marvellous to Blanche, as she gazed at the heathery heights so near the sky, which the little brown feet had scaled, and she began to feel ambitious to be able to perform similiar feats. "It would be such fun to climb one of those hills to the very tip-top, quite alone by ourselves," she would sometimes say. "I shouldn't tell Miss Prosser, you know, because she would be sure to say it was out of the question. I should coax Mrs. Worthy to give us a lot of sandwiches, and we would take a bottle of milk with us, and that would be having a flask like papa. Oh! it would be so nice, Morag; I really think we must set out the first chance we can find."

But Morag was scrupulously faithful to her post as guardian and guide, and always loyally disapproved of any proposal that might meet with disapprobation; and she had, moreover, a quiet power over the impulsive little Blanche, which generally prevailed.

The cavalcade had started this afternoon on the same road which Blanche and her father took on the first day when they rode together in Glen Eagle. The ground was not so quickly gone over on this occasion. There were many objects of interest which Blanche wanted to examine, now that Shag had not to be kept up to the swinging trot of her father's hunter. Occasionally the little Shetlander got rather tired of such a loitering pace, and would shake his mane, and give his tail a whisk, as if to say, "Come on, my little mistress! This slow state of affairs is excessively tiresome; let's have something lively;" and off they would start on a sharp trot, leaving Morag far behind, but presently returning to her.

Shag and his mistress had now started in one of these frisky fits, and Morag seated herself at the roadside to wait till they should re-appear again. Left to her own meditations, she began to think of something which Blanche had been reading to her yesterday in the fir-wood. She would fain have heard more, but the little lady had closed the book with a yawn, and stretching herself on the soft turf, said, impatiently, "O Morag! I do wish I had my 'Illustrated Fairy Stories' here; I should be so glad to read them to you, and I'm sure you would like them—they are so nice;" and then she began, in glowing words, to tell one of them, and Morag thought it very delightful, indeed; but still her thoughts would wander back to a wonderful story which she had heard for the first time that afternoon. Blanche had happened to read in the end of St. John's Gospel, where we hear about Mary Magdalene finding the rocky grave of the Lord empty, to her great wonder and grief, till she recognized the dear familiar voice of the Master, who had risen again from the dead, and drew near to comfort her.

Morag had been able to gather from Blanche's reading a little about our Lord's life on earth, and all the wonderful things which He went about doing; and she knew that at last He had been killed by wicked men, and laid in the grave still and dead; but from this story it would seem that He was alive again; and Morag could not understand it at all. Often she wandered into the little graveyard in the Glen, and among the worn mossy head-stones peeping from the long rank grass, which told the names of the quiet sleepers below. Sometimes, too, she watched a little company of mourners, with their sorrowful burden, wending their way along the white hilly road; and when she went to see her mother's grave next time, she would notice a fresh green sod somewhere near, and she knew that another dweller in the Glen was laid there, in his long home, never to be seen among them more.

But this good Lord, who died on the green hill, and was laid in His rocky grave, seemed to have come back to the world again to speak loving words to everybody, as He had done before He was crucified. Could He, then, be alive in the world now? Morag's heart gave a great throb when she thought of it. Perhaps one day He might come to the hut and speak kind words to her, as Mr. Clifford had done on that rainy afternoon when she was so wet and miserable. Perhaps He might offer to get the roof of the hut put right too, since the laird wouldn't do it, and even to give her father a new house, which he wanted so much. But Morag thought, that to hear His voice speaking beautiful kind words, as He used to do to the people long ago, would be better than anything else; and as she thought of it, her hope grew stronger every minute, that one day He might come to the Glen, and she might see Him and hear His voice.

Blanche came galloping back at last, her face all aglow with happiness, and her long curls floating about her.

"O Morag!" she cried, excitedly, "I want you to come and see the prettiest little cottage I ever saw in my life, with delicious lumps of green moss growing out of the brown roof, and pretty roses climbing up the wall. Papa and I passed it before, when we rode this way, and we saw such a nice old woman in the cornfield behind the house. She was tall and stooping, and looked so very tired all alone at work among the sheaves of corn. She looked up with such kind beautiful eyes when Shag and I passed. I should like so much to see her again; but I've been looking into the field, and she isn't there, and it's all bare now." Blanche had been prattling on, not noticing Morag's flushed cheek and perfect silence. "Did you ever see the cottage, Morag?" she continued. "Do you know if the old woman really lives there, or anything about her? Do you hear, Morag?"

"Ay! I'll be whiles seein' her when I'll be passin' this road. It's Kirsty Macpherson's hoose," replied Morag, in low, reluctant tones, as if she were unwilling to volunteer any information on the point. Blanche noticed that there was something wrong, and they went slowly on without speaking, till they came to another winding of the road, and the cottage in question came in sight. Blanche looked longingly across the old grey dyke from the dusty road into the pleasant little garden, with its sweet-smelling, old-fashioned flowers and herbs growing side by side with the gooseberry and currant bushes shaded by one or two ancient rowan-trees. Morag was evidently trying very hard to avert her eyes, and kept steadily gazing into Shag's glossy mane, when Blanche exclaimed, as if inspired by a new and pleasant idea—

"Look here, Morag! suppose we knock at the door, and ask the old woman to give us some water to drink? that would be a good way to see her again, you know; and, besides, I'm really thirsty, after my gallop. Do let's go at once; it will be such fun."

"Ye'll need to ask it yersel, then, leddy. I'll no darken the door," replied Morag, with flushing face, and an expression about her mouth which suddenly reminded Blanche that she was the daughter of the sinister-looking keeper, under whose glance she had felt so strangely uncomfortable on the evening of the first day in the 'Glen. She felt puzzled and annoyed at Morag's reply; but she was a wilful little person and loved to have her way at any cost. So she pulled up Shag, and prepared to dismount, saying, rather impatiently, "Well, Morag, if you don't wish to go, you needn't; though I really can't think why you shouldn't want to see such a nice old woman

But there isn't any harm in my going to the door surely? and besides I'm really thirsty. You won't come then?" added Blanche, who had now dismounted, and was gathering up her habit as she moved towards the little rustic garden-gate. But Morag made no reply; and taking hold of Shag's bridle, she went slowly on along the road with a dogged expression on her face.

The cottage door was ajar, and Blanche could see into the room at one end, and there, seated at the low fireside in a high-elbowed chair, quietly reading, she recognized the old woman whom she had seen in the field binding the sheaf. The little girl knocked gently, but the moment she had done so, she began to wish that she had not come, especially when Morag seemed to be so opposed to her going. It was too late to repent now, however. The old woman had heard her knock, and laying down the spectacles on her open book, she rose to go to the door. She looked at the little girl with the same placid face and kindly look in her gray eyes as she had done across the dyke in the cornfield, and waited quietly to hear what she wanted. Blanche stood silent for a few seconds, feeling rather foolish, and forgetting in the confusion of the moment the mode of address which she had previously arranged, but at last she managed to gasp out nervously, "Oh! please, I was only passing this way with Morag and Shag, and I felt rather thirsty, and thought perhaps you would be so very kind as to give me some water to drink?"

"That will I, my bonnie bairn. Jist ye step ben here," said the old woman, smiling kindly. Blanche followed her, looking round this new interior with considerable curiosity. There were only two rooms in the cottage, the *but-end* and the *ben-end*, as they are called in Scotland. Within, as without the cottage, everything was beautifully trim and neat. The floor of the room was earthen, but it was smooth and dry, and looked quite comfortable. The tables and chairs were all of clean white wood, and on the shelf above the table were ranged rows of white and blue and yellow shining delf. The fire was on the earthen floor, kept together by two blocks of stone; and on either side, in what is called the *ingle-neuk*, there stood one or two little stools, and near the big arm-chair, where the solitary inmate had been seated.

Blanche had time to note all these surroundings while the old woman took a pitcher and went to fetch some water. It was rather

an exertion for her now to go down the steep
steps to the well, and indeed she had a supply
of water in the house which was meant to
serve for the day; but Kirsty always liked to
give the best she had, and she went gladly to
fetch a draught of cool, clear water from the
mountain spring for the thirsty little maiden.
Presently she returned, and setting the pitcher
on the earthen floor, she took a shining delf
jug from the shelf, and filling it she gently
offered it to Blanche, saying, with a smile—

"Here noo, my bonnie lambie, is a drap o'
cauld watter to ye. Ye're welcome tilt. May
ye get a lang draught o' the watter that He
gies, afore ye try a' the broken cisterns o' this
warl.'"

Kirsty's dialect was more difficult for
Blanche to understand than even Morag's.
She came originally from that part of Scotland
where a rough, harsh dialect is spoken, almost
as difficult for English people to understand as
a foreign language would be. Blanche, however, understood sufficiently to make her reply
eagerly—

"Oh! that is the water we read about in
the Bible, is it not? I suppose you are very
fond of reading the Bible, and know all about
Jesus Christ? I do wish Morag had been

here; you might have told her some of the things she is so anxious to know. She's so fond of the New Testament,—so much more than I am. She's such a nice little girl, Morag. I'm sure you would like her if you knew her," added Blanche, eagerly, on peace-making thoughts intent. "She is the keeper's daughter, you know, and often goes out with Shag and me."

The old woman, in her turn, had difficulty in understanding the little English girl's rapid, silvery flow, and Blanche had again to explain that the keeper Dingwall's daughter was waiting outside.

"Alaster Dingwall's bairn, say ye? I hae heard tell she wasna an ill bairnie, puir thing. She's ootby there, is she? I wad like richt weel to tak' a look o' her. It's mony a lang day sin' I hae lookit intil her faither's face. Weel div I min' upon the last time, though," continued the old woman, with a sad look in her calm gray eyes.

"She's at the gate with Shag; do come and see her," said the impulsive little Blanche, forgetting how unwilling Morag had been to make any advances to Kirsty.

"Do you live quite alone in this cottage? Aren't you very lonely sometimes?" asked

Blanche, as she watched the old woman moving about her solitary habitation. "I'll come back and see you again soon, if you would like; and perhaps Morag may come in with me, next time," added Blanche, in an encouraging tone.

"'Deed, an' I'll be richt glad to see ye, my bairn, gin yer folk kens ye're here, and doesna' objec. I'm thinkin' ye're fond o' a bit flouer, like mysel," said the old woman, smiling, as she pulled a pretty yellow rose from the wall beside the cottage door, where it had been carefully fastened, to preserve it as long as possible, and gave it to the little girl, who had stopped to admire it.

Meanwhile, Morag and Shag were waiting on a shady bit of the road, a few yards off. Blanche ran eagerly forward to meet them, whispering in an excited tone to Morag—

"O Morag! you'll like her so much. She is such a nice, kind old woman; and besides," she added, in a lower tone, "I think she knows all about Jesus Christ—just what you are so anxious about. She's coming now to talk to you; she knew your father once, she says, and wants to see you."

The old woman came slowly along the road towards them, but Morag's face wore a more dogged expression than ever, and she turned away from Blanche, and began to plait Shag's mane in dumb silence.

"So ye're Alaster Dingwall's dochter, my bairn," said the old woman, slowly, as she looked at the little hot-cheeked girl. "Ye maybe dinna ken auld Kirsty, but yer faither will min' o' her, fine. Will ye tell Alaster Dingwall that Kirsty Macpherson is willin' to forgie him, though he brocht sair trouble upo' her ance. But it's lang syne,—and we maun forgie, as we hope to be forgien," and the old woman held out her long, thin hand to Morag

The little girl glanced at her with a mixture of curiosity and surprise, and her face worked nervously; but she gave no hand in return, and preserved a dogged silence.

Blanche wondered greatly how the good little Morag could ever have grown so naughty all of a sudden, and there followed an awkward silence, only broken by some manifestations of restlessness on Shag's part, as if he thought it was more than time to start for home. At last Blanche thought there was no use of waiting longer for any rift in the cloud, and going up to the old woman she laid her little fluttering hand in the thin fingers, saying, "Good-bye, Kirsty, and thank you very much for the nice drink of water, and for this pretty rose. I'll make Ellis' fix it in my curls when I'm dressed for the evening. I shall come back to see you again, at any rate," she added, with an emphasis on the personal pronoun, as she mounted Shag, and turned to go, while Morag followed silently, with downcast eye and lingering step.

The old woman shaded her eyes with her long thin fingers, and stood watching them till they were out of sight, and then she returned with slow steps to the cottage. She sighed as she glanced round the room, which a few minutes ago had been filled by the child's bright presence. It seemed more solitary than usual now, Kirsty thought, as she looked wearily round. "She said she thocht I maun be some lonesome. Sic a bonnie bit blink o' a lassie! I wad like richt weel to see her agin. I liket the look o' Alaster Dingwall's bairnie. Surely he couldna hae pitten her agin me? She lookit some dour like, and wouldna speak ava'."

Like persons who live much alone, Kirsty nad the habit of thinking aloud; and, indeed, her thoughts were so often with a living, listening Friend, that the practice seemed quite a natural one. As she pulled out her rough blue stocking, which she was knitting, and seated herself on the doorstep, in the yellow afternoon sunlight, she continued—" If I didna mistak that wee leddy wi her sweet tongue, she said that the bairn was wantin' to ken aboot the Lord Jesus. Eh! Lord, but Thy thochts are wonderfu' and Thy ways past findin' oo.. Puir lambie! may the gude Shepherd lead her til Himsel. It's a pity gin her faither has pitten her agin me. I wad like to see the lassie, whiles. There's been nae bairn i' the house sin he gaed away. My puir, lost laddie! fat's come o' him? O Lord! I wad fain ken aboot the wanderin' sheep afore I gang hame mysel," and the old woman covered her face with her withered hands, and rocked to and fro in silent grief, at the memory of a life-long sorrow which was ever present with her.

In the meantime Blanche and Morag had been going on their homeward way. The afternoon was beautiful as before, and the soft cool breeze made the road through the heather very pleasant indeed ; still neither of the girls felt so happy or light-hearted as they had done when they started.

> " The little rift within the lute,
>   That soon must make all music mute,"

had this afternoon shown itself for the first time

since they became friends. With Blanche, however, it was only a momentary feeling of unpleasantness and perplexity as to how Morag,
the wise and good, should on this occasion
have behaved so badly. It was not her habit
to keep her thoughts to herself, so she presently exclaimed, " Well, Morag, I really can't
understand what makes you dislike such a nice
old woman. You were really quite sulky and
rude when she held out her hand."

A host of bitter feelings were surging in
poor little Morag's breast, and she made no
reply to Blanche's remark. She had tried so
hard to do what was right, much against her
own inclination, and now everything seemed
wrong. Her bonnie wee leddy, whom she
loved so well, and wanted so much to please,
had called her rude; and very rude, ce. in ,
must Kirsty have thought her.

Little did Blanche know what a familiar,
enchanted spot this cottage was to Morag.
How often she had glanced wistfully into the
little garden with its sweet-scented flowers—the
nicest she ever saw in her life, and how she
had longed to speak to the old stooping woman
moving about among them. On one eventful
occasion, as she happened to pass along the
dusty road, Kirsty stood knitting at the gate,

and, looking at the little girl with her kindly smile, she had said, "It's a richt bonnie day, my bairn."   That was all; but poor little Morag went home feeling as if a great event had happened, and resolving that she would pass that way again, in the hope of such another salutation. She recounted the circumstance glowingly to her father, but as he listened, his face wore its darkest frown, and he said sternly, "Ye're no to be passin' that way agin, I tell ye, gettin' Kirsty Macpherson's clavers. Depend on't, she didna know your name was Dingwall, or she wouldna hae spoken til ye. Ye'll no be darkenin' her door agin. D'ye hear, Morag?" and the little girl had replied meekly, for she noticed that her father was in one of his darkest moods.

Morag had often pondered the matter, and wondered why her father disliked Kirsty so very much. Always when they chanced to pass by the road, Dingwall would glance uneasily at the cottage and its garden to see if the old woman was about, and presently he would make some bitter remark, and repeat his injunction that Morag should have nothing to do with the "like o' her," till the little girl had come to think that though Kirsty looked so delightful, she must surely be a very wicked woman. Still, she had a curious fascination for the little girl; she longed to see the interior of the pretty cottage, and felt a great interest in all the ongoings of its inmate which it was possible to observe from afar. She had always conscientiously avoided an encounter, however, and on this afternoon she had in loyalty to her father shaped her conduct, which Blanche characterized as rude. But now Morag began to doubt whether Kirsty could really be a bad woman after all; she looked so gentle, and had spoken such kind words,—and that strange message to her father, too, what could it mean? The little girl could not understand it, and she walked by Shag's side in silent perplexity and distress.

Blanche began to feel rather uncomfortable in having Morag walking by her side so sadly and quietly. She could not be long silent under any circumstances, and finally took refuge in a lively conversation with Chance, who had been keeping beside her with rather a depressed aspect, as if he guessed that something was wrong. At last, when he bounded off in pursuit of a rabbit which had crossed the road, Blanche felt glad of the excuse to follow, and trotted off, leaving poor little Morag companionless. More heartsore than footsore, she wearily seated herself on the heather to await their return. Her tears were not in the habit of flowing readily, indeed she hardly remembered having a fit of crying since she was a little girl; but as she sat on the bank, the bright sky and the purple heath seemed suddenly to become dim to her eyes, and hot tears rolled down the brown cheeks, and trickled through the little hands, which would fain have hid them from the day. It was so hard, she thought, to have tried to be good and obedient, and yet to feel so much in the wrong as she did now, and to be so bitterly disgraced. If the wee leddy could only know how much she would like to have gone to the cottage-door with her, and what a struggle it had been to refuse when the opportunity, so longed for, had presented itself. How nice it would have been to see what was inside those pretty curtained windows, and to watch the old woman moving about the cottage ! And the wee leddy had said something about Kirsty knowing the Lord Jesus; so she would be sure to be able to tell her all the things which she wanted so much to know.

Morag laid her head among the heather, and wept bitterly at the thought of all she had missed that afternoon. And as she lay sobbing there, the remembrance of the story which she had heard the day before for the first time flitted across her little troubled heart like a gleam of light. The Lord Jesus seemed always so very willing to help and comfort everybody in trouble before the wicked men crucified Him on the green hill. And had He not even come back again after He was laid in His grave, and spoken such kind words to the woman who stood weeping there, and might He not be able to help her now?

Hardly knowing that she spoke aloud, Morag buried her face among the bracken, and cried in her distress, "O Lord Jesus! gin ye be a frien' o' Kirsty Macpherson's, dinna let her think ill o' me for no speakin' til her; and mak' me happy again wi' the wee leddy."

When she had finished speaking, she glanced around with an expectant gaze, as if she might see a listener standing by her side. But there stretched the solitary moors on all sides, with the yellow afternoon sun shining calm and bright on everything, and sending his kind rays upon the sorrowful little girl.

Meanwhile, Blanche had been trying to enjoy her canter. She went further on her homeward way than she intended; and Shag remonstrated not a little when his bridle-rein intimated that he must retrace his steps. "What! Shag, do you really mean to say that you've the heart to go home, and leave Morag all alone?" expostulated Blanche; and at last the wilful little Shetlander was brought to a better mind.

And now Blanche began to think of the troubles which she would have to face again; for she was a little person who could not be happy unless she was the best of friends with everybody round her, winning and bestowing smiles on all sides; and she felt that it was a very uncomfortable state of matters to have Morag walking beside her, so sad and silent. It did not occur to her that her friend's broken-hearted aspect was more than half her doing; for Blanche had yet to learn how much " evil is wrought by want of thought as well as want of heart." But when she felt herself in the wrong it was a much easier matter for her, than it is for some people, to seek forgiveness eagerly and graciously. All at once it dawned upon her that it was not quite kind to have brought Kirsty to talk to Morag, who seemed so anxious not to see the old woman. Perhaps, indeed, it might have been better not to have gone into the cottage at all; and certainly it had quite spoilt a pleasant afternoon. Thoroughly penitent, Blanche resolved that peace must be instantly proclaimed between her mountain friend and herself. She quickened Shag's pace, and swept suddenly round upon poor Morag, whom she found starting up from the heather with a tear-stained face. Blanche was at her side in a moment.

"O Morag, dear, I'm so sorry! It's all my fault. I've just been thinking I shouldn't have brought Kirsty to speak to you when you didn't want to see her. Miss Prosser says I'm so thoughtless, and, you see, it's quite true. Do say you forgive me, and don't cry any more, or I shall begin directly." And Blanche's eyes filled with tears as she threw her arm round the little brown neck, and looked into Morag's sorrowful face.

"It's no that I didna want to see Kirsty, but father bid me no speak til her,—niver, and I couldna' anger him. I would hae liket weel to gang inby, though," she added, in a mournful tone. Then Morag went on to tell, with much unconscious pathos in the narrative, of the romance which had grown up round Kirsty Macpherson and her pretty dwelling, of how long she had watched her from afar, often passing by that way, in order to catch a glimpse of the old woman among her flowers, till her father's in-

junction had made it an act of disobedience;
and since then she had tried very hard always
to look the other way. Blanche could not help
thinking, as she listened, how much more good
and obedient this little untaught maiden had
proved than she was likely to be in similar circumstances.

"But, Morag, I really can't think why your
father should forbid you to talk to Kirsty. I'm
sure she can't possibly be a bad old woman;"
and Blanche gave a glowing description of her
visit to the cottage, to which Morag listened
with eager interest.

Shag was taking advantage of the pause to
snap some delicious blades of grass on the roadside, as well as his mouthful of steel would permit, while Chance had drawn near to investi-
gate the reason of this objectionable halt, and
was captured by Blanche, who began to twine
a wreath of deer-horn moss round his reluctant
neck, as she talked.

"I'll tell you what you must do, Morag,"
she said presently, jumping to her feet with
energy, as if inspired by a new idea. "Tell
your father all about our stopping at Kirsty's
cottage,—how I would go to ask for some water
to drink, and how kind and nice she was to me;
and wanted to speak to you so much, if you

only might have spoken to her. And, by the by, she sent a message to your father—something about forgiving him, wasn't it? I couldn't understand her very well. Now, Morag, if you only tell your father the whole story, and coax him a little, you know, he will be sure to allow you to speak to her next time. I do want so much to go and see her another afternoon; but I shouldn't care to, if you didn't come with me."

Morag shook her head; she had not the same belief in her own coaxing powers as she had in the bonnie wee leddy's.

"I'll maybe try, but I'm thinkin' he'll no bear the soun' o' Kirsty's name," said Morag, in a desponding tone, as she rose to recapture the straying Shag. Then she reminded Blanche that they had still a long way to go, and pointed to the sun, which was fast westering; so the cavalcade moved on, and both the little hearts felt happier than they had before the halt.

Blanche felt certain that Morag's story would melt her father's prejudice, whatever it might arise from; and Morag, though less sanguine, began to be more hopeful, and listened with delighted smile to the castles in the air which her companion was building concerning a visit to the cottage; how they would tie Shag to a paling where he could find some nice grass, and deciding that Chance must really be left at home, being much too outrageous for a small room like Kirsty's. Besides, as Blanche thoughtfully suggested, she might very likely have a cat, in which case, Chance would be a most unwelcome guest, for his sentiments regarding cats were only too well known to his anxious mistress.

Morag was still very shy and timid, and it was only on rare occasions that even the little English maiden's pleasant prattle could put her at her ease. It was quite an effort for her still to make a remark or to ask a question; and now, as she nervously took hold of Shag's mane, Blanche felt sure that she wanted very much to say something which would come out presently. At last she asked, in quiet, eager tones, "Will ye be so kind as to tell me, leddy, what she would be sayin' about the good Lord? Is she weel acquaint wi' Him?"

"Oh! let me see. I forget exactly what she said. I think I said that I thought she must be very lonely, living there all by herself, and she said she would be if it were not for the Lord Jesus Christ—or something like that," replied Blanche, unable to give a sufficiently circumstantial account of that part of the interview to satisfy Morag, who remarked meditatively—

"I dinna' min' o' seein' nobody goin' intil the hoose, excep' auld Elspet Bruce. Will He be goin' to see her, whiles, when she's her lone, think ye, leddy?"

"Who do you mean? I never said anybody went to see her; she did not tell me so, you funny Morag," replied Blanche, looking puzzled.

"I jist thocht maybe He will be goin' inby, whiles, when she was terrible lonesome—the Lord Jesus, ye ken," stammered Morag.

"Why, Morag, what queer, odd ideas you do have! Nobody ever saw the Lord Jesus—at least not since He died and went to heaven,—and that's ever so far away beyond the sun, you know, so He couldn't possibly come back. I forget how far the nearest planet is from the earth. I had it in my astronomy lesson the other day only."

Morag relapsed into puzzled silence. She had not the remotest idea what astronomy was, and wondered if she should know about that too when she was able to read the Bible. After a little pause, she hazarded one remark more—

"But do ye no min', leddy, how we read

yestreen about the good Lord no restin' intil His grave, like other folk, and when the woman was cryin' there, how He came inby, and was terrible kind like ?"

"Oh yes," said Blanche, interrupting her; "of course 'He rose again the third day,'—the creed says so, you know. But indeed, Morag, He never comes and sees anybody now. I never heard of such a thing in my life. If I were to ask Miss Prosser, she would be sure to say, 'My dear, I'm shocked at your ignorance,' as she generally does when I ask questions." And Blanche sighed at the thought of her ignorance, which appeared so shocking to her governess in many instances.

They were coming near home now, and had reached the shady birk walk which led to the castle, when they heard through the trees Mr. Clifford's pleasant ringing tones, which Morag loved to listen to. " Well, pussy, what mischief have you been about this afternoon ? " he said, smilingly, as he lifted his little daughter from her pony.

" O papa ! I've so much to tell you. I have actually been inside Kirsty's cottage, and it looks quite as pretty inside as outside, and she's such a nice old woman," said Blanche, rapturously, forgetting that she had not introduced her new acquaintance.

"I fear I must confess shameful ignorance, Blanchie," replied her father, smiling. "Who is this Kirsty? and where does she abide—a friend of Morag's?"

And then Blanche remembered that was a question which might prove embarrassing, so she adroitly changed the subject.

"Oh, here comes Lucas for Shag. I know Morag wants to get home to make ready her father's supper," she continued, being quite at home now in all the domestic arrangements of the hut among the crags.

Morag seemed nothing loath to make her escape. She quickly resigned Shag's bridle to the old coachman and was turning to go, when Mr. Clifford, opening the luncheon basket, took a beautiful bunch of grapes, and handed them to her, saying, "Here, little black-eyes, take this to eat on the way home."

Morag lifted the dark fringes, and looked timidly up for a moment, then a pair of brown hands were held out to receive the purple cluster. The tartan skirt touched the ground in a low curtsey, and after a timid glance at her bonnie wee leddy, she walked slowly off, carefully balancing the gift in both hands.

"I hope she will eat them on the way home, and not keep them for her father," said Blanche, sighing, as she looked fondly after her little friend.

"Why, Blanche! you ungracious little person; do you really object to my gamekeeper having a share of all the good things going?" said Mr. Clifford.

"Yes indeed, I do, papa. I don't think the keeper can be a nice man at all. Only fancy, he has quarrelled with that nice old Kirsty, and has forbidden Morag to speak to her even; and she is such a good girl she will not do it, though she wanted to know Kirsty for ages."

"And so you are going to be a sort of damsel-errant, riding forth on Shag to redress all the wrongs and quarrels of the Glen," laughed Mr. Clifford, as he looked at Blanche's glowing face. "Depend upon it my keeper has some very good reason at his finger-ends for having quarrelled with this same Kirsty. Perhaps he found her poaching; who knows, Blanchie?"

"What's that, papa? But if it's anything wicked, I'm quite sure Kirsty would not do it. Is poaching wicked, papa; and what is it?"

"Just you ask the Major, pussy! Blanche has got a knotty question for you to solve, Seton," said Mr. Clifford, turning to one of his guests. "She wants to know if poaching is wicked!"

" But I want first to know what poaching is, because papa says that nice old woman Kirsty may have been poaching, and that is the reason why the keeper dislikes her so much," said Blanche eagerly, as she joined Major Seton.

"Ah! I see. You want to know what poaching is, and you reserve the right of deciding whether it is right or not. Very proper," said the old gentleman, as he looked kindly at the little eager face. " I'll tell you what game preservers call poaching; but, perhaps, if you were to ask your friend of the uncouth name, she might not give you exactly the same description of the word. You might find her sitting down to sup on a hare, which she caught in the act of dining off her nice trim row of cabbages—some of which she meant for her own dinner, probably, if the hare hadn't thought them good to eat. Perhaps she might invite you to join in her savory supper, and you might be sitting smacking your lips over it. But, suddenly, an official-looking individual might pop his head in at the door with a knowing look, and tapping your friend on the shoulder, say, in a stern voice, ' My good woman, you must come with me ; you've been poaching.' And if, in defence, you attempted to explain that the hare was treading down the trim gar-

den, and eating the cabbages when Kirsty caught
it, 'Just so, little girl,' the individual would
reply; 'I see you're in possession of the facts.
This woman is a poacher, and must be commit-
ted for trial. My prisoner,' he would say," and
the Major finished with a little tap on Blanche's
shoulder, which made her start as if the said
official were at her elbow.

"So that's what you call poaching?" she
said, with a long-drawn breath. "But, Major
Seton, how can anybody call it wicked to kill
a beast that is destroying one's garden when
gentlemen shoot them only for fun on the
hills?"

"So it may appear to our philosophical
minds, Blanchie; but I doubt whether your
papa and his gamekeeper will take quite the
same view of the matter. Clifford, your
daughter is dead set against the game-laws.
I haven't succeeded in making her view poaching in a criminal light. She's a born Radical,
I fear. You must take her in hand, and
teach her young idea how to shoot in a proper
Conservative direction," said the pleasant old
gentleman as he rolled away, but his love
for truth brought his portly figure rolling back
again the next minute. "I say, Blanchie, dear,
I'm afraid my parable was decidedly one-sided.

Remember that poachers are often no better than common thieves—stealing a gentleman's game as they might steal his watch or his umbrella, if they had the chance. So don't go romancing in your tender heart over the wrongs of poachers, little woman. They are often great rascals, I assure you."

"Well, I only hope papa won't ever put a nice old woman into prison for catching a creature that was spoiling her pretty garden. But do you know, Major Seton," added Blanche, in a confidential tone, "I don't like Dingwall. I think he could be very cruel and unkind. He has got such cruel eyes— not a bit like Morag's. I don't like him at all."

"Why, what a prejudiced little puss it is, to be sure. What ails you at the keeper? Is it a case of the unfortunate typical Doctor Fell, I wonder?" But just then Blanche was summoned to tea, and the reason, if she had one, of her dislike to the keen-eyed keeper was not forthcoming.

VII

MORAG'S VISIT TO KIRSTY, AND HOW IT CAME ABOUT.

IT was the Sabbath-day. Glen Eagle was, if possible, stiller than its wont—no shepherd shouted upon the mountains; no reapers stood among the upland, half-shorn fields; the moor-fowl had peace that day among the heather, unmolested by dog or gun. The white, motionless clouds on the deep blue sky, as well as the lower landscape, seemed pervaded by that peculiar stillness which Morag always noticed belonged to this day, though it brought to her no sound of church bells, inviting her to mingle her worship with the congregation. Sunday was always a very lonely day in the little eyrie among the mountains, and during these past weeks they had seemed specially empty and solitary to the little Morag. For then there were no rambles with the bonnie wee leddy—indeed she seldom saw her on these days, except she chanced to catch a glimpse of her from afar, as she was driven past in an open carriage, embedded in furs and dazzling with bright colors. But the little gloved hand would always emerge from the furs in friendly salute if Morag was in view, and the blue eyes look kindly, and often longingly, down on the little mountain maiden, who would stand watching the shining carriage as it swept swiftly along the winding road, and listening to Blanche's silvery laugh as it echoed among the silent hills.

But on this Sunday morning Morag did not wander down the hill, as usual, when her work was done, in the hope of catching a glimpse of the people from the castle. She sat very disconsolately on the turf in front of the hut, watching her father as he went down the hill toward the kennels.

The keeper had gone to loose the dogs, to take them for a long walk, which he always did on Sunday. He was not a frequenter of the little kirk in the village, and somewhat disliked the cessation from his ordinary work which the day of rest imposed. This morning he had gone off in one of his darkest moods. Morag was used to his periods of grim silence; but, of this one, she thought that she could trace the cause, and she pondered ruefully over the utter failure of the wee leddy's sanguine plan for softening the keeper's heart towards Kirsty. The story of the visit to the cottage, and her share in it, had been narrated on the previous evening to her father without any other result than a bitter sneer, as he said, "Ye did weel, Morag, my lass, no to darken Kirsty Macpherson's door; and gin ye be yer ain frien', ye'll jist better keep that chatterin' bit leddy outby."

Morag felt as if she had received a blow, but there still remained one other arrow in her quiver, and she drew it at a venture. "But, father, though I didna speak wi' Kirsty, I couldna shut my ears when she was speakin', ye see. I hae a bit o' a message for ye frae her—I'm thinkin' I min' upon ilka word that she said—this was it: 'Will ye tell Alaster Dingwall that auld Kirsty is willin' to forgie him?' There was some more I'm thinkin', but I didna hear right," she added in low, troubled tones, lowering her eyelashes, and not daring to look into her father's face.

He was smoking his pipe at the time, and he sat gazing gloomily into the red embers on the hearth till he had finished. Morag knew that he had come in for the night, so she was not a little surprised to see him refill his pipe again and prepare to go out; but he gave no explanation, so she did not venture to ask any questions. It was a fine moonlight night; Morag came to the door of the hut, and stood watching him as he sauntered slowly down the hill, and went in the direction of a larch plantation, some distance off, which looked pale and shadowy in the clear shimmering light, with its background of dark fir-trees that stretched beyond.

These larches were young seventeen years ago, when Dingwall had known the place well; and a crowd of strange memories, conjured up by Morag's random shot, drew him towards it to-night. The little girl had sat watching and waiting by the whitening peat embers till she grew very sleepy; and before her father returned from his night walk, she crept away to bed.

So this bright Sunday morning opened very gloomily for the inmates of the hut among the crags. Morag had taken the old Bible from the depths of the *kist*, and it lay open before her on the turf, but somehow to-day she felt disinclined for the slow spelling of the words, and rather disheartened with her progress generally. She began to fear that her eye would never be able to go swiftly down the pages, understanding every word like her little teacher, or as Blanche had said, Kirsty was able to do; and then her thoughts went back to the events of yesterday. How sorry the wee leddy would be to hear of the plan for melting the keeper's prejudice, and perhaps she might be angry and call her rude again the next time she refused to go into the cottage. It all seemed very hard, Morag thought; and, as she sat gazing up into the calm sky with its motionless clouds, she could not help thinking how very far away it seemed from her and her troubled ways. Presently these sad meditations were interrupted by the reappearance of her father, who, to her great surprise, seemed to be coming up the hill again, with the dogs all scrambling round him. He had only been gone a few minutes, and it was his custom to take a long walk, so Morag wondered what could have brought him back, but she did not venture to ask any questions. He seated himself on the turf beside her, and after playing with the dogs for a little, he glanced at her with a half smile, and said, hurriedly—

"Weel, Morag, lass, is yer heid as sair turned as iver aboot that auld Kirsty Macpherson?"

"She looks a real nice old woman, father. I canna think why ye'll no let me speak wi' the like o' her. She surely canna be an ill woman, as ye think," returned Morag, emboldened by the smile on her father's face.

"Wha ever said she was an ill woman?" said the keeper, looking dark again, and ignoring all the bitter things which Morag had often heard him say concerning Kirsty. "We did ance quarrel, but I'll no say I wasna maist to blame. Gin Kirsty Macpherson speaks a ceevil word to ye agin, ye needna jist athegither haud yer tongue, lass. D'ye understand, Morag?" asked the keeper, getting up from the turf as if he had said what was on his mind.

Morag could hardly believe her ears. She sat watching her father go down the hill again, as if she were in a dream. Presently an idea seemed to seize her, and she bounded off after him, and all trembling with eagerness, she said—

"Father, I'm feert Kirsty will be thinkin' me terrible rude for no speakin' yestreen. Would it anger ye if I jist ran past the cottage to see if she was outby? I needna speak gin she doesna, ye ken."

"Oh ay; ye can gang if ye like, lass. I'm thinkin' that Kirsty is atween ye and yer wits,

Morag," he added, smiling at the earnest face. " Jist tak' a brace or twa o' the grouse hangin' there wi' ye. The auld wife will think mair o' them than us." .

. Morag was bounding back to the hut in wild delight, when her father called again, " Bide a wee, lass. Ye mustna tak' the birds. I dinna think she would athegither like sic a present frae me."

Morag stood rather discomfited. The idea of a peace-offering had been very pleasant, and it was disappointing to be obliged to abandon it. She suddenly remembered the purple cluster of grapes which Mr. Clifford gave to her the day before. She had hidden it away as a delightful surprise for her father, during some period of to-day, and she said, doubtfully—

" I was keepin' some bonnie berries for ye that the maister gied me yestreen ; but maybe ye wouldna min' if I gied them to Kirsty ? "

" That'll do fine, my lass," cried Dingwall, in his most good-humored tone, as he disappeared down the hill, surrounded by the scrambling pointers and setters.

In a very short time after, Morag might have been seen hovering near the little gate of Kirsty's cottage, with her peace-offering carefully balanced in her little brown hands. A few of the precious moments previous to setting out had been spent in performing a most careful toilette, and the opinion of a broken corner of the looking-glass was that the black locks had never looked so smooth and sleek before. Having scampered down the hill in a state of breathless excitement, she did not at first contemplate the bold step of entering the sacred precincts and knocking at Kirsty's door, as the wee leddy had done. She quite counted on seeing her "outby" somewhere, and she hung about on the roadside in that hope, but no Kirsty appeared. Then Morag remembered that it was Sunday, and she began to fear that the old woman might have gone to the kirk. The little girl felt bitterly disappointed; for she felt sure that this must be the case, since Kirsty was not visible anywhere, and no smoke came from the tiny chimney of the cottage. If she lost this opportunity, she might never have such another. What if her father changed his mind again? she thought. Indeed it seemed hardly possible to believe that she was here with his permission when she remembered his stern command on the previous evenings that she was never to darken Kirsty's door. At last, with exhausted

patience, she resolved to take the bold step of
entering the little gate and tapping at the door,
for had she not a peace-offering ?—and it was
just possible that Kirsty might not have gone
to the kirk after all.

Many a time in after years Morag Dingwall
remembered that first knocking at Kirsty's door
on the still Sunday morning, and smiled a quiet,
thankful smile as the vision of the eager, breathless little girl, standing on the threshold of Life,
rose before her in the shadowy distance of the
Past.

The outer door stood open, but nobody
answered the knock, though Morag fancied
that she heard some movement within. The
doors of both *but* and *ben* were closed, but she
ventured to knock again, and this time a voice,
which seemed to sound feebler than the old
woman's did on the previous day, called " Come
ben."

Morag obeyed the call, and at last stood inside the pretty cottage which she had so longed
to see. The room looked as pretty as the wee
leddy had described it, but the arm-chair at the
ingle-neuk was empty, and there was not the
faintest glow among the white peat embers on
the hearth. The little girl looked round in
dumb surprise, but presently a voice came from

the bed in the dark-panelled wall, " Eh, lassie, but is this you ? Ye're the keeper Dingwall's bairn 'at I saw yestreen—arna ye ?" and Kirsty raised herself in bed, and holding out her hand, smiled kindly on the little Morag.

"Are ye no weel, Kirsty?" she asked, in low, sympathizing tones, as she drew near the bed.

"I'm nae jist verra weel the day. I had a bit blastie i' the nicht. 'Deed, bairn, I some thocht He was ga'en to tak' me hame til Himsel. An' fat's brocht ye here the day, my lassie?" said Kirsty, turning kindly to the shy little Morag, as she held her hand in her long thin fingers.

"I brought ye some bonnie berries the castle folk gied me yestreen. Maybe ye'll tak' some," said the little girl, as she lifted the grapes from the table where she had laid them, and put them on the bed.

" Eh, bairn ! but that was terrible mindfu' o' ye. They're richt bonnie graps, and will cool my mou'. 'Deed, they'll be the first thing I hae tasted the day." Morag felt immensely gratified when Kirsty plucked a grape from the purple cluster and put it into her parched mouth. She was now seated at Kirsty's bedside, by her invitation, and began, already, to feel quite happy and at home in this enchanted interior of her dreams.

"I'm richt glaid to see ye, Morag," said the old woman, smiling kindly on her. "The sicht o' a blythe young face does a body guid—and it's a rare ane to me, sin' mony a lang year," she said, sadly; and then, brightening, she added, "But we canna say we're unca lonesome, when we can hae a sicht o' His ain face, gin we lat Him in. Eh, bairn; but He's aye keepit His word wi' me. 'I'll no leave ye comfortless, I will come to ye,'" said Kirsty, as she closed her eyes and laid her head on her pillow again.

"Ye'll be meanin' the Lord Jesus, arna ye, Kirsty?" asked Morag, her face all quivering with eagerness. "Then He does come, efter a'?" she added, triumphantly. "The wee leddy o' the castle said how it wasna possible. I would like richt weel to see Him, mysel. He maun aye come i' the nicht, surely, for I'll whiles be passin' o' this road, and I never saw Him goin' inby."

Kirsty looked at the eager, young face, with a shade of perplexity in her calm, gray eyes. Morag noticed it, and felt a chill, but she would not give it up yet. "It will be the Lord Jesus who comes cheerin' ye when ye're feelin' some lonesome like, isna it, Kirsty?"

"Ay is't, my bairn. And He's willin' to come til ye, just the same. It's ane o' His ain sweetest words, 'Suffer the children to come.'"

"But Miss Blanche says naebody iver saw Him, and that He doesna go aboot healin' and comfortin' folk, as He did lang syne. I dinna understan' it richt; for just the ither day she read til me i' the fir-wood that He cam' oot o' His grave efter wicked folk killed Him deid on the green hill, and was speakin' real kind to the woman that was cryin' inby there. I would like weel to see Him, Kirsty. I dinna think I would be feert."

"Eh, my bairn, but I see fat ye would be at, noo. But ye're jist for a' the earth like the onbelievin' Thamas, that wouldna rest satisfeid till he pit his fingers intil His maister's verra side. We mauna forget that He says Himsel, 'Blessed are they who dinna see, and yet believe.'"

Kirsty's Biblical illustration was too much advanced to suit the little untaught maiden, but she gathered enough from it to begin to fear that the wee leddy must be right after all, and presently she said, in a mournful tone—

"Then, Kirsty, it's true that we canna see His face nor hear Him speakin' no more at all?"

"No wi' the eye o' sense, my bairn. 'The warl seeth me nae mair; but ye see me,' He says Himsel', and He aye keeps His word. Jist ye get a sight o' Him wi' the eye o' faith, bairn, and it will mak' ye rejoice and be glaid a' yer days;" and the old woman turned with a radiant smile to the little girl, who sat gazing wistfully, with folded hands.

It was evident that this good Lord was a real present person to Kirsty, however shadowy might be the conception which Morag could at present form of Him. But to understand in any degree that He was a real, present friend, though unseen, was more than Morag could know, just then.

The yellow autumn sun came streaming in at the little window, and shone on Kirsty's face, showing how wan and wearied it was after her sleepless night. Morag was full of motherly, ministering instincts, and it made her little heart ache to see the kind old woman look so ill and feeble. Glancing at the cold hearth, she remembered, wondering how she could have been so long of thinking about it, that Kirsty could not have had any breakfast yet, and must be cold and faint for want of it.

"Wouldna ye be better wi' a cup o' tea, Kirsty? I'll jist licht a bit fire, and be puttin the kettle on," said Morag, as she rose and began to break some dead branches which Kirsty's careful fingers had gathered in the gloaming on the evening before.

"'Deed, bairn, I would tak' it richt kin' o' ye," replied Kirsty, who had always the good grace to receive a favor simply.

The branches soon began to crackle merrily, the peats caught the glow, and the kettle commenced to sing in the midst of the cheerful blaze. Morag moved quietly about, filled with contentment that she was able to be of use to Kirsty. She had shut her eyes, and was lying quietly, so Morag did not trouble her with questions, but seemed to know by instinct where all the component parts of a cup of tea were to be gathered. When Kirsty opened her eyes again, it was to see the little maiden standing by her bedside with the restoring beverage all ready, and a bit of beautiful toasted bread into the bargain.

"Eh, but it's unca kin' to be comin' ministerin' til an auld body like me," said the old woman, as she sat up in bed. "But winna yer faither be wonderin' what's come ower ye? ye mauna anger him, ye ken."

"Wha wad hae thocht that Alaster Ding wall's bairn would be makin' a cup o' tay til

auld Kirsty?" continued the old woman in a
soliloquy, as Morag washed the cup and plate
when she had finished her breakfast, and re-
placed them among the rows of shining delf.
How very clean and pretty they looked, Morag
thought; and she resolved that she would immediately arrange the slender stock of unbroken
dishes belonging to the hut after the same
fashion, and make them look bright and shining
too. Then she proceeded to build up the fire
with skilful fingers, and surveyed the room,
with a thoughtful air, to see what the possible
wants for the day might be. The pitcher
which held the supply of water was almost
empty, so Morag ran quickly down to the
spring under the tree, and brought it back re-
filled, and then she poured some into a cup and
set it by Kirsty's bed. "Thank ye kindly,
bairn. The Lord reward ye for yer helpin' o'
an auld frail craeter. Afore ye gang, wad ye
jist rax me that Bible, an' maybe ye wad read
a bittie til me; my eyes are some dim the
day?"

"I would be richt glaid to read to ye,
Kirsty, but I canna read ony," replied Morag,
sadly, with an ashamed look; and then she
added, "the wee leddy's been tryin' to learn
me, though, and maybe I'll be fit to read to ye

some day, but it'll no be for a lang time yet, I'm thinkin'."

"Eh, my puir bairn, I never thocht but ye could read. 'Deed it was ill dune o' the keeper nae to sen' ye til the schule," remarked Kirsty, in a more severe tone than she generally used.

"How could he sen' me til the schule, and it such a lang road frae this,—and him aye needin' me forby," replied Morag, kindling up in her absent parent's defence.

"Weel, weel, bairn ; maybe I shouldna hae been judgin'. We're a' ready eneuf at that. But gin ye'll come to see me, whiles, when I'm a bit stronger like, I'll gie ye a' the help wi' the reading 'at I can. I've a gey curran buiks there."

"I'll be real glaid to come back and see ye, and I'm thinkin' father will no hinder me, noo. I maun be goin' hame, but I'll try and get back the morn, to speir how ye're keepin'. I'm real sorry to leave ye yer lone, Kirsty," said Morag, pityingly, as she glanced at the lonely, frail old woman. Then she remembered what Kirsty said about not being lonesome when the Lord Jesus was with her, and she added, " I'm thinkin' when I'm awa, ye'll jist be speakin' til Him—the good Lord, ye ken."

"Aye, that will I my bairn; an' I houp ye'll learn to speak wi' Him yersel. It's His ain blessed Word, that them that hungers efter Him will be filled. 'Deed but I'm richt glad ye're ta'en up aboot Him, Morag. There's whiles He stands at the door o' bairns' hairts and knocks, and they winna lat Him in; but tak' their ain foolish, sorrowfu' gait. Keep on seekin' Him, and ye'll surely get a sicht o' His face or lang. It's jist as plain as gin ye saw Himsel' i' the body, like the woman at His grave. Now, bairn, ye mauna bide a minute langer. Yer faither will be wonderin' what's come ower ye," said Kirsty, looking uneasily at Morag, who had seated herself again, and seemed inclined to linger. "Tak' this bonnie word wi' ye oot o' His ain Beuk," she added, smiling on the little, grave, perplexed face that looked into hers. "'Them 'at seek me early shall fin' me.' Good-day, Morag, and haste ye back."

Morag was soon crossing the breezy heather road on her way home, with a very happy heart, only disturbed by a slight feeling of anxiety lest her father should have relapsed into his old state of feeling towards Kirsty, and she should be hindered from another visit to the cottage.

VIII

THE GYPSIES AT LAST.

ONE pleasant day, when the woods and hills of Glen Eagle were lying in the yellow afternoon sunshine, Morag and Blanche wandered into their old trysting-place, the fir-wood, which they had rather deserted of late.

The precious holiday afternoons had most frequently been spent in the *ben-end* of Kirsty's cottage, and a staunch friendship had sprung up between the old woman and the little girls. These visits had become a great and daily happiness to Morag. Kirsty's illness lasted for some time, and Morag often thought that but for it she should never have felt so much at home in the cottage, which she had so long watched from afar with a mingled feeling of curiosity and dislike; and now she knew every stone and cupboard of it by heart. For had she not helped Kirsty on her recovery to make a thorough cleaning of both *but* and *ben*, for which the old woman's active fingers had longed, as soon as she was "to the fore" again. Already, the little untaught maiden had learnt from her old friend many useful household arts and wise maxims, and the keeper's home began to bear traces of Kirsty's thrifty ways and cleanly habits. Every morning during the old woman's illness, Morag had started for the cottage after her own work was done, taking the short cut through the heather, and gathering, as she went, a little bundle of sticks for the fire-lighting. Then, after Kirsty's morning wants were supplied—and she was not an exacting invalid—Morag would take her seat on a little low wooden stool which Kirsty named "Thrummy," from its being covered with shreds of cloth fastened to the wood. It was made by her long ago for a vanished child, who once had been the light of that now lonely home. Morag often sat on it in these days, listening with eager, upturned face to Kirsty's solemn reading of the book she loved. Her rough northern tongue sounded very different from the silvery flow of the little English lady; but Morag felt that the words which she heard in the cottage were no mere tale to Kirsty, "no vain thing, but her life."

Slowly, the words of Jesus began to sink into the little girl's heart, and gradually she came to understand, after the first chill of disappointment was past, that though the earthly voice of the Son of Man was heard no longer, nor His ministering touch felt among the people, as it used to be in those early days of which the Gospels told, yet He was still the loving, listening Helper of all who came to Him. Kirsty's belief that He was not dead, nor very far away, but a very present Friend to be listened to and spoken to at all times with a certainty that He would both hear and help, had in some degree penetrated Morag's soul; and she, too, ventured to bring her little cares and troubles to this new-found Friend, and had already a spiritual record of help given and difficulties met in the name and strength of Jesus.

And so it happened that Kirsty's cottage became quite a rival to the fir-wood, which seemed to Morag like a dearly-loved, but neglected friend, as she trod among the soft moss and brown fir-needles on this afternoon. After visiting a few of the historical spots sacred to the memory of the first days of their acquaintance, Blanche proposed that they should make an exploring tour to a part of the forest which she had never visited; and the little girls made their way through the fir-trees to where the shadows were darkest, and the arching green boughs almost shut out the day. Blanche was gay and talkative as usual, dancing hither and thither, singing snatches of songs, and making the great aisles of pine re-echo with her laughter and fun. She kept stopping as usual to gather various treasures from the great floor of the forest—"specimens," she called them; but it is to be feared that they never reached a calm state of museum classification. Blanche meant that these "specimens" should travel to London with her—and stowed them away in corners of her room with that intention, though her design was frustrated in most cases, however, by their being deposited in the dust-bin by Ellis, while she remarked to cook that she "never did see the like of missy for fillin' her room with rubbage of all kinds."

Chance had chosen to remain at home on this afternoon, notwithstanding Blanche's pressing invitation that he should accompany them. He had replied to it by shaking his head, knowingly, as if to say, "No, no, my little mistress, I'm not going to be taken in. Shag is not going, I see; so you are only going to loiter about in an aimless manner, and I should certainly be bored. Much nicer here," he thought, as he stretched himself lazily on the warm stones of the old court-yard, where the sun was striking, and snapped at a fly,—pretending to look the other way when Blanche made her final appeal to his honor and conscience. Perhaps he felt a few twinges of remorse at having so determinately chosen to neglect his duty, for he rose presently and stood looking after the girls as they disappeared among the birk-trees; but he did not repent, evidently, for he went and lay down again, deciding that there was no use of a fellow putting himself about for two silly little girls on a hot afternoon like this.

Morag and Blanche wandered into the forest till they reached the old road skirted by a low, lichen-spotted wall, which was the entrance to the glen, and divided the forest. And now Morag's clock—the afternoon sun—told her that it was more than time for them to be turning their steps in a homeward direction,—especially since, that very afternoon, before they started, she had received strict injunctions from Miss Prosser to see that her charge was not again late for tea, since the flight of time seemed to pass quite unnoticed by Miss Clifford. It was by no means an easy matter to be time-keeper to such an inconsequent young lady as Blanche, who never realized the unpleasantness of being late till she was brought face to face with Miss Prosser. She was now wandering about in all directions, adding to her lapful of gatherings, and talking pleasant nonsense, while Morag's rare laugh was sometimes heard joining in her merriment.

At last they started on their homeward way, and Morag was congratulating herself that she would be able to present her erratic wee leddy in time for tea, when Blanche noticed a plantation of larches, which looked so pretty and feathery through the dark firs that she thought she should like to inspect them more closely, and coaxed Morag to come on with her.

An old grey dyke separated the fir forest from the larches. The girls followed its windings for a little, and presently Blanche climbed across the loose stones, and went a little way into the larch plantation to explore. Morag felt impatient to proceed, and walked on to try and discover which would be the most direct route home through the firs. Presently she heard a sound, which her accustomed ear detected as an unusual one in that silent sanctuary of hers. She hastily turned a sharp corner to see what the next winding of the dyke would disclose, and, in doing so, she almost ran up again a sort of tent. It was a very rude erection, and consisted of a few large branches which had been driven loosely into the ground, and partly rested against the old wall for support. A tarpauling was thrown over them, but it was evidently too small to cover the abode, and was supplemented by a tartan plaid, which hung across the front stakes, so that no entrance was visible. This was not Nature's doing, evidently, and Morag was seized with a great panic when she saw the unexpected human habitation. She had heard wild stories of terrible deeds done on lonely moors and in lonely woods, and felt more frightened than she had ever done in her life when she thought how far they were from home, and that the precious wee leddy was unprotected, save by her. However, she saw no terrific personage as yet, and she began to hope that the inmates of the tent might be from home. But there was that sound again, and this time it seemed like the moaning of a voice in pain. Morag felt that safety lay in immediate flight, and she quietly turned to meet Blanche, and to make a sign of silence. But, before she had time to do so, the wee leddy's voice rang out in gleeful tones, concerning the varied delights of the larch plantation, which the dwellers under the tartan could not fail to hear. Whenever Blanche caught a glimpse of Morag's startled face, she knew that there must be something very far wrong, and she stood looking at her in questioning silence. Presently, a rustling sound made them both turn, and Blanche's eye caught sight of the rude tent. For a moment she stood riveted gazing at it, while Ellis's stories and prophecies concerning the gypsies chased each other through her mind, and she thought with terror that they had all come true at last.

Presently there was a fluttering of the tartan awning, and a hand appeared among its fringes, as if to make a passage out.

Blanche's face grew white with fear, and she clutched Morag's arm with a scream of terror. The little mountain maiden kept quite silent, though her face looked as terror-stricken as that of her companion. Seizing Blanche's arm, she began to pull her along, running as nearly as possible in a homeward direction. On they galloped, breathless and speechless ; but the fir needles were slippery, and the trees were in the way.

At last Morag felt that the wee leddy's steps were beginning to flag ; and, worse than all, she fancied that she heard footsteps behind. It was a terrible effort, but the suspense began to be insupportable, and without slackening her pace she turned to look. There, sure enough, was a man behind them, gaining ground upon them very fast, too. Poor Blanche kept up bravely in the race for a while, but now she began to fail. First, her hat fell off, and even Morag did not venture to turn to pick it up; then her lapful of gatherings dropped one by one, tripping her as they fell; finally she stumbled, and the golden crown was down, down among the fir-needles, and the tears were falling fast. No entreaties of Morag's could persuade her to move, and the footsteps of the pursuer sounded nearer every minute. The little mountaineer could have outrun almost anybody, but she never dreamt of leaving Blanche; and now she seated herself quietly beside her bonnie wee leddy, determined to protect her to the death. In her distress she cried to the unseen, listening Friend, whom in these last days she had been learning to know: "O Lord Jesus, dinna let the gypsies get hand o' us; and may no ill come ower the bonnie wee leddy here," she added as she seized her hand, and made a last effort to rouse her to run again. She knew that the pursuer, whoever he might be, must be close at hand now, but she did not dare to look back. Blanche at last raised her head, and now, for the first time, she heard the sound of the footsteps behind. With a shriek of terror she rose to run again; Morag followed, but this time she did not feel quite so frightened, somehow, as she had done before, and, at last, a sudden impulse caused her to turn round to face her pursuer, and await her fate.

Hurrying through the fir trees, she saw, not a terrific-looking gypsy, but a pale, slender boy, with a gentle-looking face, considerably taller than herself. He was signing to her, and called something when he saw her turn round at last. Morag's terror began to abate in some degree, and the boy presently joined her, breathless after his chase, and rather frightened-looking also. He was holding Blanche's hat in his hand, which he shyly restored to Morag. "She dropt it," he said, pointing to Blanche, who still continued to run at full speed without turning to look. The restoration of the dropped hat looked promising; Morag began to feel reassured, and at the same time rather ashamed of herself.

"Will you be so kind as tell me where I can find some water?" asked the boy in a quiet tone; "we are strangers, and mother is very sick;" and his voice faltered.

Morag's little motherly heart was melted in an instant. "I'm real sorry yer mother's no weel," she replied in sympathizing tones. "I'll maybe find a drop o' water for ye, but it's some far frae here. The wee leddy and me were terribly frightened, and we couldna jist help runnin'," she added apologetically.

Blanche had halted in her flight, not hearing Morag's step behind, and her astonishment was as great as her terror had been the previous moment when she turned and saw Morag calmly engaged in conversation with the object of their fear. She did not venture to join them; but a feeling of curiosity, which is a great dispeller of fear, took possession of her, and she stood waiting breathlessly to see what was going to happen next.

Presently Morag came running to her to explain and consult. The lad slowly followed, looking rather more abashed than before, when he saw Blanche. He turned to Morag again and said, eagerly, "Will you not come and see my mother? I think it might cheer her to see you. We have come a long way, and the water is done, and she is so tired and thirsty. I'm afraid she is very ill—she says she's dying." It was a fine manly face; but the gray eyes filled with tears as he looked imploringly, first at one and then at the other of the little girls.

"Oh yes, certainly; we shall be glad to go and see your mother. I do hope she is not so very ill. And, of course, we must find some water, though we have to go right home for it, Morag," said the impulsive little Blanche, every trace of her former fear having vanished in a moment. "You must have thought it very queer of Morag and me to run away as we did. But, indeed, we were dreadfully frightened, and quite thought you were dangerous gypsies, you know."

The boy's face flushed, but he made no reply. Meanwhile, Morag was silently planning what would be the best thing to do. It was now more than time that Blanche should have returned to the castle, and yet here was an appeal which it would require a harder heart than Morag's to resist.

"Of course we must help him, Morag," whispered Blanche, noticing her hesitation. "Don't you see how sad he is about his sick mother? I really don't think there could be any harm in going to see her. He seems so very anxious. Come, let's go for one minute."

And so they turned to retrace their steps

along the path over which they had hurried in such terror a few minutes before, with their dreaded pursuer walking calmly and inoffensively by their side.

When they reached the tent, Morag recognized the moaning voice which had at first roused her alarm. The boy drew aside the tartan folds and stepped in before them, and presently they heard a feeble voice say, "Kenneth! Kenneth! you've been long away. Don't leave me, my boy—it won't be long now you'll have to stay. I would like to have lived to see her, though. We must surely be near the place now. The last milestone said three miles from the kirk town of Glen Eagle, didn't it? The Highlander said she was still alive, you know. You'll seek her out when I'm gone—she's good and kind, he always said. Bring her here, and she'll help you with everything there will be to do—after I'm gone. I would fain have seen her once before I died, though; but you'll tell her I have gone to meet her long lost Kenneth, who is safe in the happy home of God. You will follow Jesus, and He will lead you safe home, my boy."

Morag had been listening intently to the feeble, broken sentences, and now she could

hear that Kenneth gave a great sob, as he said,
'O mother! don't speak like that! I'm sure
you'll feel better again, when we find grandmother. You've often been nearly as ill before.
There's a nice little girl I met in the wood,
going to try to get some water, and maybe
you'll be better after you get a drink."

"A girl did you say, Kenny? where is
she?" asked the sick woman, turning restlessly
about.

Kenneth drew aside the tartan screen, and
beckoned to Morag, who stepped in softly, followed by Blanche.

In a corner of the tent, on some loose straw,
lay the dying woman, with her head resting on
one of the lichen-spotted stones of the old dyke.
She turned her large, bright, restless eyes on
the little girls as they entered the tent. Raising herself a little, so that she might see the
strangers, she said, in a feeble, though excited
tone, "I'm very ill, you see. I've come a long,
long way to die in this lonely forest. I didn't
think once that I should end my days like
this." A fit of coughing came on, and after it
was over she lay back exhausted.

Blanche had never seen anybody very ill
before, and she felt rather afraid of the bright,
hollow eyes and the strange sound of the short,

gasping breath, and was much relieved when Morag stepped forward and put her little brown hand into the white, wasted fingers. The little girl could not think of anything to say, but she stood, with a pitying look, holding. the hand of the sick woman, who seemed pleased, and smiled kindly on her. Suddenly she seemed to recollect something, and starting up, she asked Morag, in an eager tone, "Can you tell me where Glen Eagle is? it surely can't be far from here;" and before Morag had time to reply, she added, "Did you ever hear of a Mrs. Macpherson who lives near there, in a little cottage all alone?"

Morag pondered for a moment, and then, turning to Blanche, she said, " Will that no be Kirsty?"

" Yes, yes; it is Kirsty! Christian was her name. He used to say they called her Kirsty," exclaimed the sick woman, eagerly.

Kenneth had been mending a fire which he had kindled between two of the loose stones. As he got up from his knees to listen, a ray of hope flitted across his pale, anxious face.

"Oh, we know Kirsty perfectly well!" burst in Blanche, glad to be able to say something pleasant. "Morag and I go to see her almost every day. She is such a nice old woman, and lives in such a pretty cottage!"

"Do you think you could bring her here to see me?" said the sick woman, entreatingly. "I do so want to see her once before I die."

Morag glanced doubtfully at Blanche. "It's no jist terrible far frae here til Kirsty's cottage; but she hasna been weel, and it's a lang road for her to come, I'm thinkin'. But I wouldna be long o' runnin' to see."

"God be thanked. He has granted me the desire of my heart," said the dying woman, clasping her hands. "The Lord reward you, child. Tell Christian Macpherson that her Kenneth's wife is lying dying here, and wants to see her—to come soon—soon," and she sank back, exhausted with the effort of speaking.

"We had better start at once, Morag," whispered Blanche, eagerly. "I do hope Kirsty will be able to come. It is certainly very far for her to walk. Never mind me, Morag," she added, seeing her friend look perplexed as to the best course of action. "Of course I shall be hopelessly late; but I'll tell papa all about it, and I'm sure he won't be angry. He will have come from the moors, I daresay, by the time we get home."

"I'm so thirsty; do you think you could

find me some water? It might keep me up till she comes," said the woman, turning wearily to Morag.

And then a new difficulty arose; for the nearest spring was quite half-way to Kirsty's cottage, and Morag foresaw that there could not possibly be time before dark to fetch the supply of water, and bring Kirsty too; and Kenneth could not go, for the poor woman was evidently too ill to be left alone.

"I'll tell you what we must do," said Blanche, quickly perceiving the difficulty. "I can't go to Kirsty's, because I shouldn't know the way through the wood, you see! But I can stay with your mother," continued Blanche, turning to Kenneth, and trying hard to look as if she were making an ordinary arrangement, she added; "and you can go with Morag and fetch the water, while she goes on to the cottage."

It was certainly a great effort for Blanche to make this proposal, but she was very anxious to be brave and helpful in the midst of this sad scene, and she insisted on its being carried out, though Morag felt very doubtful as to the propriety of leaving her bonnie wee leddy all alone there. Still there seemed no help for it, so she consented at last, and was soon hurrying towards the spring with Kenneth. They walked along the narrow path through the forest for a long time without breaking the silence. At last Kenneth said in a stammering tone, "You've been very kind to us, strangers; I'll never forget it, and I'm sure mother won't. I think she'll be all right again when she has seen grandmother. She has been fretting so about finding her."

"Is Kirsty Macpherson your grandmother?" said Morag in a surprised tone, raising her downcast eyes, and looking at Kenneth. "She never telt me about ye," she added, musingly.

They had now reached the spring, and Kenneth having quickly filled his pitcher, and looking gratefully at Morag, turned to retrace his steps in the direction of the tent.

The little girl ran on eagerly, more anxious than ever to fulfil her mission. Emerging from the forest at last, she crossed a small hillock, and came down at the back of Kirsty's cottage. She found the old woman seated at the door, knitting busily, as she watched the sunset. The amber clouds were beginning to gather round the dying sun, and Kirsty sat watching the cloudland scene with a far-away look in her tranquil gray eyes.

"Na! but is this you, my dawtie? I'm

richt glad to see ye. I some thocht ye might be the nicht; but how cam' ye roun' by the back o' the hoose?" asked Kirsty, smiling as she welcomed her little friend, when she appeared round the gable of the cottage.

Instead of answering her question, Morag asked, hurriedly, "Kirsty, will ye be fit for a good bit o' a walk the nicht, think ye?"

"Weel, bairn, I wouldna min' a bittie, in this bonnie gloamin'; but I'll no say I'll gang sae fast or sae far as I ance could hae done," replied the old woman, smiling at Morag's breathless eagerness.

"D'ye think ye could gang as far as the other end o' the fir-wood, Kirsty?"

"Na, bairn; but I'm thinkin' ye're makin' a fule o' me the nicht. Ye ken brawly I hinna gaen that length this mony a day," said Kirsty, looking up with a shade of irritation in her calm face at the thoughtlessness of her usually considerate little friend.

"Weel, Kirsty, I'm thinkin' ye'll need to try it the nicht. There's somebody lyin' there that's terrible anxious to see ye." Morag's voice trembled, as she continued, "I've a message for ye, Kirsty. Your ain lost Kenneth's wife is lyin' i' the firwood, and wants to see ye afore she dees!"

For a moment Kirsty looked bewildered; but there' was no mistaking the slowly spoken words of the message. Presently she held. out her hand to Morag to help her from her low seat, with a sigh; and, leaning against the door, she stood thinking. Her usually calm eyes looked hungrily at the little .messenger, and her voice sounded faint and hollow as she asked, "Is he there himsel?" And then she added, shaking her head, mournfully, "Na, it couldna be; he would hae come til his mither surely."

"There is a Kenneth, but I'm thinkin' he's no yer ain, Kirsty," replied Morag, with a pitying glance at the poor mother's yearning face.

"Tak' me til her, Morag. Kenneth's wife! —she's dyin' i' the fir-wood! The Lord grant me the strength to gang." And the old woman laid her trembling hand on the little girl's shoulder as she moved to go.

Very soon they were toiling across the hillock together, and not till they were far into the forest was the silence broken.

Meanwhile, Blanche had seated herself on the grey dyke, and was keeping watch beside the sick woman. It was a strange vigil to keep, alone in the darkening fir-wood, beside this tossing, wild-eyed, dying woman; but, somehow, Blanche did not feel frightened in the least degree. Since she had taken her post, it began to seem the most natural thing in the world that she should be there. The sick woman took no notice of the little girl for some time, and, indeed, seemed hardly aware of her presence, till, turning round suddenly, she saw her seated there, her fair curls gleaming in the half darkness. She looked at her restlessly for a little, and said presently, "How came you here, my pretty dear. You're surely far from home. Will your mamma not be getting anxious about you? It seems so dark in that wood."

"I haven't got a mamma," replied Blanche, vivaciously. "Miss Prosser will be cross, I daresay; but I don't think she'll mind when I explain. I'm sure Morag won't be longer than she can help in bringing in Kirsty," added Blanche in a comforting tone, for she noticed that the weary eyes wandered restlessly toward the entrance of the tent.

Presently a terrible fit of a breathlessness came on, and the poor woman sank back exhausted on her hard stone pillow when it was over. Blanche gazed pityingly at the sufferer, and longed for the morrow, when she meant

12

to return with various needful comforts. She
had made up her mind to enlist Mrs. Worthy's
sympathy, believing her to be more amiable
than Ellis.

Meanwhile, she took off her soft jacket, and
folding it, she slipped it under the poor restless head on the hard stone. The sick woman
noticed the pleasant change, and smiled grate
fully.   And as Blanche looked at her, she
thought how pretty she must once have been,
before the cheeks had got so hollow, and the
eyes so sunken.

It was beginning to get very dark within
the tent, and Blanche was not sorry to see
Kenneth make his appearance with his pitcher
filled with clear water from the spring. The
sick woman seemed greatly refreshed by the
draught, which she drank eagerly. But presently, she began to get very restless, and kept
moaning, "Kenny! Kenny! are they not within sight yet? It's so long since that little girl
went away."

At last, after Kenneth had drawn aside the
tartan folds several times, he brought back the
news that the little girl and an old bent woman
were coming through the trees.

"Oh, it's all right!—Kirsty and Morag—
here they come!" cried Blanche, joyfully, as

she sprung out to meet them, saying eagerly to Kirsty, " Do come quickly ; she's so very anxious to see you, Kirsty ! "

The old woman made no reply, but walked silently towards the tent, looking intently at Kenneth, who stood in front of it. " My ain Kenneth's bairn," she murmured, as she laid her trembling hand on his head. Morag heard him say, " Grandmother, we've found you at last ! Mother will be so glad ! " and he led her to where the dying woman lay, and the tartan folds shut them out from sight.

In the meantime, two figures might be seen wandering through the forest, searching hither and thither in all directions. They were Ellis and the keeper, who had started in company to look for the missing girls. Blanche's maid was in a state of high nervous agitation concerning her little mistress. She had been consigning her to various imaginary harrowing fates since she left the castle in search of her, but the keeper had smiled his grim smile, and assured her that girls were like kittens, and had nine lives. Nevertheless, he too began to feel rather anxious about them, after he had reluctantly led the way to Kirsty's cottage, where he expected to find them safely housed ; but, to his surprise, they found it quite tenantless. Ellis began to wring her hands in despair when she detected a shade of anxiety on the keeper's face, after the neighborhood of the cottage had been searched without any result. Then Dingwall decided that the fir-wood must be thoroughly explored, for he knew that it was one of Morag's favorite haunts. They wandered on, searching everywhere, till at last the keeper's keen eye discovered, through the fir-trees, the dark tent resting against the old dyke, with its back-ground of pale larches. He began to feel rather uneasy, and to wish that he had brought some defensive weapon with him, for there was no trace of the girls, and it was more than likely they had been picked up by the gypsies, and sharp measures might be necessary for their recovery. He did not, however, confide his fears to Ellis, but went forward to take a nearer inspection of the encampment.

Meanwhile, the little girls were hovering about the tent, wondering what would happen next. Morag had quite made up her mind that the wee leddy must instantly be conducted homewards, and was relieved to find that she was not unwilling to go—the reason being that Blanche was full of hospitable ideas concerning the dwellers under the tartan, and she felt impatient to get home again to enlist all the sympathy possible in their favor.

Morag, before starting for the castle, had gone to reconnoitre a little round the tent, to try to find an opportunity of whispering to Kirsty that she would return presently, provided her father would allow her. Just at that moment, Blanche spied Ellis and the keeper hovering about among the trees, and ran forward to meet them.

Ellis's anxiety immediately changed to indignation when she perceived that her little mistress was safe and sound, and she was about to break forth in angry words of remonstrance when Blanche held up a warning finger and pointed to the tent, which the little fire within was making more visible in the darkness.

"Gypsies, I declare!" shrieked Ellis. "You've been kidnapped. We're just in time to save her!" she added, wringing her hands, and turning to the keeper, who in his turn began to feel a shade of anxiety regarding his Morag, as she was nowhere visible.

"Hush, Ellis; they aren't gypsies a bit. There is a very sick woman lying there—dying, she says, but I hope she isn't quite that. They are strangers, and have come a long way."

"Didn't I tell you? They always come

from the hends of the earth. Gypsies, as sure's
my name's Ellis.   Are you kidnapped, missie—
tell me now?"   But Blanche appeared still in
possession of a wonderful amount of freedom,
and glanced with an amused smile at the keeper
as she listened to her maid's suggestions. So
Ellis continued, in an angry tone—

"What have you ever been about so long,
missie? Miss Prosser's well-nigh into a fit
about you, and Mrs. Worthy says she can't sit
two minutes in one place for anxiety. And
there's cook, as declares she has miscooked master's dinner for the first time in her life—all on
account of her hagitation concernin' you."   And
Ellis went on to give a chronicle of the various
distracted feelings of each separate member of
the household.

"Has papa come home, then? and what
did he say about my being so late?" interposed
Blanche at last.

"Oh, well, you see the master is a quiet
gentleman, and never does make much ado,"
replied Ellis, rather crestfallen that she had
nothing sensational to narrate from that quarter.
"But he said we would be sure to find you
at that old woman what's-her-name's cottage,
where you're so fond of going to; and you see
we didn't. Really, missie, it's too bad! I'm

near wore off my feet between the fear and the draggin' after you. I only hope you won't be let go out at the door again without Miss Prosser—that's all I've got to say."

Blanche hoped it was, but she feared not. She had a painful consciousness that she was jacketless, and felt certain that, sooner or later, that fact would be discovered and inquired into.

Meanwhile, Morag joined them, not having been able to get a word with Kirsty, though she could hear her voice mingle soothingly with the eager, gasping tones of the dying woman, who appeared to have a great deal to say to this long-sought friend. Morag seemed to feel more relief than alarm at the sight of Ellis in possession of her little charge. But when she discovered her father's tall form leaning against one of her pillars of fir, she started, and looked nervously towards the tent. The keeper accosted her rather sternly, saying, "I wonder at ye, Morag. I thocht ye had mair wit—takin' up wi' a set o' tinkers, and bidin' oot so lang, forby."

Morag did not venture to explain the cause of their delay, nor did she mention that Kirsty Macpherson was so near at hand. She observed that, though her father seemed quite willing now that she should go to see the old woman, yet he evidently wished to avoid meeting her; and Morag felt sure that to disclose the fact that Kirsty was one of the alleged tinkers within the tartan folds, would not help to smooth matters.

"Missie! wherever is your jacket?—well, I never!" screamed the maid, with uplifted hands, when, for the first time, she observed the absence of that garment.

"My jacket? Oh, never mind, Ellis; it isn't cold," replied Blanche, looking rather un·easy, but attempting to assume a careless tone.

"Never mind! Did I ever know the like! Where's your jacket, missie? I insist on knowing!" screeched the excited Ellis. "Stolen by them vagrants you've been a-takin' up with, I'll be bound," and the maid looked at the keeper, as if she thought he ought to take immediate steps towards the recovery of the stolen property.

Morag glanced anxiously at Blanche. She did not know what had become of the missing jacket, and she began to wonder whether it could have been dropped in their flight from the supposed dangerous gypsy. She was about to suggest that she might go to look for it, when the indignant Ellis continued—

"Well, keeper, what *is* to be done? You see Miss Blanche doesn't even deny that they've stolen her jacket—her beautiful ermine one, too. I gave it her on because she sneezed this morning. Pity there isn't a policeman to set at them," snorted Ellis, in great wrath, as she glanced at the keeper, who stood stolid and immovable, looking at Blanche.

The little lady began to feel at bay, and, being again challenged by her maid to tell what had become of the missing garment, she planted herself against a fir-tree, and flinging back her curls, she folded her arms, saying in a dramatic tone—

"Now, Ellis, listen! I'd rather suffer all the tortures we read of yesterday at Kirsty's, in Foxe's Book of Martyrs, than tell you where that jacket is!"

Morag had been about to expostulate with the wee leddy; but now she felt much too awed to utter a word. As she stood gazing at her, the fir-tree was immediately transformed in her imagination to a stake, and visions of lighted faggots and rising flames coursed through her brain. Ellis, too, seemed rather impressed, and Blanche took advantage of her position to remark in·her most imperious tone, as she quitted her dramatic pose, "Now, Ellis, if you say another word about that jacket, I shan't go home with you a step. Perhaps to-morrow I may tell you what has become of it," she added, bending her head graciously, as she volunteered to start for home under these con-ditions.

At this juncture, Kirsty suddenly emerged from the tartan folds. She had been reminded that the little girls still waited by hearing the sound of voices, and she came now to urge them to return home at once.

The moon was now giving a clear, plentiful light. It shone on Kirsty's placid face, and showed her another face which she had not looked on for many a year, and it seemed strange that she should see it to-night. The keeper looked as much startled as if he had seen a ghost, when the old woman moved slowly towards him, and holding out her hand, said, solemnly, " Alaster Dingwall, is that you ? " and still holding his hand, she added, ".. Weel do I min' the nicht I saw ye last. But come ben, and hear o' the goodness o' the Lord frae this dyin' woman. Eh! but He's slow to anger, and plenteous in mercy. The soul o' my lang-lost Kenneth is safe wi' Himsel'. He has granted me the desire o' my hert. Com. ben, and see Kenneth's wife ! "

Dingwall's usually inflexible face showed traces of strong emotion as he listened to Kirsty. He made no reply, but was about to follow her into the tent, when Ellis, more mystified than ever by these strange dealings with these disreputable gypsies, who had already given her so much trouble that afternoon, shouted in angry tones, "Well, keeper, if you're going to stay in this wood longer, I'm not. Come along, missie, we must find our own way as best we can." And without waiting for a reply, the indignant maid hurried off with her reluctant charge.

Morag stood watching her father, as he followed Kirsty, bending his tall figure to creep into the low tent, and then she sat down on the old grey dyke outside, to await the next scene of this strange evening. She could not help feeling very glad that her father and Kirsty were going to be friends at last, though it was such a sorrowful occasion which seemed to have brought the reconciliation about. Presently she saw Kenneth slip out of the tent, looking very grave and sad. He came and leant silently against one of the fir-trees, and stood gazing into the pale larch plantation, with its long dark grass shimmering in the white moonlight. Morag knew that he was looking so sorrowful because his mother was going to leave

him, and she felt very sorry too, and longed
to be able to do something to comfort him;
but she thought that perhaps it was best to
keep quite quiet there, and let him think his
own thoughts. She wondered whether Kenneth knew and loved his grandmother's Friend,
and was able now to tell Him all his trouble.

When the keeper entered the tent, the dying woman fixed her great restless eyes upon
him, and looked questioningly at Kirsty. The
old woman stooped down, and said, "It's Alaster Dingwall—him, ye ken, that was Kenneth's"—friend, she was going to say; and
then she glanced sadly at the keeper, and did
not finish her sentence. But presently she added, "Eh! but He's been good and forgien us
muckle, and we maun be willin' to forgie," and
taking the thin, white fingers, she laid them in
the keeper's broad, brown palm.

"Yes, yes," gasped the woman; "I remember the name. My husband said something
about him when he was dying, too; but I can't
recollect now." Her memories of the troubled
past were growing dim in the haze of death.

"My boy, where is he?" she asked, presently, turning to Kirsty. "I've brought him
to you—you'll love him for your own Kenneth's sake, won't you? He's a good boy; it's

hard to leave him in this wicked world alone; but you will look to him, won't you?" and she looked beseechingly at Kirsty. "We've travelled many a weary mile to reach you—he'll tell you all about it after. But it's all over now—all past, and the rest is coming," she murmured, and then she lay quite still for a few minutes, and her lips moved as if in prayer.

Presently she seemed to remember something, and, putting her hand into her breast, she drew out a little bag with one or two gold pieces in it. Handing it to Kirsty, she said, "It's all there is left—he's very ragged I'm afraid, and I'll be to bury. But you are good and kind, he always said, and you'll be kind to my boy, for Christ's sake, and for your own Kenneth's, grandmother, won't you? I haven't remembered all his messages, I'm so tired to-night. He wanted your forgiveness so much—but you'll see him again—we'll both be waiting you and Kenny!"

"Eh! my bairn; but ye mauna forget that a sicht o' Christ's ain face will be better than a' the lave," said the old woman earnestly, as she wiped the cold damps of death from the white forehead.

"It's so cold, and gets so very dark," she

moaned restlessly. "There was a candle left in the basket, I think; why doesn't Kenny light it? Where is he? why does he go away?"

The candle was already burning near its socket, and Kirsty saw that the haze of death was fast dimming the eyes that would see no more till they awoke in that city "where they need no candle, neither light of the sun, for the glory of God doth lighten it; and there shall be no night there."

The old woman went to call Kenneth, who was still leaning silently against the fir-tree. "Come ben to yer mither, my laddie! Ye winna hae lang to bide wi' her noo, I'm thinkin'." And the boy came and knelt beside his mother. The keeper had been standing with folded arms, looking silently on, but now he crept away, and sitting down in a corner of the tent, he covered his face with his hands. The sins of his youth came crowding to his memory; one dark spot stood out in terrible relief, and made him cower with shame and remorse in the presence of this boy, and his mother on her lowly dying bed.

Meanwhile, Kirsty went out to look for Morag, whom she had not forgotten. Seeing her seated on the old dyke, she beckoned to her, saying, "Come awa, dawtie, dinna bide there yer lane! Puir thing, she winna be lang here, noo. It's a sair sicht for a young hert, but come ben, Morag. 'Deed they're best aff that's nearest their journey's end," murmured the old woman, as she stepped under the tartan folds again.

Morag followed, and stood gazing sorrowfully at the dying woman. She had been lying quietly for several minutes, but presently she looked wildly round, and, stretching out her arms, she cried, "Kenny, Kenny, lift me up!"

Kirsty stepped forward, and raised the weary head on her arm, saying, in her low, firm tones, "Dinna be feert, my bairn. The valley is dark eneuch, but 'there's licht on the tither side. Jist ye haud His han' siccar, and ye'll see His face gin lang." For a few moments she lay peacefully, with her hand resting on Kirsty's breast, but presently a great spasm of agony crossed the wasted face, some lingering breaths were drawn, and the poor, quivering frame lay at rest.

Neither of the children knew that it was death. After a long silence Kenneth rose from his knees, and whispered to Kirsty—"She's gone to sleep; we must not wake her for a while—it's so long since she slept before."

"Ay, ay, my laddie," replied Kirsty, shaking her head, mournfully; "she's gane to sleep, til her lang, lang sleep. Nae soun' o' ours will waken her noo; it will be His ain blessed voice i' the Day that's comin'."

Poor Kenneth understood now. With a low cry of agony, he knelt beside the body, which Kirsty had laid tenderly on its lowly bed among the brown fir-needles again. And as she did so, Morag caught a glimpse of the wee leddy's missing jacket; she understood now why she was so vehemently unwilling that it should be searched for.

The keeper had been a silent spectator of the sad scene. At last he turned to Kirsty, and brushing a tear from his eye, he said, in a husky voice—"Kirsty, woman, I've whiles afore rued yon dark nicht's work sore eneuch, and all that came o't, but I niver rued it sae muckle as I do the nicht."

"Dinna say nae mair, Alaster Dingwall," replied Kirsty, holding out her hand. "I'll no say that it wasna sair upo' me for mony a day, but I see it a' the nicht. Ye were jist the instrument in His hands for sendin' the puir prodigal safe hame til the Father's hoose. Will you no come intilt yersel', man? The far countrie o' sin is an unca lonesome place, Alaster Dingwall," and Kirsty laid her hand on his arm, and looked earnestly into his face.

" It's no easy wark for an auld sinner like me, Kirsty ; but, I'll try," Dingwall replied, as he glanced kindly and pityingly at the orphan boy, and lifted him from his dead mother's side.

" Noo, keeper, ye and Morag manna bide a minute longer. The puir lassie maun be deid tired," said Kirsty, rousing herself to think what must be done next. " I'se watch aside the corp ; and maybe, when the morn's come, ye'll hae the kindness to speir gin the wricht i' the village will come ootby here, and we'll lay her in her lang hame, and the puir laddie will come hame and bide wi' me."

The keeper would not hear of leaving her, and Morag seated herself on the dyke, saying quietly, " I canna be goin' home and leavin' Kirsty, father."

The poor boy seemed so faint from grief and fasting, that Dingwall at last decided to take him away from the sorrowful scene, and to leave Morag, who determinately clung to her old friend.

Kenneth stood gazing mournfully at the silent form, murmuring, " Mother, mother!" in a low monotone of agony. He would not be persuaded to quit the spot till Kirsty unfastened the tartan plaid from the stakes, and laying it reverently on the body, she covered the dead face out of sight. And as she unwound the plaid from its fastenings, she remembered with a sharp pang of sorrow the morning on which she had last seen that old plaid. While the keeper and Kenneth are wandering through the fir-wood on their way to the shieling among the crags, and the old woman, with Morag by her side, keeps her strange, lonely watch beside the dead, we shall explain why it was so terrible for the keeper to remember, and so difficult for Kirsty to forget, the events of a certain night long years ago, which had driven the older Kenneth from the Glen an outlawed man, and left his mother a desolate, childless woman.

Kirsty's husband had been the village smith. He was a much-liked and respected inhabitant of the little hamlet. He was suddenly cut off by fever at a comparatively early age, leaving his wife one son, who was henceforth to be her sole earthly hope and care. The smith had been a sober and diligent man, and Kirsty was a frugal housewife, so a little money was saved, and the widow had been able to move to the pretty cottage in the Glen, which had been her home ever since.

Kirsty had one earthly ambition, and one which she shared in common with many a Scotch peasant—namely, that her son should become a scholar. This desire seemed, however, to meet with no response from the boy himself. He hated books, and loved, above all things, to roam about the Glen, finding his pleasure there, frequently, when he should have been at school in the village. Thither every quarter-day his mother duly went, full of anxiety to hear about his progress, and with the school fees wrapt in a corner of her pocket-handkerchief, while a small offering for the schoolmaster's wife, from the garden or barn-yard, was never forgotten. But she always returned from these visits crestfallen and grieved. "He does not take to his books, Mrs. Macpherson; I fear we'll never be able to make a scholar of him," the parish schoolmaster would say, shaking his head, and adding, as he noticed the mother's disappointed face, "He's a fine, manly, truthful boy, though; you'll find he will be good for something yet."

But Kirsty was not satisfied, and went on praying that God would give her son a hearing ear and an understanding heart in things intellectual and spiritual. And so the years of boyhood passed, and Kenneth grew up a great anxiety to his widowed mother. Sometimes he would leave home for whole nights and days of rambling among the hills with other lads. He was an immense favorite among his companions, and their chosen leader in every wild exploit. Bold and frank and fearless he certainly was, and possessed much of seeming unselfishness, but it was a quality of a very different kind from that which his mother practised at home. Nobody could wile so many trouts from the river as Kenneth; and nobody so generously shared his basketful among his comrades. He knew every foot of the Glen by heart, every lonely pass, each deceptive bog. He had set his heart on being a gamekeeper, but his mother looked upon it as an idle trade, and always hoped that he might yet show some leaning towards another employment.

Alaster Dingwall was many years older than Kenneth, though a great friendship sprang up between the two. Dingwall had been under-gamekeeper at some distance from the Glen, but he had lost his situation, and returned to lounge about the village, on the outlook for work. He admired the bold, reckless young Kenneth, and the boy was greatly attracted by his older companion, and felt flattered by his appreciation. Kirsty noticed that the companionship only served to foster Kenneth's idle habits, and she did all she could to discourage it, but in vain.

One Sunday evening Kenneth had been induced to stay quietly indoors, and sat reading to his mother, who was feeling intensely happy in having him with her. But presently she heard a whistle outside, which she had learned to know and dread, for she knew that it was a summons for her boy to join his idle companions.

"That's Dingwall's whustle; I ken it fine. Dinna gang out til him, Kenny—bide wi' me the nicht, my laddie. He'll no want ye for ony guid."

But the warning, "My son, if sinners entice thee, consent thou not," fell unheeded on the foolish Kenneth's ear, and a sorrowful reaping-time for all after-life was the result of this brief sowing-time of folly.

"It's only for a bit o' a walk, mother. There's no ill," pleaded Kenneth, as he hurriedly shut the book; and taking his bonnet, he prepared to go out. "I'll no be long, mother," he added, as he went out whistling, and Kirsty could hear through the clear frosty

7

air his merry laugh re-echoing among his
companions, and stood listening to it at the
door of the cottage till the sound died away in
the distance. Then the mother went back to
the empty room, and prayed for her son till
the grey morning broke, and still he did not
return.

At last she crept away to bed, and in the
morning she was awakened from her troubled
slumbers by a loud knocking. On opening
the door, she saw Kenneth standing, pale and
haggard, with blood-besmeared clothes, between two strange men. One of them stepped forward, and said to the bewildered Kirsty—

"Sorry for it, missus; but this chap must
go with me. Found a snare set in the larch
plantation yonder—all but caught him at it, in
fact. It's not the first offence, I'm thinking.
There's been a deal of poaching lately in the
neighborhood; but we've caught the thief at
last."

"Mother, I didna do it! I never set the
snare! I didna even ken that it was amang
the grass!" gasped Kenneth, looking plead-
ingly at his mother, as if he cared more that
she should not think him guilty of the deed
than for the serious consequences which seemed

to threaten him, whether he was guilty or not. And his mother looked into his eyes and knew that he was innocent, as indeed he was. He had been simply used as a tool by his false friend.

Since he had been out of employment, Dingwall had gained his livelihood by poaching. But, having reason to suspect at last that he was being watched, he resolved to shift the suspicions on Kenneth by enlisting him in the service, and offering him a share of the gains. He thought, too, that if the offence were discovered, it was more likely to be lightly treated if the offender were a mere boy, like Kenneth, so he resolved on that evening to divulge the plan to his boy-friend, who, as yet, was entirely ignorant of the way in which Dingwall gained a livelihood, and little guessed on what mission he was being led into the larch plantation.

Kenneth had seated himself on the lichen-spotted dyke to smoke, while the more cautious, because guilty, Dingwall stood darkly by, having slipped his pipe into his pocket long before they reached the wood. He was pondering how he should best confide his secret to Kenneth, and was about to propose that he would show him the snare which he had set, when his keen eye detected traces of danger and discovery. He immediately crept away in base silence to hide himself, and presently his innocent boy-friend was seized by the emissaries of the law. Then Kenneth understood that he had been betrayed; but he would not betray in return. He simply asserted that he had not set the snare, and knew nothing whatever about it.

"Come, come, now; that's all very fine—didn't do it, forsooth. Strange place for a walk on a winter night—the larch plantation," said the man, smiling sneeringly to his companion, as he listened to Kenneth assuring his mother that he was innocent, while they stood at the cottage door.

"Come along with us. In the meantime," he continued, as he laid his hand on Kenneth's arm to drag him away, "if you're able to prove that you didn't do it, all the better for you, my boy, I can tell you."

Kenneth turned with a look of anguish to his mother, who stood gazing at him with a face of marble. She asked no questions; it was no time for reproaches then, and, somehow, Kenneth felt that she understood how it had all happened, she looked so pitiful and so loving. When she saw that the men were really going to take him away, she went and prepared him some breakfast; but Kenneth said he could not eat, and turning to the men, volunteered to accompany them at once. He looked cold and faint in that chilly November morning: and just as he was starting, his mother brought his father's plaid, and wrapped it tenderly round him, but she did not utter a word.

"Come now, there must be no more coddling of this bird, old lady! Time's valuable, and there isn't a minute to spare!" said the man roughly, as he led the boy away.

When Kenneth had got beyond the garden gate, and was being hurried along the highway by his jailer, he turned and looked with unutterable agony and remorse toward his mother, who stood, stricken and desolate, at the door of his home, which was to be blighted during so many years for his sake.

A few weeks afterwards he was tried, and sentenced to a short term of imprisonment. He had pleaded not guilty; but could not explain how he came to be in the larch plantation at such an hour, and declined to give any information concerning the real offender.

Kirsty knew him to be none other than Alaster Dingwall. In her anguish she went to him, and implored that he would not sacrifice the innocent, speaking burning words from the depths of her broken mother's heart; but she only met with the sneering rejoinder that she would find some difficulty in proving that he had anything to do with the matter.

And then the news came that the wretched boy had escaped from prison; and from that day forward Kirsty heard nothing of her son. Seventeen long years she sat at her lonely fireside, waiting, and hoping, and praying! For a long time she left the door nightly open, in the hope that he might at least come and visit her in the dark. But he never came; and long ago Kirsty's deferred hope had changed itself into a prayer, that wherever he might be roaming throughout the wide world, they might meet in the home of God at last.

Sometimes, after a long night of prayer for her lost son, the mother felt as if she heard a voice, saying, " I have seen his ways, and I will heal him;" and she would begin the lonely day with lightened heart. And now, at last, she had the joy of knowing from the lips of his dying wife that the wanderer, who feared to come again to the Glen, and had sought refuge for his blighted life in distant lands, had, at last, been led unto the fold above, and had learnt to know the Shepherd's voice, and to follow it in the midst of many earthly trials and hard experiences through which he had to pass.

So this sorrowful night was mingled with great joy to Kirsty, as she kept watch in the fir-wood. Morag felt sure that she must have much to say to her unseen Friend, as she sat resting her head on her long thin hand, and gazing into the red embers among the stones. The little girl crouched silently by her side, often glancing at the tartan folds that covered the weary sleeper below, and pondering over the events of this strange afternoon.

And as she sat keeping vigil, there came to her memory the story of a very sorrowful night, of which she had been reading with Kirsty only the day before. It was the scene in the old garden of Gethsemane, where the Lord Jesus Christ spent those terrible hours, "exceeding sorrowful even unto death."

It was the first time that Morag had heard of it, and the hot tears of pity stole down her face as she listened. Kirsty had looked up, and said gently, as she laid her hand on her head, "Bairn, I dinna wonder though ye greet. It was a sair dark nicht i' the history o' the warl'. But jist ye read a bittie farther on, aboot how they garred Him tak' His ain cross up the brae; the women grat for verra pity, and syne He turned Himsel', and spak' til them, sayin', 'Daughters o' Jerooslem, weep no for me, but for yersels and for yer chil- dren.'" And Morag thought that she under- stood why Jesus was called the " Lamb of God, who taketh away the sin of the world."

At last the chill grey morning light came stealing through the dark green boughs and among the tall fir-trees. Presently the lonely watch was broken by the arrival of messengers from the castle, bringing with them every comfort which could be stowed away in a huge hamper.

" 'Deed it's richt mindfu' o' the wee leddy o' the castle to sen' sic a hantle o' things," said Kirsty, rising slowly to receive the ser- vants. "An' I'm thinkin' she left her bonnie white coatie yestreen to mak' a safter heid for the puir lamb. Ye'll jist tak' it wi ye noo, gin it please ye, sirs—and a' the ither things, forby. We dinna need them here. Tell ye the wee leddy that the puir weary craeter she saw lyin' sae low yestreen i' the fir-wood is awa this mornin' among the green pasters and the still waters o' the Father's hoose, where there's nae mair hunger, nor sorrow, nor cryin', for the auld things hae passed awa."

IT was nearly the end of September now, the air of Glen Eagle began to feel chilly, and the purple bloom was fading from the hills, but the interior of Kirsty's cottage looked as warm and bright as ever, when one afternoon Blanche Clifford came bounding in with glowing cheeks, after a race across the heather, followed by Morag, to pay a visit to their old friend.

Kenneth had just been piling one or two sturdy birk logs on the peat-fire, in preparation for their arrival. His grandmother's cottage was his home now; the cheery fire which he had just made was quite a fitting emblem of the brightness which he had brought into the lonely dwelling. His mother had been laid in the quiet grave-yard on the hillside, and the boy often stole out in the gloaming to hover round the fresh-laid turf. He seldom, however, spoke of the past, and already began to lose his careworn expression, which had so touched the hearts of the little girls in the fir-wood. Indeed he appeared daily to gain strength and manliness; while Kirsty watched the change with mingled feelings, remembering a Kenneth of other days, whose strength had once been her pride.

"How nice and cosy you do always look here!" exclaimed Blanche, glancing round the room, as she seated herself on Thrummy at Kirsty's feet. "When I'm an old woman, I mean to have a room exactly like this. I couldn't endure to live in a house with so many rooms as papa's, or as Aunt Matilda's. One never knows in which room they may be sitting, and can never picture them to one's self if you are away, and want to think of them. Now, Kirsty, when I go back to London, I shall always be able to think of you just as you are now," said the little girl, as she laid her hands on the lap of her old peasant friend. Kirsty was seated in the ingleneuk in her high-elbowed chair, knitting placidly. Her fingers moved rapidly round the rough blue stocking which she had in progress, but her eyes rested kindly on Blanche, and she smiled as she listened to her pleasant prattle. She, too, as well as Morag, had learnt to love this little English maiden, with her pretty, gracious ways, who had made herself so happy in the Highland glen, and showed such warm friendship for them all. Since the weather became colder, the scene of the reading lessons had been transferred from the fir-wood to the *ben end* of the cottage, and the old woman was always an interested listener, often unravelling knotty points by her shrewd remarks and wise decisions.

Sometimes, too, Blanche would entertain her Highland friends with descriptions of the world beyond the mountains, and expatiate on the many marvels of the great city she lived in. Morag's eye would dilate with wonder and awe as she described the grand old Abbey, filled with the dust of kings and statesmen, soldiers and poets, or dwelt on the varied delights of a day at the Crystal Palace or the Kensington Museum.

After Morag's fingers had laboriously travelled over a few pages of the " Pilgrim's Progress," she begged that Blanche would read a little. The little mountain maiden's reading capacities did not at all keep pace with her desire to know ; and now she sat, coiled up at Kirsty's feet, listening with eager interest, as the wee leddy's clear voice flowed pathetically on, concerning the cruel treatment which the

Pilgrims received from the people of Vanity Fair.

"Vanity Fair!—how funny!" exclaimed Blanche, as she tossed back her curls and looked up. "Do you know, Kirsty, there is a place in London, called Hyde Park, where I sometimes go to drive and ride with papa, though not nearly so often as I should like. Well, Kirsty, I remember one afternoon when we were there, papa met an old, very old gentleman—rather queer looking—whom he hadn't seen for ever so long. He held out his hand to papa, and I remember he said, 'Well, Arthur, you didn't expect to meet me in Vanity Fair, I daresay?' and then he laughed; and I wanted to ask papa afterwards what he meant, but I suppose I forgot. But, Kirsty, it surely can't be the same place where they were so unkind to the poor pilgrims, and called them names, could it?"

"'Deed, bairn, but I'm nae sae sure o' that noo. The Apostle Paul says that the carnal hert is enmity agin' God. And dinna ye min' how the Maister says Himsel', 'Marvel not though the warl' hate ye. Ye know that it hated me afore it hated you.' But forbid that I should say He hasna a remnant o' His ain in-tilt, bairn," said Kirsty, as she noticed Blanche's troubled face. "It's His ain prayer til His Father, ye ken, no to tak' them oot o' the warl', but to keep them frae the evil," she added solemnly.

"Oh! but indeed, Kirsty, I am sure that none of the people in the Park could possibly be cruel to the poor pilgrims," replied Blanche, rather on the defensive. "There are such pretty ladies and gentlemen, riding and driving about; I'm sure they wouldn't hurt anybody. I like so much to go to the Park! and papa says, when I'm grown up and have quite finished lessons, that I may go there to ride or drive every day, if I like. I'm sure I wish the time were come!" and the prospect seemed so inspiring that Blanche jumped up, upsetting Thrummy in her progress round the earthen floor in a gleeful waltz.

Morag's eyes followed her bonnie wee leddy wistfully. Somehow her heart sank at the vista which seemed to stretch out, so fair and pleasant, in Blanche's eyes. They were play-fellows now, but how would it be in these days to come, when her little friend merged into one of these grand ladies whom she had been describing?

Presently Blanche picked up her stool, and came to seat herself at Kirsty's feet again.

14

"Eh, my bonny lambie!" murmured the old woman, as she stroked the little girl's golden crown. "May the Guid Shepherd Himsel' gather ye in His ain arms, and carry ye intil His bosom a' thro' the slippy places, and keep ye a bonnie white lambie, til he tak's ye safe hame til the fauld!"

Morag did not say "Amen" audibly, for she had not yet learnt that conventional ending to a petition. But none the less did she join Kirsty in fervent asking, that the Lord Jesus Christ would preserve their bonnie wee leddy amid all the dangers of this terrible Vanity Fair, which had proved so full of perils for the pilgrims in the story.

A shade of seriousness stole across Blanche's face as Kirsty's long thin fingers played among her hair, while she uttered this blessing-prayer; but the shadow did not linger long there. The little girl had never thought of life as being difficult and dangerous, and did not feel the need of a friend and guide. Moreover, she did not like anything that made her feel serious, so she quickly closed the book, and, restoring it to its place on the shelf, ran away to the cottage door, warbling a gay song, as she plucked some berries from one of the old rowan trees to make a wreath for Morag, and crown her queen of gypsies.

Presently the old woman came and seated herself on the door-step. Her knitting was in her hand, but it lay idly on her lap, and she sat watching the little girl with tear-dimmed eyes. She trembled for the many snares and dangers which the days to come would be sure to bring to the beautiful high-born child. But Kirsty forgot that there were shorter, safer, smoother paths to the golden city than through the many windings of Vanity Fair.

"I have just been to old Neil's, grandmother," said Kenneth, as he walked in at the little gate on his return from a message to the carrier of the Glen. "He says he'll be happy to oblige you with the cart on Sunday for the kirk. He'll not be able to go himself, because of his rheumatism; but he is to lend the cart if I'll yoke the horse."

"I'm richt glaid to hear't, laddie," replied Kirsty. "It's mony a Sawbbath day sin' I ha' been i' the kirk. 'Deed I thocht never to sit at His table upon the earth anither time."

"Morag, hae ye speird gin yer father be gaein' to lat ye gang wi' me til the kirk?"

"Ay, Kirsty, I've been askin' him, but he hasna said yet. I'm no thinkin' he'll

do't, though. But he said he would see yersel' afore that time. Maybe he'll be up the
nicht."

"Oh, Kirsty, are you really going to that
pretty little church in the village on Sunday?
Do let me go with you; I want so to see the
inside of it," chimed in Blanche, eagerly.
"It will be so much nicer than reading prayers with Miss Prosser in that dreadful school-
room."

"Weel, I'se be richt glaid to tak' ye wi'
me, bairn, gin yer folk doesna objec'; but I'm
no thinkin' they would lat ye gang ava. It's
a lang road, and, ye see, we'll jist hae Neil's
cartie, wi' a puckle strae intilt, and that'll
maybe no be fit for the like o' you."

"Oh, yes, of course it would—-perfectly
delicious," cried Blanche, clapping her hands.
"I must really go with you, Kirsty. I shall
ask papa to-night, if I have a chance; it would
be such fun, wouldn't it, Morag?"

"Sawbbath 'll be a gran' day. It's the Sac-
rament wi' us, ye ken," said Kirsty looking
up from her knitting. "But I'm thinkin' it
wad be ower langsome like for you bairns,—
though I'se houp there's a day comin' when
ye'll be sittin' doon til the table yersels, and
meetin' wi' Himsel' there," continued the

old woman, as she gazed kindly at the little group.

"Oh, is it really the Holy Communion ; and may we children stay ? I should like above all things to see it ; shouldn't you, Morag ? Miss Prosser always sends me home with Ellis when she stays to Communion. But then it doesn't last very long at all. For by the time that I've spoken to Chance and my birds, she has always come home again. But, perhaps, it is something quite different here, is it not, Kirsty ? "

"Weel, I'm thinkin' there will be some differ from what I hae heerd tell. But eh, bairn, I mak' nae doobt that He feeds His ain folk the richt gait, in ilka part o' His warl'."

"Here's yer father comin' inby, Morag ! " said Kirsty, as she rose to welcome the keeper, whom she saw leaning against the garden gate, looking at the group round the cottage door.

The keeper had become a frequent visitor at Kirsty's cottage since that eventful evening in the fir-wood. . Often, when the work of the day was done, he might be seen wandering across the moor in the gloaming, in the direc- of the abode which he had viewed for so many years with mingled feelings of dislike and fear.

Many a pleasant talk the old woman and he seemed to have together, and the keeper appeared more at ease and happy in Kirsty's society than he had been with any mortal for many a day. His face already began to lose the sinister expression which had made Blanche distrust him on that first day when she saw him. He did not say the bitter things which he used to do about his neighbors in the Glen, and no longer prided himself in looking dark and mysterious and self-contained, but seemed more happy with himself, and, consequently, with the rest of the world.

Morag felt, with a daily, hourly, silent gladness, that a change for the better had come to her father. To her he had never been positively unkind, but now he was more gentle and genial than she had ever known him. Already the little shieling among the crags began to show traces of the brighter days which were dawning. The evenings were no longer dreary and monotonous as they used to be. For the company of books had been summoned from the old *kist*, where they had been buried so long, and they proved very pleasant companions to both father and daughter. Dingwall would occasionally read aloud to Morag as she worked; and thus finally proved that his former dislike to reading had not arisen from an ignorance of the art, as Morag had sometimes suspected.

Occasionally, a bundle of old newspapers from the castle found their way to the hut, and were eagerly scanned by the keeper as he smoked his pipe; and his remarks to his little daughter showed her that he knew more about the world beyond the mountains than she ever guessed.

And now he seemed to notice favorably Morag's efforts after domestic reform, which he had sneered at, or completely ignored before. He commended her on her attempts to improve the interior of the hut, and occasionally teased her laughingly about her imitation of Kirsty's domestic arrangements, which was everywhere visible.

It seemed suddenly to occur to him that since the laird would not have the hut mended, he possibly might make some effort towards its restoration himself, and he began to make plans for the repairing of the porous roof, after the shooting party should have taken their departure.

Morag could date this happy change in her life from that eventful evening in the fir-wood, and she often thought that, whatever the old quarrel had been, the healing of it had proved a very blessed thing for all of them.

Sometimes Morag overheard Kirsty talking

to her father in low, earnest tones, as he stood
beside her, listening quietly, and more than
once she caught the name of Kirsty's Lord and
Master mingling with their talk; and then the
little girl's heart was filled with gladness. She
never yet had the courage to tell her father
about that new Life which she had been finding during these autumn days; but she often
longed to do so, and was only prevented by
her extreme shyness and reserve. She felt
very anxious that her father should come to
know and love that unseen, but real Friend,
who had been the light of Kirsty's lonely
home for so many years, and whom she was
now learning to know and love.

Occasionally, when her father and Kirsty
were engaged in these conversations, Morag
would start with Kenneth on an expedition to
some of their moorland haunts, to introduce
them to the stranger lad. They often wandered into the little graveyard on the hillside,
and stood silently beside the fresh-laid turf,
while Morag tried to recall the face of the
quiet sleeper below; and Kenneth's thoughts
went slipping back to the time when he played
at his mother's knee, a merry little boy.

It was rather a grief of mind to Kirsty
that she never could induce her grandson to

talk of the past, nor to give any chronicle of his former life, which she fain would have heard; but she was both wise and kind, and did not seek to elicit confidences which were not freely bestowed, hoping that the time would come when they might be voluntarily given.

But, sometimes, on the way home from these visits to the little graveyard, Kenneth would talk to the quiet Morag as he never had done to Kirsty. And as he told of his past chequered life, the eyes of the little maiden were filled with wonder and pity at the strange experiences through which her boy-friend had passed in the world beyond the mountains.

Kenneth was daily gaining in vigor and manliness. The bracing mountain air seemed to put new life and strength into him; and in Kirsty's comfortable dwelling he had parted with those wearing anxieties which had so long darkened his young life,—though with a darkening that had not been evil.

Kirsty was very anxious that her grandson should at once choose a trade and begin to work. She dreaded idleness for him, above all things, and was somewhat dismayed to find his love for mountain roamings, and to notice his intense enjoyment in a day with the keeper

at the moors.   The boy little knew what pain
it gave to his grandmother when one day that
they were talking about his future work in life
he frankly acknowledged that he should like
nothing half so well as to be a gamekeeper like
Dingwall.

But seventeen years of growing trust in the
wise love and gracious leading of her Heavenly
Father enabled her to commit the boy to His
care, and to bid him go and prosper in the
path of life which he had chosen.

THE KIRK IN THE VILLAGE.

"HAVE you heard your pupil's latest request, Miss Prosser?" asked Mr. Clifford, laughingly, as he turned from Blanche, who had been pleading her suit in low, coaxing tones. "She actually wants to go to the kirk in the village for some high festival occasion next Sunday—and in company with that wonderful Kirsty, too, whom we hear so much about just now. She refuses with disdain my kind offer of the carriage for herself and party—wants to go in a wheel-barrow, or something of that description —is it not, Blanche?"

"Oh no, papa! how can you think such absurd things? We are going in Neil's cart, of course. It will be such fun! Kirsty says there will be lots of straw for seats, and Kenneth is to drive. You know you have more than half promised to let me go, papa," added Blanche, beseechingly clinging to her father in the hope of an immediate decision in her favor, for her governess had raised her voice in strong disapproval of such an irregular proceeding.

Mr. Clifford had noticed with pleasure how much his little daughter seemed to be enjoying these autumn days in the Highlands, which he feared might prove duller than she expected. It was evident, too, that her enjoyment of them consisted chiefly in the companionship she had made with those peasant friends in the Glen.

Blanche's glowing description of Kirsty, and her repetition of several of the old woman's shrewd sayings, gave Mr. Clifford a favorable impression of Kirsty. And for the little Morag he had always entertained a special liking since the stormy day on which he had found her, all alone, at work on the soaking earthen floor of the hut, and he congratulated himself on having secured her as an appendage to the little Shetlander. He frequently assured the doubting Miss Prosser that the child would get no harm from her intercourse with these dwellers in the Glen; and, in the present instance, he did not object that she should see a new phase of life, in company with her Highland friends.

Before Blanche went to bed, she had gained her father's consent to the Sunday project. She lay awake for a long time, thinking how very delightful it would be to go to church with Kirsty and Morag—and in a cart, too; and to be obliged to stay so long away that she should not be at home either for early dinner or afternoon lessons with her governess, so that the latter would have to be dispensed with altogether. Blanche thought it would be the most delightfully out-of-the-way Sunday which she had ever known; and she fell asleep at last, to dream that she and Morag, with Kirsty and Kenneth, had come rumbling in Neil's cart into Westminster Abbey while service was going on.

Morag, too, on that same evening, after a more brief and tremulous suit than her wee leddy's, had gained her father's permission to go to the kirk, for the first time in her life.

To the little English girl the prospect was merely a pleasant ploy; but to Morag Dingwall it was the fulfilling of a dream of years. How often she had watched, and how much she had longed to join, the little straggling companies wending their way along the white hilly roads from all parts of the Glen to meet in that little kirk in the village, which she had never seen but closed and silent. Kirsty often told her that the Lord Jesus Christ loved to have His people gather to worship Him. Only a few days ago she had been reading to the little girl the story of how He had once come, after He rose from the dead, into the midst of a little company which had met to worship, and of how He had stretched forth His hands, saying, "Peace be unto you."

Morag had remarked, in a mournful tone, " He never does the like noo, Kirsty; would ye no like to see Him, jist ance?"

"An' have I no seen Him?" answered Kirsty, triumphantly. "'Deed, bairn, I've whiles felt as near 'til Him as gin His fingers were wavin' aboun' my heid, wi' the verra words i' His mou', an' 'Peace be wi' ye.' I aye gaed oot o' His hoose wi' a blither hert an' o lichter fit than I gaed tilt."

The old woman had never been strong enough to go to the kirk since Morag's acquaintance with her, and she mourned over it as a great privation. Neil's cart was a rare luxury, only procurable indeed on Communion Sabbaths, which were held once a year in the Glen, when the scattered inhabitants came from its remotest parts,—many of them across miles of pathless hills, to share in the services of the day.

Never did Jewish peasant go up to the Holy City on the great day of the Feast with more joy and hope than did Kirsty Macpherson to the yearly communion at the village kirk. And, to the present occasion, she looked forward with special gladness; for had she not to give thanks for a dear one whom she knew, at last, to be safe in the home of God—the homeless wanderer, whose name had often been borne by her in agony from that communion-table to the ear of Him who came to seek and save the lost?

Morag was waiting in the castle court-yard on Sunday morning, long before the little *châtelaine* had completed her toilette to her maid's satisfaction. At last the door was swung open, and the wee leddy came running out to meet her friend, looking fresh and dainty in her spotless white dress and pretty blue hat, with which Ellis had adorned her—not without many regrets that such elegant garments should descend to such degraded uses as a seat in a cart; but, since she was going to church, her maid concluded that, of a necessity, she must wear her best attire.

"How bonnie ye look!" exclaimed Morag, gazing at her wee leddy with unfeigned admiration. "Ye're jist like the sky itsel', a' blue-and-white like."

"So I am! how funny! But oh, Morag, is not this a glorious morning? Won't Kirsty

be pleased? I really think it's the finest day
we've had since I came to Glen Eagle. I'm so
happy," and Blanche danced gleefully on the
soft turf. "Now, Chance, you needn't be wagging your tail. You are not to be invited to
come with us to-day, my dear dog. It's Sunday, you know, and we are going to church
with Kirsty and Kenneth; and dogs never do
go to church you know, Chance."

"Ay do they, whiles!" interrupted Morag,
patting the pleading Chance sympathizingly;
"they gang to the kirk onyway. For I've
often thought I wad jist like to be auld Neil's
collie, when I've seen him passin' wi' Neil on a
Sabbath mornin', and I was feelin' terrible lonesome at hame. Kirsty says, 'The dogs are
mony a time quaicter than the bairns at the
kirk, and that attentive-like.'" But Morag
agreed that since Chance was not a dog of
church-going habits, it would be wiser to leave
him at home.

Neil's cart already stood on the road at the
cottage gate when the little girls reached it.
Kenneth was waiting at the horse's head, and
Kirsty came forth in all the glory of a spotless
white *mutch* (a high cap of muslin, worn by
the old peasant women of Scotland). She wore
also a pretty scarlet cloak, which had been her

best attire for the last fifty years. In her hand she held her big, worn Bible, carefully wrapped in her ample white pocket-handkerchief, and from it there projected some stalks of thyme, and mint, and southernwood, as a preventive against possible drowsiness, during the long services of the day.

"Welcome til ye, my bairns," said she, greeting the little girls kindly, as she closed the little gate behind her. "Havna we gotten a bonnie Sawbbath-day? It's jist an oncommon fine mornin' for this time o' the year. May the Sun o' Richtyousness arise wi' healin' intil His wings the day, lichtin' up a' the dark herts, —jist as the bonnie sun this mornin' garred the drumlie licht weir aff the glen," added Kirsty, with a glad light in her calm gray eyes.

Blanche had already mounted into the cart, and was jumping about among the straw, greatly to the destruction of Ellis's careful morning toilette.

"O Kenneth! isn't this so very jolly? It will be such fun going to church like this. I'm sure I shall never forget it all my life. I do wish papa could see us start. Do you know I almost think he wanted to? Doesn't Kirsty look beautiful? I wish she'd always wear that red cloak; don't you, Kenneth?"

The old woman came leaning on Morag's shoulder, and stepped into the cart, followed by the little girl. Kenneth cracked the whip with an air of business, and the little company started.

It was certainly a perfect autumn day, and Glen Eagle was looking its loveliest. Kirsty's face wore a look of holy peace, as she sat silently with folded hands, and gazed upon the calm, still scene around. "I hae jist been minin' o' that glaidsome word o' David's," she said presently, turning to Morag, who was seated by her side. " 'The Lord is good til a', an' His tender mercies are ower a' His warks.' I'm thinkin' it maun jist hae been on some bonnie quaiet day like this, when he was awa' frae the din an' the steer of Jerooslem, 'at he thocht on makin' that bonnie psalm."

Morag had never heard the psalm, but she resolved she would try to find it that evening, and perhaps her father might help her. She said the verse over to herself, and thought Kirsty must be right in imagining that the poet-king would think his beautiful thoughts on such a day as this.

But Kenneth, who had been listening quietly, as he walked by the side of the cart, presently looked up, and said, "I'm not so sure of

that, granny. Don't you think King David
would just be as likely to say that after a long
day's fighting at the head of his soldiers, or
after a busy day in his palace, as among sunny
green fields when he had nothing to do but
enjoy himself? Do you no think, granny, that
folk maybe need to believe in the tender mercies of the Lord most in the din and the fret
of big towns, when, besides perhaps being
lonely, and in want one's self, you see so many
people still more sad and worse off? D'ye no
think, granny, that it would be more comfort
to think of the tender mercies of the Lord, living in such dreary streets, than in such a bonnie
glen as this?" said Kenneth, smiling sadly as
he remembered how much he and his mother
had needed, and how often they had found,
these tender mercies in such places.

"'Deed, laddie, I'm thinkin' ye hae the richt
o't efter a'; I'm glaid ye thocht o' that," said
Kirsty, looking down at her grandson with her
most pleased smile.

As Morag sat silently listening to the conversation, she thought how good it was that
these "tender mercies" seemed to be over all,
—among the busy, crowded haunts of men, as
well as with the lonely dwellers among the
mountains. And as the cart rumbled slowly

along the winding road, the little girl repeated the verse to herself till she knew it well.

Many a time in after days that verse came back to her memory, sometimes as a prayer, but more often as a thanksgiving. Across the waste of years, with graves between and many a sorrow, she would look back and remember this still Sabbath morning when she went for the first time to the little village kirk, and the vanished faces that were round her then; and she would sum up the tender mercies of the Lord.

The sound of the old church bell now began to be heard across the still moorland. The little straggling companies quickened their pace at its sound, and the nearer roads began to stir with assembling worshippers.

Blanche looked with eager interest at the gathering groups, occasionally asking whispered information from Morag concerning them. Among them were old bent men and young children, who had come many a mile through the pathless hills that morning. There were shepherds in their plaids and broad bonnets, with their collie dogs following, just as Morag had said, Blanche noticed; and she resolved to keep an eye on their behavior in church, and perhaps give Chance a similar privilege another

time if her impression of the conduct of the
collies was favorable.

The kirk stood in the centre of the village
green, and when Kirsty and her young party
came in sight, there were already many groups
gathered round it. The old minister was threading his way among them, and there was many
a broad bonnet raised and many a curtsy dropped, as with kindly, gracious, though silent
greeting he passed into the church.

The old bell was still pealing, sweet and
musical, just as it used to do centuries ago in the
convent chapel down in the hollow, from whence
it had been taken when the ancient chapel became a roofless ruin; and now it called the
dwellers in the Glen to the kirk with the same
soothing chime as it used to summon the nuns
to matins and vespers, and remind the scattered
peasants that the hour of prayer had come.

Suddenly it ceased to chime, and the thronging groups on the greensward moved quietly
in at the open doors of the kirk.

Many eyes were turned on Kirsty and her
young friends as they passed slowly up the
aisle. Some recognized the bonnie wee leddy
of the castle; and not a few knew the nut-
brown Morag by sight, and smiled kindly on
her. The story of the poor woman, who had

come to the Glen to die on such a lowly bed,
was known to many, and they looked with
interest on Kirsty's grandson.

The kirk was almost filled when they
entered. Two long, narrow tables, covered
with white, stretched from the pulpit the whole
length of the church, at which the communi-
cants were to sit. Before taking her place
there, Kirsty led the children to seats at the
side of the church; and then she moved away
slowly to take her solitary post at the long
white table.

Morag did not venture to raise her eyes for
some time. The scene was so new and strange
to her that for a moment she felt something of
the terror-stricken feeling which possessed her
on the evening when she was brought before
the party at the castle. But when, at last, she
ventured to look up, she caught a glimpse of
Kirsty's calm, wopshipping face, and she began
to feel more reassured. Meanwhile, Blanche
kept gazing about in a vivacious manner, taking
notes of everything. On the whole, she felt
much disappointment with the interior of the
little kirk. It looked so bare and stern, she
thought, as she searched in vain for the altar,
or the organ, which she expected to peal forth
every minute.

At last the silence was broken, not by the organ, but by the grave, deep voice of the minister, who reared his gray head from the pulpit, and began to read a grand old psalm, which the congregation joined in singing. Then followed a prayer, and all the people rose, the men covering their faces with their broad bonnets.

Morag stood listening with closed eyes and moveless posture. Blanche tried very hard to do so also, but she could not help opening her eyes occasionally to see what the dogs were about, and presently she began to wish that the prayer was done and they would begin to sing again. She occasionally made exploring tours with her eyes over the church, and at last she caught sight of Kirsty's red cloak and familiar face, and by her side she saw a figure which she thought she recognized. To facilitate observations, she raised herself on tiptoe; and at last she was satisfied that the stalwart form at the long white table, beside Kirsty, was none other than the keeper Dingwall. She could hardly restrain an exclamation of surprise at this discovery. The keeper, she knew, was not in the habit of going to church; and, certainly, Morag would have told her if she had expected him there to-day. Very impatiently did she listen to the concluding petitions, for she could not get Morag to open her eyes till the prayer was done. At last, while the congregation were engaged in turning the leaves of their Bibles, in search of the chapter about to be read, Blanche contrived by a variety of signs to make Morag's eyes alight on the spot where her father stood. If Blanche's astonishment had been great, Morag's was still greater, when she caught sight of her father's tall form rearing itself beside Kirsty's bent head. This, then, was the reason why he had smiled so strangely that morning when she laid her hand on his arm, and said, with a great effort to break through her reserve, "O father! I would like richt weel gin ye were comin' til the kirk wi' us. I ken fine the Lord Jesus Christ would be glaid to see ye. Kirsty says He's aye weel pleased to see folk intil His ain hoose."

And now he was seated beside Kirsty at the communion-table, where, as the old woman had told Morag, none but those who loved the Lord might come. The little girl felt a thrill of delight, greater than she ever did in her life. She felt sure that her father must have begun to know and love the Lord Jesus Christ, or he never would have come there. So happy and thankful was she, that she could not wait till the minister prayed again, but said, low in her heart, words of deep thanksgiving.

There were many besides Blanche who noticed with astonishment the tall form of the keeper in his unwonted place at the communion-table; and many along with Morag gave thanks to Him who " turneth men's hearts as rivers of water whither He will," and who had brought this proud, rebellious spirit to the foot of His cross.

Dingwall had been welcomed to the place he occupied to-day by the old minister some evenings before in the manse. He disclosed the picture of his past life, with its darkest shadows unrelieved; and had told of his late repentance. The pastor recognized it as genuine, and there was a light in his eye to-day as he read his Master's message, " This is a faithful saying, and worthy of all acceptation, that Jesus Christ came into the world to save sinners."

After the usual service was over, Blanche's interest, which had been flagging, began to revive, and she felt glad that her maid was not in attendance to take her home, as she felt curious to know what was coming next.

Presently a hymn was sung to a sad wailing tune, which suited the words. It told of that

night on which the Son of Man endured the
" eager rage of every foe ; " and Blanche felt
a knot rise in her throat as she listened to it
and tried to join.   Never before, she thought,
had she felt so sorry for the Lord Jesus Christ,
who was " crucified, dead, and buried," though
she had heard all about it so many times.
And then she suddenly remembered Morag's
anxiety to know all about the " good Lord who
died on the green hill," and how many questions she used to ask about Him during the
first days of their acquaintance; but she never
mentioned the subject now, so Blanche concluded that she could not care so much as she
did before.

The words of the hymn had brought tears
to Morag's eyes, too.   But then she quickly
remembered the joyful side of the sorrowful
story, and thought of Him " who liveth, and
was dead, and is alive for evermore."

While the hymn was being sung, four old
men, the *elders* of the kirk, walked slowly in,
carrying the plates of bread and cups of wine,
which they placed reverently on a white-covered
table, where the minister now sat, and which
Blanche supposed must be the altar she had
been in search of.

The children watched with mingled curiosity and awe while the symbols were passed to all who sat at the long white tables, after the minister had given thanks and read to the congregation the Master's words which He spoke in the upper room at Jerusalem when He commanded that this Feast should be kept by His disciples till He should come again.

Perfect stillness reigned throughout the church; almost every head was bowed, and many a heart went up in silent adoring gratitude to Him who had loved them and given Himself for them.

When the elders had again reverently placed the symbols on the table in front of the pulpit, the stillness was broken by the deep, grave voice of the pastor, speaking words of exhortation to his flock, that they should be " blameless and harmless, the sons of God." A sweet psalm of thanksgiving was sung, and then, with uplifted hands, the minister prayed that the peace of God might rest on the little company; and, at last, the peasants moved away from the long white tables to scatter to their distant homes in the Glen; some of them never to meet again till they gather to the Feast above.

The children sat and watched them as they passed slowly out of the kirk, and then they, too, rose to go. Morag sought her father immediately. She gazed eagerly into his face, as if she expected him to say something; but he only pressed her hand, and turning to Kirsty, he said 'Good-bye,' and then walked away.

"Lat him gang hame his lane, bairn," whispered Kirsty, as she noticed Morag's disappointed look, and her movement to follow, when her father started to go home alone. "I'm thinkin' he'll hae better company wi' him than ony o' us wad mak' Morag, lass."

And then surveying her little flock, Kirsty said, smiling kindly, "Noo, bairns, I'se warrant ye're hun'ry eneuch. Jist ye come doun til a quaiet burnside 'at I ken fine, and we'll hae a bit o' a rest—and ye'll eat a piece I hae brocht for ye a'."

So the old woman led the way to a quiet nook behind the village, where the yellowing birk-trees drooped round a pleasant bit of greensward, hiding it from the dusty highway, while the splashings of a little burn, rolling merrily among the white stones, kept the turf smooth and green all the year through.

Here Kirsty seated herself, with her merry little party round her. From underneath her red cloak she then produced a basket containing some delicious cream-cakes, which she had baked on the previous evening for this occasion, and of which she now invited the children to partake.

Never did lunch taste so nice; and never was there such a pleasant Sunday, Blanche thought, as she sat at Kirsty's feet, eating her piece of oat-cake, and talking to her old friend.

Morag was perched on a stone, with her sunburnt feet paddling in the brown water, and Kenneth stood watching the fate of twigs, meant to personate his friends, which he occasionally tossed into the water, where presently they got among the tiny rapids of the burn, some of them being finally entangled there, while others were able to extricate themselves from their difficulties, and were borne onwards to the river.

Blanche prattled away merrily, as usual, upon a variety of topics; sometimes asking questions about the services of the day, and comparing notes with the arrangements of the church where she went in London. Morag listened with wondering eyes as the wee leddy glowingly described the beautiful, many-colored picture-windows, the pretty gilded altar, and the great organ, with its surpliced choir. The little mountain maiden had looked upon the interior of the village kirk as very beautiful; but this church, described by Blanche, must be much more so: and Morag began to think that perhaps the Lord Jesus Christ liked best to be worshipped in a fine church like that, since He was so high and holy. But, with the thought, there came a pang of disappointment, and, whenever she had an opportunity, she confided her trouble to Kirsty.

' After pondering a little, the old woman slowly replied, " Weel, bairn, I'll no say but that the Maister likes a' thing that's bonnie and fair to see. A fine bigget hoose o' worship, wi' the best wark that the fingers o' man can mak', canna be onacceptable til Him. But I'm thinkin', efter a', the thing that'll please Him maist is to see ilka hert worshippin' Him in speerit and in trowth,—nae maitter whither it be intil a gran' bigget kirk, or amang the bracken upo' the hillside, as oor folk ance did, lang syne, Morag, lass."

" Oh yes, Kirsty, I know. You mean in the time of the Covenanters, don't you?" said Blanche as she broke off a branch from the bog-myrtle, and threw it into the burn, in imitation of Kenneth's amusement. " I know all about the Covenanters. By the by, I've got a book in London with some rather nice stories about them. I wish I had it here, Morag; I think you would like it. The sol diers certainly were very cruel and rough to the people they found making a church among the heather. I'm sure I could never see why," continued the little English maiden, as she went to extricate her twig from among the rapids with her umbrella; because that twig was Morag she said, and she must give her a little poke on.

"Ay, ay!" said the old woman meditatively. "They were the dark days o' oor kirk, but wha kens 'at they warna the brichtest days, efter a', i' the eyes o' Him 'at walks amang the seven golden cawnal-sticks we read o' i' the Revelations. He aye telt His kirk nae to be feared at onything it had to suffer."

"Weel, Morag, lass! so ye're thinkin' yet ye wad like to worship i' the gran' hoose in Lou'on, 'at the wee leddy tells o', better nor in oor wee kirkie?" said Kirsty, turning smilingly to the crestfallen little Morag, as she divined her thoughts. "D'ye min' far the Laist Supper was keepit—i' the upper room in Jerooslem? Weel, I'm no thinkin' there could hae been onything very braw intilt; and yet the Maister thocht it guid eneuch for sic a Feast as the warl' niver saw."

Blanche did not remember about it, so

Kirsty handed her the old Bible, and she read St. Luke's account of the Last Supper, finishing with the words—"And when they had sung a hymn, they went to the Mount of Olives."

"Why, Kirsty, how funny! That's just something like what we've done to-day. And I'm sure the Mount of Olives couldn't be half so nice as this burn-side; could it, Morag? I shall be sure to remember this Sunday when I go to Holy Communion, Kirsty. But that will be ever so long yet. I've got to be confirmed first, you know. Miss Prosser says it's proper to go to Holy Communion when one is about seventeen; but, oh dear! it's a long time till then. I do wish I were grown up," said Blanche, with a sigh over the slow progress of Time.

"Eh, but my dear lambie, ye maun let Him intil yer hert lang afore that time comes roun'. Will ye no listen til the Guid Shepherd's voice callin' ye the day? There's a hantle o' rough slippy bits o' life afore ye, my bonnie bairn, I'm thinkin'. Will ye no lat Him tak' ye intil His arms, and carry ye safe through them a'?" said Kirsty, as she looked fondly at the little girl.

Blanche did not reply, but sat nervously

plucking blades of grass. Presently she jumped up, and ran to join Kenneth, who had gone to catch the old cart-horse grazing by the waterside, to yoke him in the cart again, and prepare for the homeward journey.

Then Morag gave Kirsty a shoulder to help her from her low seat on the greensward ; and as she stooped to pick up the basket, she said in a low, eager tone, " Kirsty, werna ye richt glad to see father i' the kirk the day ? I never thocht he was comin' tilt."

" Ay was I,—glaider than ye can ken' o', bairn," replied Kirsty, her gray eyes beaming with joy. " 'Deed I'm thinkin' there maun hae been joy amang the angels themsels, the day when they saw yer father sitting at the table o' the Lord—a bran' plucked frae the burnin'. Eh, bairn, ye that's ain o' His ain lambs yersel', arna ye glaid to think that yer puir father's nae latten bide oot i' the cauld."

Morag's face flushed with joy to hear Kirsty call her a Christian, and she was going to make some reply when they heard Blanche's clear, silvery tones calling them to come—that the cart was all ready to start.

" There's that bonnie wee leddy, wi' her sweet tongue," said Kirsty, as she moved to go. " Dear lamb ! may the Guid Shepherd mak'

16

goodness and mercy to follow her a' the days o' her life. She's a winsome bit thing as I ever set eyes on. I wad like richt weel to ken that she gied her young hert to the Lord, Morag. There's a heap o' snares and dangers o' the great warl' for the like o' her. They tell me she's fat they ca' an heiress, and has heaps o' hooses and lan' in Englan' belongin' til her-sel'. It wad be a richt sair maitter gin she were like the young man—him ye ken that we read o' i' the Scripter, wha turned awa frae the Lord sorrowfu'-like, because his hert was set upon his gran' possessions. She has sic a hantle o' bonnie ways aboot her, and as sweet a like natur' as ever God made. Ye maun be earnest wi' the Lord for yer wee leddy, Morag, my lass."

This was a subject about which Morag longed greatly to talk to Kirsty, though she had never yet been able to break through her shyness and reserve. She looked up eagerly in the old woman's face, and was about to reply, when Blanche pushed aside the fringing birk-trees in search of them, and they left the quiet green nook, and turned into the dusty high-way.

Many a time in after years, when these autumn days lay far away in the dim haze of dis-

tance, Morag Dingwall would leave the beaten
path, if she chanced to pass that way, and wander in among the whispering birk-trees and the
scented bog-myrtle, to stand and gaze at this
little spot of mossy-turf. Time having brought
many changes for her, she would stand pensively
and gaze at this still unchanged spot, where the
little singing burn flowed on in its sparkling
glee, heedless of the vanished voices which had
once mingled in its sport. And as she stood
there her thoughts would go slipping back—

"By the green bye-ways forgotten, to a stiller circle of
time,
Where violets faded for ever, seemed blooming as once
in their prime,"

till her bonnie wee leddy's voice seemed again
to ring out clear and silvery, and she could hear
Kirsty's low, earnest tones, as she spoke of the
Master she loved so well.

THE LOCH.

A COLD north wind that smelled of winter had been sweeping through the glen for several days, making the great fir-forests creak and swing, and the ash and birk-trees down in the hollow shiver and drop their leaves at each gust. The nights had begun to draw in visibly, and the mornings felt chilly, and looked sad and grey. Everything seemed to proclaim that the pleasant autumn days at Glen Eagle were nearly done. The purple bloom had quite faded from the heather, and the hills began to look stern and bleak in the cheerless afternoon.

> " Red o'er the forest peers the setting sun,
>   The line of yellow light dies fast away
>   That crown'd the eastern copse ; and chill and dun
>   Falls on the moor the brief October day."

To two young hearts that wintry wind and its accompaniments sounded dirge-like and sad, for it told of happy days that had passed all too soon. Blanche sighed as she remembered the dull London school-room, and the measured promenade in Kensington Park; and Morag's lip grew tremulous as she trotted by Shag's side along the familiar roads, and sighed to think how desolate they would seem without his little mistress.

The shooting party at the old castle had already begun to break up; and the day for general dispersion to warmer latitudes was fixed, when, one afternoon, Blanche and Morag stood together in the old court-yard, trying to decide what would be the very pleasantest way of spending it. They had promised to spend the last afternoon with Kirsty; and now the last but one had come, and the hours seemed so very precious that they feared to " squander one wavelet " of them.

Shag had returned to his winter quarters that morning, not without a tearful parting on the little girl's side. The little Shetlander manifested no emotion on the occasion ; indeed Blanche fancied that she could detect a merry twinkle of satisfaction in his bright eye when he recognized his master, and heard his native Gaelic, and he certainly moved off with him in his readiest trot. Chance, too, had been sent

southward along with the first detachment of
servants, so the little girls were able to make their
plans irrespective of their quadruped friends.

It seemed this afternoon as if the setting in
of bad weather was likely to prove a false alarm
after all. The bleak wind that had been sweeping through the strath ceased to blow to-day,
and the bright sunshine was once again lighting up the desolate ravines, and sending its
glory upon the autumnal tints down among
the hollows. Never had the Glen looked more
lovely, Blanche thought, as her eye wandered
over the now familiar landscape. The loch lay
shining in the sunlight, like a looking-glass
framed in the heather; and as she looked across
to it, Blanche suddenly remembered that she
had promised to go there before she left to
find a water lily, as a model for one of a group
of wax flowers which Miss Prosser had been
making during these holiday afternoons, while
her pupil was rambling among the hills.

It was a satisfaction to be able to find an
object for the walk, and the girls set out briskly
along the winding path which led from the
castle grounds to the moorland road. The
drooping birk boughs were quite golden now,
and the rowan berries a coral red. Blanche
kept plucking them as she went cheerily along,

warbling in the sunshine. Feeling very happy for the present, she did not allow the shadow of the coming separation to throw its gloom over her, as it seemed to do with the grave little Morag, who walked silently by her side. Everything looked bright and smiling, and her wee leddy appeared in one of her most joyous moods; and Morag wondered why she should feel so sad, that the surrounding brightness seemed to jar upon her, rather than chase away her sorrowful mood. And as she listened to the little birds, who took up the refrain of Blanche's warblings, and merrily chirruped odes of welcome to the returned sun, Morag was reminded of a sentiment expressed in one of Kirsty's songs. She had never understood the reason of its saying—

> " Why will ye chant, ye little birds,
> And I sae weary, fu' o' care?"

and had once remarked to her old friend that " even though a body was feelin' some sad like, it wad surely do their hearts guid to hear the birdies sing sic bonnie."

But Kirsty had smiled and said, " 'Deed, bairn, but ye're wrang there, I'm thinkin'. No a' the birdies' bonnie sangs, nor a' the sweet warks o' God, can pit glaidness intil broken, sorrowfu' herts. Naething can do that, I'm

thinkin', excep' a sicht o' His ain face, and a
soun' o' His ain voice. I've whiles thocht 'at
the poet-chiel' wha made the bit sang maun
hae kent fine what it was to hae a richt sorrowfu' sair hert mony a day;" and Morag thought
that she was able, from to-day's experience, to
catch a glimpse of the poet's meaning.

Presently Blanche caught the infectious
sadness of her friend, and became quiet and
meditative also. Flinging away her bunches
of rowan berries, she came and put her arms
round Morag's sunburnt neck, saying, gently,
"You won't quite forget me, Morag, dear,
when I'm far away, will you?"

A great glow of love rose in Morag's heart
as she felt the soft curls about her neck and
Blanche's lips on her cheek. She felt as if she
could have died for her bonnie wee leddy then
and there, but she only answered quietly, " I'm
no thinkin' we'll forget ye that ready. Kirsty
and me will be min'in' on ye ilka day. But
I'm some feared whiles that ye'll no be min'in'
o' the Glen when ye gang back to the gran'
muckle toun ye bide in."

There was something else which Morag
longed to say to Blanche that afternoon, and
many times before, but she had never been able
to summon up courage to speak about it. She

wished to tell her of the new feeling that had been taking possession of her heart, and which she longed to share with Blanche.

Since those first days of wonder and perplexity—which hearing the hymn in the fir-wood caused—Morag had never talked to the little English girl of those things which had been slowly sinking into her heart. Kirsty had been her Evangelist, Morag sometimes thought, as she read the " Pilgrim's Progress." It was she who had pointed out the way to the Wicket Gate when the little girl was groping blindly; and to her alone could she speak freely as yet. But now that she had come to understand what a real, living, listening Friend the Lord Jesus Christ is, though unseen by earthly eyes, she longed intensely to share this new faith and hope with her wee leddy, whom she loved so well. And since Kirsty had hinted at the many dangers which the world beyond the mountains might have in store for her now guileless friend, she longed the more to ask her to take this unseen Friend for her Saviour and Guide. But somehow the opportunity passed, and they had reached the loch before Morag could find words to say what she wanted.

Blanche did not like the sombre mood which appeared to have fallen on them both;

and seemed bent on talking herself and her friend into a gayer mood by 'castle-building. She began to prattle about all that she meant to do next summer, of the many ambitious feats in the way of climbing which she meant to perform, and of the familiar places—written over with memories of those pleasant autumn days which they would have to revisit.

The yellow afternoon sun was shining on the rippling water of the loch, and the blue sky, with numberless white fleecy clouds, lay like heaps of snow reflected on its clear depths. On the soft mossy banks, sloping down to the loch, there grew masses of scented bog myrtle, and alder bushes, while yellow flags and rushes fringed the edge of the water. The broad dark leaves of the water-lilies rocked about in tangled masses on the loch; but Blanche looked in vain for a lily to take to Miss Prosser. At last she gave up the search, and throwing herself lazily on the sunny bank, she lay watching the circles made by the trouts in pursuit of flies hovering upon the surface of the water.

Morag meanwhile spied a wild rose-bush at some distance off, on the bank, and she clambered up to gather the brilliant scarlet berries; and Blanche presently started off again on a fresh search after the water-lily; for she was unwilling to return from her last expedition without the flower which she had promised to find. At last she was rewarded by discovering a beautiful lily lying hidden away among the dark leaves. It seemed to be at a convenient stretching distance, so she knelt down on the moss, and put out her hand to grasp it, which she did with difficulty, for it was further off than she had thought. She was about to spring back in triumph at having captured the prize, when she felt the ground suddenly give way, and in spite of her efforts to save herself, she went slipping into the water—down, down among the roots of the floating lilies.

In her terror she gave a plunge to try to grasp some reeds growing near and to regain her footing, but she only landed herself further from the bank than before. All happened in the twinkling of an eye—so quickly that Blanche raised no cry. But now that all footing was gone, and she felt herself being fast submerged in the deep water, she shrieked with terror, and threw up her arms in wild dismay.

Morag was at the water's brink in a moment; but she only came in time to see the ripples closing over Blanche's golden crown. She stretched out her hands towards her, but saw in a moment that she had been carried too far out for any such help. Morag looked round in silent despair, for she could not swim, and she had presence of mind to realise that it would be impossible otherwise to save her; but she could not let her bonnie wee leddy die all alone there, and, in an instant two little girls, instead of one, were struggling for life among the rocking lily-leaves. Morag's wild plunge brought her alongside Blanche, who, with her remaining consciousness roused, clutched her arm, but very soon both the girls were sinking, sinking, and the cruel water closing over them!

Once again Blanche's hands were thrown up, and her closing eyes looked on the calm afternoon scene—the sun-lighted grass, with the scarlet berries scattered over it, dropped by Morag in her wild plunge towards the bank— once again, and then—

But what is that rustling among the alder bushes, and these sounds of heavy breathing after a hard race?

Kenneth Macpherson stands on the grassy bank just as the long, floating curls went under the rippling water, and Blanche Clifford's last struggle for life seemed over. She had loosened her hold on Morag's arm, who now began to make convulsive efforts to find her again, as she was drifted away. In a moment, Kenneth's arm was round Blanche, and with a few vigorous strokes he laid her on the bank—or all that remained of her, for his hasty glance gave him little hope that life was there.

Morag's consciousness partially returned as soon as he grasped her, and very soon she, too, was laid on the grass by the panting Kenneth. But the most difficult part of his work was yet to come, he thought, as he glanced at the motionless figures on the turf. Kneeling down, he began to chafe Blanche's cold hands, and vainly tried to detect some sign of life. Presently Morag got up from the turf, and stood shivering, gazing blankly round, as if she were at a loss to know what had happened. The sight of the water recalled everything with terrible vividness; she looked wildly round in search of Blanche, and saw her lying pale and motionless on the bank. her fair curls all drenched and tangled. With a cry of agony, Morag sprang to her side.

"I don't think she's dead, Morag!" whispered Kenneth, who still knelt beside her. "Do you think you are able to stay here while I go to the castle to get help? But I'm afraid you must be very wet and tired, yourself, poor Morag!"

"Oh, rin ! rin to the castle ! I'll easy bide wi' her ! My bonnie wee leddy, speak but ae word til me ! " And Morag bent eagerly over her ; but the lips were silent and bloodless, and the eyes gave no sign of life. It was terrible to be so helpless to do anything, Morag thought, as she kept chafing the cold fingers, while, in a low monotone of agony, she prayed that her wee leddy might come back to life again.

Meanwhile, Kenneth flew like lightning to the castle. On the way, he met the wearied remnant of the shooting party sauntering homewards, after their last day at the moors, all unconscious of what had been going on at the loch. Their pace was quickly changed as they hurried towards the water, while servants followed with a supply of blankets and all other necessaries. Mr. Clifford hardly listened to Kenneth's incoherent words, when, flinging down his gun, he hurried towards the bank where his child lay still unconscious.

"Blanche, darling, speak to me ! " he cried, lifting her in his arms. But the head fell back, and the motionless frame gave no sign of life. The dearly won trophy, the water-lily, dropped at last from the unclasping fingers, and the white arm hung listlessly down.

All restoratives were eagerly tried, and at

length the anxious group on the greensward fancied they could detect a slight quiver through the frame, and Blanche slowly returned from the borders of the far-off Land, as the last rays of the evening sun were gleaming upon the loch. The blue eyes opened wearily, and she glanced shiveringly round, evidently unconscious of where she was.

"Morag, Morag! don't let me go!" she cried, with a look of terror. "The river is so dark and cold! Do you not see the Golden City yet, Morag?"

"Hush, Blanche, darling! You must not think of the river any more. You are safe in papa's arms now!"

Gradually Blanche returned to consciousness, and remembered what had happened. After a bewildered glance at the group on the turf, and Miss Prosser seated at her side, she began to understand what had brought them all there. Presently she sat up among the blankets in which she was imbedded, and began to look eagerly round for one familiar face which she did not see. "Morag!" she whispered, looking inquiringly at her papa, and then she glanced towards the rippling water, all tinged with the gorgeous sunset hues, and there she saw floating the wreath of rowan berries which she had twined among Morag's black locks that afternoon. "Morag! where is she? Oh, surely not *there?* She jumped into the loch! I remember seeing her! I remember it all now!" and Blanche clasped her hands, and looked wildly into her father's face.

Morag was, meanwhile, seated farther up on the bank, where she could catch a glimpse of her friend, though she could not be seen by her. With her usual shyness, she had fled when the castle party surrounded Blanche; and hiding behind some alder bushes, she watched with intense anxiety the movements within the circle. But when, at last, she heard her own name called by Blanche, her heart gave a great throb of joy, and in an instant she was at her wee leddy's side.

"Morag, darling! it's all right then? I never felt so happy in my life," said Blanche, clasping the little brown hands in her trembling fingers. "Oh, I was so frightened when I woke up. I couldn't see you anywhere, and felt almost afraid to ask, when I saw the rowan-wreath floating about. Oh! it was too terrible. But do tell me, how did it all happen? how did we ever get out of the water?"

"We were droonin', ye ken, leddy; but Kenneth cam' runnin' doun the bank frae the peat-moss, and took's baith oot o' the water."

"Oh yes; by the way, where has the brave fellow gone?" asked Mr. Clifford, getting up from the turf, where he had been kneeling by his daughter's side, and looking about for Kenneth.

"But Kenneth—I don't understand," said Blanche, looking perplexed. "He wasn't with us, Morag. How did he ever come here?"

It was, indeed, a strange coincidence that Kenneth Macpherson should have been within sight and hearing of the loch this afternoon. It was the first time he had been so near it since he came to Glen Eagle. He had come to a peat-moss in the vicinity to-day in Kirsty's winter supply of peats, having borrowed Neil's cart for the occasion. Early in the afternoon he noticed the little girls pass on their way to the loch, as he conjectured. He stopped his work for a moment to watch them, and wished he had been a little nearer, so that they might have spoken to him, as he heard Blanche's ringing silvery tones through the keen air. And not long afterwards, when he heard the wild shriek from the loch, he thought he recognized

the voice, and leaving cart and peats, bounded
off in the direction from which it came, reaching the spot, as we know, just in time to rescue
the little girls. After his return from the cas-
t e he had hovered near the watching group
till he satisfied himself that Blanche had recovered, and then he went again to work at the
peat-moss.

Morag had watched him slip quietly back
to his work, unheeding of thanks or praise; and
from that hour he became enshrined as a hero
in her little woman's heart. She longed to see
the joy and pride which would be reflected in
Kirsty's gray eyes when she heard of her grandson's share in the doings of this afternoon; and
she felt a glow of pride when Mr. Clifford called
him a brave fellow.

As soon as Blanche had recovered sufficiently, they prepared to carry her away from
the scene of the catastrophe. She was looking
as pale as the water-lily lying on the turf beside
her. Catching a glimpse of it, she picked it up,
and handed it to Miss Prosser, saying, "You
see I have got it for you. Isn't it a beauty?
It was the very last one I could find; I remember holding it so tight when I was in the deep
water. I suppose Kenneth fished it up with
me," she added, smiling, as Miss Prosser took

the dearly-won trophy from the trembling fingers, and kissed her little pupil with more tenderness than she was wont to do.

Poor little Morag watched her bonnie wee leddy being borne away to the castle with the desolate feeling of being left out in the cold. The reaction had come after the intense experiences of these past hours. She stood watching the glad procession set out with wistful eyes, and then she moved away in the direction of her solitary home, for she felt cold and weary enough now. Her father had gone to the kennels before the shooting party heard of the accident, and he now sat at home in the hut, wondering what had become of his little daughter.

" Papa, I remember it all now!" exclaimed Blanche, who had been lying pale and meditative in her father's arms, as he carried her home. " I slipped into the water just as I got hold of the lily. Morag wasn't in sight, I remember, and I got very frightened when I felt the dark water coming all round, and carrying me quite away from the bank. I recollect hearing myself scream quite well, and then, in a minute, Morag stood on the bank, stretching out her hand ; but I couldn't reach it, and only got further away than before. And just as the water was going right over me, I saw

Morag jump in, and then I don't remember anything more. Dear, brave Morag! it was just like her, wasn't it, papa? I'm sure I should have been much too frightened to jump into the water. But she must be as cold and tired as I was, papa! Where are you, Morag?" asked Blanche, looking round.

"Yes, to be sure, pussy; we should have thought of that before. You have been absorbing all our attention in a such troublesome manner, you see. Where are you, little black-eyes? I saw her flitting about quite briskly a little while ago, as if the ducking in her native waters had not affected her unpleasantly. I declare, if she hasn't redeveloped her propensity for scudding, Blanchie! She's nowhere to be seen," said Mr. Clifford, glancing round the group.

Blanche was so distressed at the disappearance of her friend, that one of the servants was despatched in quest of her, and the little girl being presently recaptured, she was, in spite of her entreaties, carried off to the castle, and put under the old housekeeper's care.

She was made quite a lion of in the servants' hall that evening, though she was somewhat at a loss to understand why. She recounted, quite eloquently for her, how Kirsty's grandson had saved them both, and seemed much surprised when somebody commended her for her efforts to save their little mistress; for it never occurred to her that any other course would have been possible than to die with her bonnie wee leddy.

Ellis had never taken the little native to her heart, in spite of her little mistress' frequent triumphant reminders that the ragged maiden of the fir-wood had proved no dangerous gypsy after all; but to-night she was most gracious, patting the trembling little Morag condescendingly on the head, as she led the way to Blanche's room, where Morag was summoned in the course of the evening.

The little bare, weather-beaten feet trod much more uneasily on the soft carpet than among the bracken; and the friendship which had sprung up and flourished among the woods and braes did not seem likely to thrive in the atmosphere of a luxuriantly-furnished apartment. Blanche was lying on the sofa, wrapped in a blue flannel dressing-gown, looking very feeble and subdued, when Morag entered the room. She looked wistfully at her little mountain friend, but did not speak, and Miss Prosser, who was seated at her pupil's side, noted the mutual shyness, and considerately withdrew.

Beckoning to Morag to come and sit beside her, she took the little brown hand into her fluttering fingers, and said, nervously, " Morag, dear, I want so much to speak to you. Do you know, though it was only such a moment of time, I thought so much when I felt going down, down among the dark moving water all alone. And you left the pleasant, sunny turf, and came to drown with me in that dreadful water. How could you venture, Morag? It was too brave and kind!" and Blanche's lip quivered.

Morag was going to interrupt her, but she went on. " Do you remember that chapter of the Bible we were reading to Kirsty yesterday, Morag? I'm afraid I didn't care much for it at the time, and only read it to please her; but since I've been lying here, I seem to hear one verse of it always. Wasn't it Jesus Christ who said that it was the greatest love to lay down one's life for a friend? Morag, that's what you did for me. I saw you do it. Oh, Morag, when I awoke and saw the rowan-wreath floating about in the water, and you not anywhere to be seen!" and Blanche covered her face and sobbed.

All Morag's shyness seemed to vanish when she had to take the part of a comforter.

The little brown arm was quietly slipped round the bent head, and she whispered gently, " Ye mustna think nothing o' my slippin' in efter ye til the water. I couldna hae bidden ahin' for onything. But ye see if it hadna been for Kenneth, none o' us would hae been gotten oot o' the loch." And after a pause she continued, "I'm no thinkin' that word frae the Bible would even mean the like o' Kenneth, though. Will it no be meanin' the Lord Jesus Christ, that died o' the green hill,—as ye're bonnie hymn speaks o'? I weel min' the day I heard it;" and then she added, with an evident effort, "and I've aye been wantin' to tell ye that I love Him richt weel mysel' noo, sin' yon day i' the fir-wood."

" And is it because you love the Lord Jesus so much that you were so brave at the loch to-day, Morag?" said Blanche, looking questioningly at her.

" I'm no thinkin' that exactly," replied Morag, slowly, as if she were pondering her motives; "I'm thinkin' it was because I looed you, little leddy, and forby, life wouldna hae seemed muckle worth gin ye had been awa."

" D'ye min' the bonnie picter oot o' the ' Pilgrim's Progress?' I was jist thinkin' to mysel', on my road hame the nicht, that gin

Kenneth hadna come, we would hae gotten thegither to the bonnie toon lyin' i' the sun,—like the droonin' folk i' the picter," and Morag looked at Blanche, and smiled brightly.

The little girl shook her head sadly. " You would have gone to the Golden City, Morag; but I'm afraid I shouldn't. You see I never really thought I should like to go to heaven. It seemed to me that it would be so much nicer to stay always here, in this beautiful world we know and love, than to be sent away to an unknown land. Do you know, Morag, I thought of all that to-day, as I looked at the pleasant sunny banks of the loch, just before the cruel, creeping water covered me all up. It made me feel so terrified."

There was silence for a few minutes. At last, Morag said, quietly—

" But I'm no thinkin' heaven isna a kin' o' land we dinna ken, when Jesus is there Himsel', waitin' for us. He made ilka body so happy-like when he was i' the warl'; and though we canna see Him, I'm thinkin' He's jist the same yet. When we get til the golden gates o' the City we read aboot i' the hinner en' o' the Bible, he wad jist be puttin' His han's on us, and sayin' something kin' like, and we wad be feelin' at hame. He speaks that plain like til folk here, tho' we canna see Him. I dinna think I would be feared to gang til get a sicht o' Him."

There was a light in Morag's eye that made Blanche feel she was speaking of what she knew.

" He never speaks to me like that, Morag. I don't think He can love me at all. I'm sure He doesn't. I'm so dreadfully wicked. Besides, I'm afraid I never cared to know about Him at all; indeed, I never felt as if He were a real person."

" I thocht that ance, till Kirsty telt me different," said Morag, interrupting her. " I'm weel sure He looes you richt weel, leddy. I'm thinking He's no far frae us, jist this minute. Will ye no speak til Him yersel' in yer ain bonnie words, leddy? I'm thinkin' He would like weel fo be listening til the like o' you," whispered Morag, eagerly, as she knelt by Blanche's side.

" O Morag! do you mean that I should pray in my very own words? I couldn't, indeed. Of course I say my prayers every night—one of the Collects generally."

" I dinna ken what a Collec' is," replied Morag, looking perplexed.

" Oh, well, it's a written prayer we use in

church. If you'll bring that case of books to me, I'll show it to you."

Blanche turned the leaves of her daintily-bound Church Service, and read some of its strong, thrilling words of prayer, which rang like the music of a psalm in Morag's ear.

"That's jist terrible bonnie—a hantle bonnier than onything a body would make up themsels. I like richt weel to hear't. Would ye jist read a bit more, gin ye please?" and the little girl's face glowed with pleasure as she sat listening.

After looking meditatively into the fire for some minutes when Blanche had finished reading, she said, slowly—

"Ay, that is richt bonnie; and I'm thinkin' sic sweet words maun please Him weel. But there's jist something mak's me think He wad like a body's verra ain words best o' a'. Now, d'ye no think, gin ye was wantin' onything frae yer father, it wouldna be sic nateral like to read it oot o' a bonnie buik as jist to pit your arms roun' his neck, and plead wi' him a bittie, as I've seen you do, whiles,—and ye ken fine ye aye get the thing ye're wantin'," she added, smiling archly; and then she continued—"Weel, I'm thinkin' that maun be what He would hae us to do, frae what He

says Himsel'. · D'ye no think that yersel',
leddy ? " asked Morag, looking earnestly into
Blanche's troubled face.

"I think I understand what you mean,
Morag; but I never thought of speaking to
Jesus Christ like that. Why did you not ever
tell me that you did till to-night, Morag ? "
asked Blanche, reproachfully. "You remember you wanted so very much to know all
about Him when I knew you first. Dear me,
Morag, you must have found out a great deal
about these things since then," added Blanche,
regretfully.

"Ay have I," replied Morag, smiling brightly. "But it was frae yersel' I first heard His
name. D'ye mind on't, leddy ? I'm thinkin'
I'll min' upon't as lang as I live—and maybe
efter-hin. Kirsty was jist sayin' yestreen,
she's richt sure folk dosna forget the travellin'
days when they win safe hame til the Golden
City."

"Oh! I remember. You mean that morning when I was gathering cones in the fir-
wood, and began singing a hymn. I had been
singing for a long time before I looked up and
saw you. I was so astonished to see you leaning against the tree, and so glad that I had
found you again," and Blanche laughed mer

rily at the recollection of the scene. Presently she became grave again, and taking Morag's hand in hers, she added, in a low tone—"But, Morag, you must not think I was singing about Jesus Christ because I loved Him, or cared for the words of the hymn. I think I chose them because they seemed to suit the air I wanted to sing. I think I do care now, though. O Morag! you might speak to Jesus Christ yourself just now, and I'll try, too. Perhaps he will listen to us both. Do ask Him to teach me to be good when I go back to London. I used to be so naughty often—you've no idea. Do, please," added Blanche beseechingly, for she knew Morag's extreme shyness, and feared that her request might not be complied with.

The little mountain maiden seemed quite lifted out of her reserve. At once the dark tangled locks went down among the bright chintz cushions, and Morag spoke in low, reverent tones to the listening friend she had come to know and love during these autumn days.

Morag was still kneeling when Ellis came bustling into the room to say that the keeper had come to fetch his little daughter. Blanche looked much disappointed. The time had passed so quickly, and there was still much she wanted to talk about, but she had to content herself with arranging a meeting at Kirsty's cottage on the following afternoon.

"We shall have so much to tell her, shan't we? And only fancy, Morag, papa is coming, too! He says he will drive me there—that he wants to see Kenneth to thank him. Is it not funny to think that papa has never seen Kirsty? He says he is quite anxious to be introduced to her. Won't it be fun to see them together? I have been telling him all the things I want him too look at, and what chair it will be best to sit on—it would be a pity if he took Kirsty's chair, you know. I'm only afraid he may be too tall to get in at the door. I've been telling him he'll have to stoop ever so much." And Blanche laughed merrily at the idea, as Ellis hurried Morag away, saying that her father would be impatient.

The next day was cold, and wet, and scowling. Blanche seemed very tired and feverish, and was not allowed to leave her bed, to which, indeed, she made no resistance—the loch adventure seemed so completely to have exhausted her. She dozed comfortably till evening, when her papa came to sit beside her, and she became quite lively as she listened to his account of his visit to Kirsty's cottage, which he had paid that afternoon.

"Now, Blanchie, is there anything more you can possibly think of asking concerning this visit?" said Mr. Clifford, laughingly, as he replied to Blanche's eager questioning. "I couldn't have endured a greater fire of cross-questioning if I had come from one of Her Majesty's drawing-rooms, and you wanted a description of each toilette. Did I .see a stool called 'Thrummy?' Well, I was almost precipitated into the fire-place, just as I was going to make my bow to Kirsty, by stumbling over a bundle of rags which answers to your description, so I suppose I did see the historical 'Thrummy.' Smiling, he continued: "Then I sat down—I hope on the right chair—but you may be sure I was dreadfully afraid of making a *faux pas* after all your instructions, Blanchie. I ended by having quite a long talk with your friend Kirsty, though I had considerable difficulty in understanding her dialect. She is really a very fine specimen of a peasant woman. I quite admire your taste, pussy. There is a wonderful amount of sense and pathos in her way of viewing things in general, notwithstanding that atrocious northern dialect."

"Oh, papa! don't say it's atrocious! I like to listen to it so much now. I'm sure I could never like an old woman half so well if she did not speak like Kirsty. She is the first I have ever known,—and I love her so much," added Blanche with a sigh, when she thought how soon she would be far away from the *ben-end* of Kirsty's cottage, where she had spent some of the pleasantest hours of her life.

"Yes; she is a first-rate old woman, I allow; but she has put me in the embarrassing position of absolutely refusing to accept any reward for her grandson's brave conduct yesterday. Unfortunately, one is not much accustomed to such delicacy of feeling, so perhaps I did not manage the matter rightly. I began to see what kind of stuff she was made of, and I did try to approach the subject as carefully as possible. But she shook her fine old head resolutely, and would not hear of anything more substantial than thanks."

"Ah! that was so like Kirsty! I don't really think she would care a bit for anything you might give her; only I do think she will be well pleased that you went to see her, and said nice things about Kenneth. She does always look so glad to see Morag and me," added Blanche, smiling at the recollection of the warm reception which they never failed to receive at the little cottage.

"But did you not see Kenneth himself, papa?"

"Yes, I did. The bright idea occurred to me that the grandson might be more amenable, and before the old woman went to fetch him, I took the precaution of asking her not to lay any commands on the boy, at all events. She replied, in that wonderful voice of hers, 'Na, na; I'se houp the laddie winna need nae comman's o' mine anent sic a maitter.' So Kenneth was produced, and I thanked the brave fellow, in your name and mine. His face quite glowed with pleasure, I saw; but when I added, 'Now, Kenneth, my little daughter wants to give you something more than thanks for saving her life and her little friend's, though we know money can't pay for a brave deed like that,'—or something to that effect, his countenance fell directly, and he was quite as inexorable on that point as his old grandmother. So we must set our wits to work to manage the matter. I'll speak to Dingwall about it."

"I'm so glad Kenneth didn't want to take anything," exclaimed Blanche. "I'm sure Kirsty will be glad. She is so very anxious he should grow up a really good man. Don't her gray eyes look so pretty when she smiles, papa?"

"Now, pussy, I'm not going to join in any more raptures concerning Kirsty's eyes, or her other perfections. Good-night, darling. You are looking quite feverish again. We shall have plenty of time to talk about Kirsty when we get back to London, you know," added Mr. Clifford, as he saw that Blanche looked disappointed to close the conversation.

At last Blanche went to sleep, thinking how very nice it was to have her papa all to herself, for a whole evening; and that, after all, though it was very sad to leave Glen Eagle, it could not be dull in London when her papa was to be there, as he evidently meant to be, when he spoke of having talks about Kirsty.

18

XII

THE EMPTY HUT.

IT had been arranged that the journey southward should be postponed for a few days on account of the loch accident; but the next morning was so bright and pleasant, and Blanche looked so fresh and well, that there seemed no reason for departing from the original plan, and it was hastily decided that she and her governess should start for London, travelling by easy stages.

Great was Blanche's dismay when she heard of this arrangement. She had been rejoicing over another pleasant day in the Glen, and began to think that the loch adventure had some advantages after all, seeing it was going to secure a few more days in the Highlands.

"It can't possibly be true, Ellis. You had better not go on with that packing till you get further orders," said the little girl, in a tone more imperious than she almost ever used, as she found her maid in a state of pleasurable bustle and excitement over boxes that were being quickly filled.

"Yes, missie; it's quite true, I assure you," replied her maid, without looking up from the box over which she was stooping. "Miss Prosser says it's a hexcellent arrangement, and, for my part, I agree with her 'eartily. It quite sets one up to think of gettin' back to civilized existence. There's cook quite a henvyin' of me, because I'm going three days sooner."

"I wish I were cook, I'm sure," burst in Blanche. "But, Ellis, I'm sure papa can't mean me to go to-day. He can't, indeed! I shall go and ask him this minute. You'd better stop putting in those things, Ellis," she added, impatiently.

But Ellis smiled confidently, and went on with her work, while Blanche ran away down the great staircase, feeling rather faint-hearted, however, as she thought of the possibility of Ellis's tidings being true. Below, she found everybody in a state of the most unpleasant pre-occupation. Miss Prosser was in the midst of elaborate packings, and smilingly assured her little pupil that they were really going. The carriage was to be at the door exactly at twelve o'clock, so she must make haste to be ready in time; and was it not pleasant they were going to have such a fine day to leave Glen Eagle?—and should they not be thankful that she was well enough to travel so soon after so serious an accident?

Blanche fled from Miss Prosser, along the winding passages towards the library, in the hope of finding her papa. There was still one last resource; she would beg him to allow her to remain, even one day, longer. There he was, seated in the library, to be sure; but surrounded by such piles of letters and papers, and with his most business-like expression on his face. Several people were waiting to speak to him and there seemed no hope of Blanche gaining an audience, unless she went boldly up to him, and made her petition before them all. She lingered about for a little time, trying to summon up courage, but at last glided away without uttering a word.

Then she wandered into the entrance-hall, and stood leaning on the old stuffed fox, watching the pile of boxes and portmanteaus in the court-yard, which increased in size every minute. The servants were hurrying to and fro in a state of bustle and excitement. Evidently, to Blanche alone these signs of departure brought a pang of regret. The thought of those pleasant vanished afternoons was too much to be borne. She had known that she must leave the Highland glen before long : but she did not dream it would be such a cruel tearing away as this.

After wandering aimlessly about for some time, she remembered that she must see Morag before the dreaded hour arrived. She could not surely have heard that they were really going to-day, or else she would have come, and there was no sign of her anywhere. Blanche wandered round the castle, among the grove of ash-trees, and into the old garden, but she did not find her friend at any of the usual trysting-places.

At last she made up her mind what she would do. Hurrying swiftly along the birk-walk, where the drooping boughs were quite golden now, she clambered up the steep ascent which led to the little shieling among the crags.

Blanche's spirits began to rise again. It would be so pleasant to give Morag a surprise. Probably she would find her at work inside the cottage. Perhaps she would be paring potatoes, as she had been on a previous occasion, which Blanche remembered well—for had she not sat down on a little stool beside her, and, being provided with a knife, had pared away delightedly. She thought it the most charming of amusements ; but when she was dressing for the drawing-room that evening, Ellis had looked suspiciously at the stained fingers, which resisted ordinary ablutions, and Blanche, having been obliged to divulge to what culinary uses they had been devoted that day, had been forbidden by her governess to visit Morag again. It was therefore many weeks since she had been within the hut; but she felt sure that Miss Prosser could not be angry at her going on a farewell visit like this.

The door stood open, and Blanche walked in on tiptoe, smiling to think how astonished her little friend would be to see her. She glanced eagerly round the room, but no Morag was to be seen anywhere. The peat fire was burning brightly, and the potatoes lay among water in a nice wooden dish, all ready pared. But these traces of the absent inmate only made the disappointment keener. Blanche stood looking round, with a very dreary feeling. It was so hard not to find Morag, and she had evidently not been gone for long; if she had only thought of coming earlier, it would have been all right. The dreaded hour fixed for leaving the castle must be very near now, and what if she could not be found before then? Blanche's heart sank as she contemplated the possibility. Before she turned to go, she cast a lingering glance round the empty dwelling, and she could not help remarking how much nicer it looked than when she saw it first.

The roof was still far from being rainproof certainly, and the earthen floor was more undulating than was quite pleasant to walk upon; but the most had been made of everything that was capable of improvement. There was a sort of imitation of Kirsty's household arrangements which was very observable to Blanche, and she smiled through her tears as she noted it. On the shelf was ranged quite an imposing row of shining delf, where there used only to stand a stray broken dish or two. Everything was spotlessly clean and neat; and, in the little window, there flourished some of the old woman's favorite flowers, of which she had given slips to Morag. All this, and more, Blanche's quick eye took in at a glance; and the thought of its being the work of a pair of little, eager hands she knew well, brought quite a glow of pleasure, in the midst of her disappointment.

Blanche stood gazing at Morag's home till it was photographed in her memory. And as

she turned away to go down the hill, she
thought that surely Morag must have sought
and found help from her unseen Friend for all
those home duties, which it must be so difficult
for a little girl no bigger than herself to have
to do ; and she longed to hear more about that
friendship, from the little mountain maiden.

Gazing wistfully in the direction of the fir-
wood, she wondered if she would have time to
go to see whether Morag was to be found at
their old trysting-place, the flat grey rock ; ·but
she dreaded that she would not, so she hurried
tearfully towards the castle, and only reached
home as the carriage drove to the door. She
found Ellis setting out to look for her in a state
of great indignation and perplexity, having,
in the midst of the bustle, only that minute
missed her charge. Some luncheon had to be
swallowed in great haste ; and then, while Miss
Prosser was seating herself in the carriage,
Blanche took the opportunity of darting off on
a farewell journey round the grey old keep,
where she had spent so many happy days.
Only at the last minute did her papa emerge
from the library to say good-bye to his little
daughter. He meant to go south by a different route, and would not rejoin her in London
for several weeks

Blanche felt as if all the waves and billows of trouble had gone over her head when she accidentally heard this piece of news, as she was at last compelled to seat herself in the carriage by Miss Prosser's side. She could not make any response to her father's cheerful waving to her as they were driven swiftly away. She felt the knot in her throat getting bigger every minute as they were whirled past the pleasant birk-walk and along the winding avenue, getting occasional glimpses through the boughs of the spruce fir-trees of the old grey. turrets, or the moorland beyond.

At last they got upon the high road, and drove swiftly on between the sharply outlined mountains that reared themselves high and solemn all round—like sentinels keeping eternal watch over the Glen, amid all the changes that went on below.

Miss Prosser was busied with the index to "Bradshaw," so that, fortunately, or the reverse, Blanche was left to her own reflections. She kept an eager watch, as they drove swiftly on in the forlorn hope of catching a glimpse of Morag. But the familiar spots were quickly being left behind, and there was no trace of her anywhere; and Blanche's hope died quite away when they got into the wider range of the strath,—away in the direction of her southern home.

If only Blanche had not buried her face for a moment among the furs as she was passing the larch plantation, which at a certain point skirted the high road, her quick eye might have discovered the person she so longed to see.

Morag stood among the larch trees, bending under a heavy bundle of faggots, which she had been gathering, and which she had just managed to strap on her back. Hearing the sound of wheels on the road, she turned to look, but was only in time to catch a glimpse of the carriage, as it passed swiftly along by the old winding dyke. Some traces of luggage were visible, and Ellis was seated on the box. Morag's heart sank. Was it possible they were leaving the Glen, to-day, after all? And she had been going cheerily on with her work that morning, in the hope of another afternoon with Blanche. For had not Ellis told her, when she went to inquire at the castle the day before, that the southward journey had been postponed for several days. Only a short time ago she had been smiling as she gathered her fire-wood, thinking how pleased Kirsty would look when the wee leddy walked into the cottage that afternoon. But now, the more she thought of it, the more sure she felt that those cruel, swift wheels were carrying her away beyond their reach, to a land that seemed terrible and unknown indeed to the little mountain maiden.

She ran to the edge of the wood, and climbing on the lichen-spotted dyke, she gazed wistfully along the winding road, where the shining carriage was rolling swiftly along. And after she had watched it till it could be seen no longer, the little girl sat down and wept bitt rly. Her bonnie wee leddy had gone without one parting word. Surely she must have utterly forgotten her, or else she could not have acted thus. Gladly would she have walked miles across pathless hills to touch her wee leddy's hand, and now she had gone without ever sending to ask her to come. And, as she sat weeping on the old grey dyke, the friendship of these autumn days seemed to grow dreamlike all of a sudden. Had she ever really walked by Shag's side with the little lady of the castle among the moors, or sat with her in the *ben-end* of Kirsty Macpherson's cottage?— or, had she been in fairyland all these weeks? The past seemed to grow so shadowy; and the bundle of dead sticks was so real and heavy, as she wearily rose, at last, to take her solitary way to the hut among the crags.

She had only gone a few steps in the direction of home, when she saw coming towards her through the larch trees Kenneth Macpherson.

"Who would have thought of meeting you here, Morag?" he cheerily accosted her. "And with such a heavy bundle of sticks, too. Let me carry it for you—do! Why it's bigger than yourself!" he added, with a pleasant smile, as he unfastened it and threw it across his own broad shoulders.

"You're going home, I suppose, Morag; ar'nt you?" he asked as he walked by her side. "I didn't know you ever came here. I often do. I can hardly ever pass the place without crossing the dyke. You mind the tartan folds, Morag?" said the boy, smiling sadly, as he glanced at the lonely spot from whence his mother's soul had gone home to God.

"Ay do I! I mind upon't weel," replied Morag, with quivering lip. The remembrance brought such a rush of mingled recollections that she could not say more just then.

"Oh, by the by, Morag, I wish I had known a few minutes ago that you were to be found here. I saw somebody who was very anxious to get a sight of you. Who do you think? The bonnie wee leddy, as you call her, on her way back to London!"

Morag stood still to listen, and as she looked earnestly into Kenneth's face, he noticed that she had been crying. "I never kent she was awa till I got a blink o' the cairage no lang syne. She never telt me she was goin' the day," and the little girl struggled vainly to keep back the tears.

"But I'm sure it wasn't her fault that you did not know she was leaving the Glen to-day, Morag. She seemed very sorry-like herself, and sent a message to you. When she noticed me on the road she jumped up from among a lot of furs, and stopped the carriage. The lady beside her was reading a book, and she looked up some angry like, and said something sharp. I think the wee leddy wanted to get out of the carriage to come and speak to me, but she wouldn't let her. Then she stretched her hand down and smiled very pleasantly, though I think she had been crying, too," added the kind-hearted Kenneth rather pathetically, as he glanced at Morag. "Then she began to thank me for what I did at the loch. I'm sure it wasn't anything to thank a body

so much for. Such a pretty voice she has.
It just sounded like the chimes of silver bells,
Morag. And after she had thanked me, she
stooped down quite low, and whispered as if
she were afraid that the lady would hear, ‘Oh,
Kenneth, do you think you could find Morag
anywhere?   I’m sure she can’t know I’ve
gone, or else she would surely have come to
see me.’   But just then the lady rose very
angry like, and said, sharply, ‘Come now,
Blanche, I cannot permit this.   Drive on,
Lucas!’ she called out to the coachman; and
then she sat down to her book again. The
wee lady seemed very vexed, and when the
horses started, she stretched down once again,
and her curls came falling about her face
and she cried, ‘Give Morag my dearest
love!’”

When Kenneth had finished his narration,
Morag began to sob again, and he felt greatly
at a loss to know how to comfort her. But
they were tears of joy now. The feeling of
bitterness was all gone.   Her bonnie wee leddy
had not forgotten her, and the friendship of
those autumn days was no bit of fairyland after
all.

Kenneth did not leave her till the bundle
of firewood was deposited in the hut, and

Morag had promised to come and pay them a visit at the cottage that afternoon.

And as he went sauntering down the hill with his hands in his pockets, whistling a tune, he thought what a very nice girl Morag was; and how glad he felt that it was not she who had gone away from the Glen. And he further decided that such a great bundle of sticks was much too heavy for a girl to carry, and resolved that, in future, he should always be in attendance to carry home the firewood.

As Morag re-entered the cottage, and glanced round the empty room, she saw something lying on the earthen floor which she had not dropped there; and stooping down, she picked up a little, half-worn glove, which told a tale. She looked eagerly round, as if some lingering presence of its owner must still pervade. Her bonnie wee leddy was leal and true after all, and she felt remorseful that she had doubted her for a moment. Kissing the token reverently, she opened the old *kist*, and slipped it between the folds of her most precious book, where it remained a sacred relic of that morning's visitor for many a long year.

XIII

BACK IN LONDON.

IT was a foggy November afternoon; the color of the surrounding atmosphere was almost as yellow as the gorgeous damask hangings which draped Mr. Clifford's handsome drawing-room. Our friend Blanche was wandering listlessly up and down the room, in one of her most restless moods, her governess remarked, as she looked up from a piece of elaborate lace-work which was growing rapidly under her diligent fingers.

It was the usual hour for walking, but the unpleasant weather had kept them indoors. Blanche seemed to find this play-hour extremely dull, and appeared to have failed in all her efforts to amuse herself. On one of the couches there lay open a beautiful drawing-room book of engravings, which she had been looking at, but she knew all the pictures by heart already, so she soon tired of turning the leaves. Then she went to the piano to try over some old chorales of her mamma's copying, which she had found among her music; but Miss Prosser presently remarked that she might play something more lively on such a dismal day as this, so Blanche, at last, glided away among the curtains, and stood looking out on the dense fog. The amber gloom enveloped even the nearest objects, so there was really nothing to see from the window, though Blanche stood gazing out intently. But there was a far-away look in her eyes which seemed to betoken that it was a mental picture which absorbed her.

Miss Prosser again glanced uneasily at her little charge; but this time she did not speak. Her pupil had been rather a puzzle to her of late, and she would gladly have shared her thoughts as she stood there. It was not her habit, however, to elicit confidences of any kind from her pupils; and, indeed, till quite lately, it had not been necessary in Blanche Clifford's case. Her nature was so frank and gay that her thoughts were generally shared by those nearest to her, whether they were sympathetic listeners or not. But, of late, a change had been stealing over the little girl. She had grown more quiet and self-contained than she used to be. Less wayward and troublesome she certainly was, but her governess sometimes thought, as she looked at her thoughtful face, that she would gladly welcome back some of the old boisterous ways which she used to characterize so severely.

Presently Blanche emerged from among the yellow draperies, and, seating herself on a low stool, looked meditatively into the fire.

"Miss Prosser, I am afraid you will think it a very silly question I'm going to ask," she said presently, as she threw herself at her governess' feet, laying her hands on her knees. "Do you think I begin to get any better at all? I have been trying so hard to be good ever since I came from Glen Eagle; but it is so difficult," added Blanche, with a deep sigh. "There now, I tried ever so hard to write that French letter correctly last night, and yet I had several mistakes to-day, you know."

"My dear child, you are getting morbid. This unpleasant fog has a most depressing effect, I know. You are a very good child, my dear. There is no reason to reproach yourself as you do, I assure you. Only this morning, in my report to your father, I stated that I was pleased with your progress, and Signor Lesbini was expressing his satisfaction with you, also," added Miss Prosser, who, however, felt rather disconcerted by the new *rôle* she had to play in taking her pupil's part against herself. It was so unlike the bright, careless Blanche of a few months ago ; and as she glanced at the wistful, upturned face, she noticed that the outline of the cheek was sharper than of old, and the delicate tracery of veins on the forehead more visible. Still the child was well enough, to all appearance, and Miss Prosser began to think that she, too, must be growing fanciful.

"But you don't see my heart, Miss Prosser, or you would not say I was good," replied Blanche, looking into her governess' face with a perplexed gaze. "You have no idea how naughty I felt to-day, when you decided that we should not go out to walk. I think I feel oftener cross than I used to do ; and yet I try so very hard to be good," sighed Blanche, despondingly. "Will you tell me, Miss Prosser, if you thought much about the Lord Jesus Christ, and tried to please Him, when you were about my age? I wonder whether my mamma did !" continued the little girl, as she looked musingly into the fire.

"My dear Blanche, of course it is proper that we should lead Christian lives. You know our parents and sponsors undertook that for us, in baptism. And one day you will be confirmed, I hope. I should like you to go up at

the same time as your cousin, Lady Matilda. By
the way, Blanche, I think I shall write and ask
her mamma if she may come and spend a day
with you. You have hardly seen her since you
came home. And you shall have a whole holiday, and do whatever you like. You quite
deserve it, for you have been a most diligent
child lately. We have really been getting over
a great deal of ground. And these harp-lessons,
which your papa is so anxious for you to have,
do take up so much time. Yes, I think I shall
write this afternoon and ask the little Lady
Matilda to come on Friday."

Blanche sighed, and continued her meditations among the glowing coals. She was thinking of another friend whom she would much
rather have to spend the day. One afternoon's
ramble in the fir-wood with Morag Dingwall,
she thought, would be worth half-a-dozen walks
in the Park with any Lady Matilda in the
world.

These autumn days already began to gather
round them that halo which seems always to sur-
round past periods. The very names and places
connected with those days thrilled Blanche like
the music of a song. But, unlike her usual
frank disposition, she never had these names
on her lips, but kept them like a stolen casket

of precious gems, only to be taken out and looked at when alone. So noticeable, indeed, was her silence concerning Glen Eagle, that Miss Prosser concluded the Highland experiences were quite out of mind; and she was not sorry, on the whole, to think that the bond had been so quickly loosened between her pupil and the little mountaineer.

The maid Ellis was absent on a visit to her friends, or probably her many garrulous memories of Stratheagle might have broken through Blanche's reserve; but, as it was, she dwelt silently among her mental pictures of the Highland glen.

When Signor Lesbini, her music master, was announced, Blanche's thoughts were far away in the *ben-end* of Kirsty's cottage. Starting up from her seat by the fire, she ran to find her music, while the servant placed her harp in its usual position, and Miss Prosser and the music master were exchanging stately salutes.

Mr. Clifford was anxious that Blanche's taste for music should be cultivated in every direction; and these lessons were inserted in the educational programme by his special desire. Blanche was very anxious that she should be able to make some pleasant sounds on the harp before her father came home; and she

was succeeding in doing so, to judge from her
master's frequent, soft, " bene,—benissimo, Sig-
norina ! "

Miss Prosser, meanwhile retired to a distant corner of the room to write various small
scented notes to her friends. Among others,
an invitation was duly despatched to the small
Lady Matilda, asking her to spend a day with
her cousin, and to go to the pantomime in the
evening. The latter part of the programme
Miss Prosser kept as a reserve treat for Blanche,
who had never been to a pantomime, and wished
very much to see one.

The invitation was duly accepted on behalf
of the little Lady Matilda. She appeared on
the day appointed, alighting from her smart
pony carriage, escorted by her maid and footman. She was a lean, dark, sallow child, very
different in coloring and expression from her
cousin Blanche. She always appeared in the
most sleek, unruffled state of tidiness and propriety; she looked, in fact, as if she had come
into the world precisely as she stood—at the
same stage of growth, and in the same faultless
toilette. At least such was the reflection which
sometimes rose to Ellis's mind as she surveyed
her with half envious, half contemptuous eyes,
side by side with her careless and often dishev-

elled little mistress, whose shoulders would somehow get out of her frocks; and one of whose shoes had been actually known to go amissing during dinner, being afterwards brought to her, on a silver tray, by her aunt's solemn butler. Of this terrible *faux pas*, the Lady Matilda's maid occasionally reminded Ellis when they quarrelled over the respective merits of their little ladies.

Notwithstanding Miss Prosser's well-meaning efforts to create a friendship between the cousins, they did not appear to draw to each other in the least. The earlier hours of the day passed in uneventful dulness—at least so thought Blanche, who shocked her governess by yawning twice in her visitor's face, and exhibiting various other tokens of her want of appreciation of her society. Finally, she disappeared for a period, and returned with the cook's white kitten rolled in her smart blue velvet dress—a trophy from among the pots and pans, and showing too many traces of its former playground to deserve its name of Snow.

The calm little Lady Matilda surveyed her companion's restless movements with a look of mild surprise, glancing up, now and then, from a piece of lace-work, on which she was bestowing great thought and care. Miss Prosser had been admiring it greatly; and commended her diligence in a way which reflected somewhat on her own pupil's want of that quality, particularly as regarded needlework.

"But what's the use of it? What do you mean to do with it, Matty?" asked Blanche, unrolling the elaborate piece of work in question.

"My dear Blanche, you are not always so practical, I am sure," said Miss Prosser, coming to the rescue. "Do you not know that it is a part of every young lady's education to be able to sew fancy work? And, besides, the habit of diligence is so good, my dear Blanche; you ought to remember that."

"Well; but it seems to me that there is no use of some people being diligent—about sewing, at all events. Don't you remember these slippers I sewed for papa, Miss Prosser? He certainly seemed very much pleased when I gave them to him; and I felt as if I had been really useful in having made a pair of shoes; and thought it would be so nice to see papa going about in shoes of my making. But, not long afterwards, I heard him say to somebody that he detested sewed slippers, and never wore them. I suppose he had forgotten all about the pair I made for him then, because I'm sure he would not have wanted to hurt my feelings," added Blanche, pathetically.

The conversation was here interrupted by the servant coming to ask at what hour the carriage would be required; and then the delightful secret came out at last. Blanche was in an ecstacy of delight at the prospect of seeing a pantomime. Some time ago her governess would have checked her glee as an unbecoming outburst, but now she hailed it as a proof that her little charge was regaining that elasticity of spirit which she had somewhat lost of late, and she congratulated herself on the success of her efforts for her amusement.

The pantomime that evening was " The Babes in the Wood," though it certainly contained marvellous variations not suggested by the old English ballad which it was meant to illustrate. In fact the Babes themselves were hardly distinguishable, so surrounded were they by moving troops of wee green folk, peeping out in all directions, and marvellously suspended from the boughs of trees. Indeed, it is doubtful whether the original robins could have found a branch throughout the forest to hop on—so covered were they by dazzling

fairies performing all manner of wonderful evo-
lutions in mid-air.

Lady Matilda surveyed the marvellous scene
with considerably more repose of manner than
her cousin. She was quite an old frequenter
of such exhibitions, so she was able to compare
it with yet more gorgeous performances, and to
feel pretty sure what was coming next.

But to Blanche, the pantomime had all the
charm of novelty. She stood entranced, gazing at the stage with eager, upturned face.
More than one frequenter of the theatre ob
served with amusement the eager little girl,
who was not content to view the scene from
her comfortable chair in the box, but kept leaning forward, in a bewilderment of happiness,
notwithstanding her cousin's mild suggestions
that she would be very tired before the end of
the play if she did not sit down.

Every scene was more charming and wonderful than the one which went before. The
fun among the wee green folks was getting
more fast and furious every minute. Blanche
thought they looked like dragon-flies in the
sunshine, as they went flitting about. It had
not occurred to her that they were real flesh
and blood creatures like herself, till, suddenly,
one dazzling little elf fell from a giddy height,

on to the stage. For a moment, Blanche fancied that the descent of the fairy was all part of the fun ; but presently a shrill cry of human pain, and a few compassionate voices from the crowd below, caused her to realize that underneath the mass of gauze and gilt there was a poor body in pain.

In an instant the poor crushed fairy was borne away from the bright scene, and the fun went on again in mad hurly-burly. But, somehow, Blanche's eyes had grown dim, and she shrank back on her seat with a shudder.

"Why, what's the matter, cousin Blanche?" whispered the imperturbable little Lady Matilda, as she surveyed her cousin's movement with mild surprise.

"Oh, didn't you see, Matty? I'm afraid it must be awfully hurt. It fell from such a height—the fairy, I mean. Didn't you hear it cry? it sounded so dreadful when we were al' so happy. I never dreamt they could feel."

Lady Matilda showed a row of pearly teeth as she replied, "Why, yes, of course. How odd you are, Blanche. Didn't you know they are poor children, who do all this for money? I should think they must be quite used to falling by this time."

Blanche was horror-struck. She tried to

avert her eyes from the stage, but, in spite of herself, she felt her glance riveted on the hovering fairies, not in delight now, but in terror, lest another of them should fall.

"Little girls who do it for bread," Blanche repeated to herself, as she leant back on her seat, and covered her face with her hands. And as she sat thus, her thoughts went slipping back to the Highland glen. She remembered the elfish-looking little form that gazed in upon her at the window of the old castle, on that autumn morning; and she shuddered to think how, under other circumstances, her friend Morag might have been such a victim. Then she began to think of the poor fairy; she wondered whether she was dreadfully hurt, and resolved that she should beg Miss Prosser to make inquiries before they left the theatre.

It was with a feeling of relief that she saw the curtain drop at last, and the people begin to move away. Then she made an eager appeal that they should go and ask after the child. The request seemed utterly outrageous when first presented to Miss Prosser's mind; but Blanche was so urgent that, at last, she consented to dispatch the maid to make inquiries behind the scenes. Then Blanche began to plead to be allowed to go, too. She was so very eager that her governess, at last, after many injunctions to the maid, gave a reluctant consent, arranging that she should wait in the box with the little Lady Matilda, who seemed to view her impetuous cousin's movements with unfeigned astonishment, not unmixed with annoyance.

Blanche was all trembling with excitement when the maid took her hand, and they began to thread their way through the corridors, which were getting emptied now. Presently they met a man who was putting out the lights, and the maid stopped to ask where they could go to inquire after the hurt fairy. Having got directions how to proceed, they went on through narrower and less luxurious passages—so dark and dingy-looking that Blanche began to feel afraid, and grasped her maid's hand more tightly. They came at last to a room, the door of which stood half open. They were hesitating whether this was the room to which they had been directed, when they heard a thin, feeble voice within, moaning, as if in pain.

"That's the fairy, I'm sure, Grant," whispered Blanche, eagerly. "Do just peep in and see."

The maid pushed open the door and walked a few steps forward. On the floor stood a paraffine lamp which shed a dim light throughout the room, showing a heap of matting in the corner, where a poor, emaciated child lay. Gleaming through the half darkness, Blanche could distinguish a pale, sharp, unchildlike face, that rested on a thin shrivelled hand. A wretched mud-colored rag seemed to be her sole garment; and, at her side, there stood a pair of big boots, or what served for them, but they seemed almost detached pieces of leather now; besides being of a considerably larger size than the wearer would require. Lying on a table, in another corner of the room, was the gauzy fairy gear, at which Blanche glanced sadly, thinking it contrasted strangely with the wretched rags for which it had been exchanged.

On hearing the sound of footsteps, the child started up, and looked wildly round, as she exclaimed, "O mother! you'll not beat me this time! I'm so bad—it's my leg! Tim said he never saw nothing like the fall I got! Oh, my! it hurts awful!" and the child began to writhe in pain.

"It is not your mother—poor thing! But I daresay your mother will be here before long," said the maid, in a compassionate tone, as she stooped down to look at the child.

In a moment, Blanche was kneeling beside the heap of matting, her pretty blue opera cloak falling on the grimy floor as she took the child's little black fingers in her hands, saying, eagerly, "O poor, poor fairy!—little girl, I mean," she added, for she could not yet divest herself of the idea of the gauzy wings and woven spangles,—"what a dreadful fall you had. I'm afraid you must be very much hurt!"

The child drew her hand away, and looked sharply at Blanche. Presently she nodded, saying, "I know; you're the pretty little girl what looked so pleased at the pantomime. We noticed you—Tim and me. Tim's the boy what hangs the lamps, you know. He's gone to fetch mother; but she aren't a-comin' yet. Drinkin' again, most likely—she's always at it."

Just then a loud-voiced, boisterous woman came staggering into the room.

"Well, young 'un, so you've been and gone and done it again! Didn't I tell you to mind your feet, you little idiot!" and the woman, stooping down, seized the child and shook her roughly.

"Oh, mother, mother, don't! I couldn't help it, noways—my head got so giddy. Oh, I'm so bad!" the weak voice wailed out; and presently the little face got more pale and pinched than before, and the poor fairy fainted away.

"You've killed her, you have—you cruel, cruel woman! How dare you speak so?" said Blanche, quivering with indignation, as she sprang to her feet from beside the matting where she had been kneeling, and almost sprang at the half-tipsy woman.

"Ho, ho! pretty bird; and who may you be? and what's your business, I'd like to know, a-comin' between me and my brat!" shouted the woman, folding her arms, and glaring at the little girl.

The maid stepped forward immediately, and said, in a quiet, firm tone, "Come, Miss Clifford, we must go at once." And then turning to the woman, she added, "We merely came to make inquiries after the poor child. We saw her get a dreadful fall a short time ago. I fear she is very much hurt. I really think you will do well to look after your child," added Grant, as she took Blanche's hand, and prepared to go. She glanced at the poor fairy, who was still lying unconscious, and discovering a jug of water standing near, the maid sprinkled some on the child's face and hands, and presently she began to show signs of returning consciousness.

"Now, Miss Clifford, we must really go at once," whispered the maid to the reluctant Blanche. "We've stayed much too long already. I don't know what Miss Prosser will think."

The woman still stood with folded arms gazing, open-mouthed, at the group. Grant again pointed to the poor little creature, reminding her that she should look after her child. And, at last, after a lingering, pitying glance at the poor little cowering fairy in her rags, Blanche suffered herself to be led away.

They found Miss Prosser in a state of great anxiety and considerable indignation at their delay. The maid explained the matter in a few prompt words, while Blanche stood by the little Lady Matilda graphically describing the sad, disenchanting scene which had followed her first visit to the gorgeous fairy pantomime.

And thus it happened that Miss Prosser's well-meant effort for the amusement of her little pupil, ended in Blanche Clifford getting a sorrowful glimpse behind the tinsel and the glitter, which only served to deepen the thoughtful shadow that had, of late, been stealing across her sunny, childish brow.

20

XIV

VISIT TO THE FAIRY.

LANCHE'S temporary maid was a very silent woman, and was therefore regarded by her little mistress as an extremely dull, uninteresting attendant. She longed for Ellis's return to her post; forgetting all the passages-at-arms which had taken place between them during her reign. And especially since the evening at the pantomime, she wanted to have somebody to talk to about the poor fairy. Grant merely replied to her remarks in the briefest possible way; and Blanche decided that she was hard-hearted as well as uninteresting, for, if she were not, she could not fail to express her sympathy for the poor little girl who seemed in such pain, and had such a dreadful mother. The remembrance of the little pinched face quite haunted her. She went over the scene again and again in her mind; and wondered where her home was, and what would become of her. Miss

Prosser assured her that she would certainly be taken to the hospital, and very well cared for; but still Blanche was not satisfied. Whenever she went out to walk, she looked eagerly, among the faces in the crowd, for the face of the terrible mother, and she resolved that however dreadful she looked, she would go to her and inquire about her little girl.

She sometimes wondered, too, whether the poor fairy knew anything about that unseen Friend whom, in these last days, she had been learning to know and love. It would be such a comfort to speak to Him when her mother was so wicked and so cruel, Blanche thought, and she did not forget to ask the Lord Jesus Christ to make the poor, bruised fairy well again, and to soften her mother's hard heart.

One day, in particular, she had been thinking a great deal about the fairy; and, in the evening, after she was comfortably tucked into bed, her maid still lingered with the candle in her hand, as if she had something that she wanted to say.

"I've been to see a little girl, to-day, who has not such a comfortable bed as you have, Miss Clifford, though her poor little bones need it sore enough."

"Ah! have you, Grant?" replied Blanche,

sitting up in bed, in a listening attitude. "Do tell me about her. Who is she, and how did you come to know her? Is she as poor and pinched-looking as the fairy, do you think?"

"She is the fairy, Miss Blanche—the poor little thing we saw at the pantomime."

"O Grant, you don't mean to say so! Have you really found her out? I'm so very, very glad. It's what I've been longing to do. Where does she live, and was she very much hurt? You must take me to see her; indeed you must, Grant. Do tell me all about it before you go."

The maid then narrated how, the day before, she chanced to meet the terrible mother, in company with another woman, somewhat less tipsy than she, and able to give Grant the information she required concerning the poor child, who, from her account, was still very ill and very destitute. Grant went immediately, in the mother's absence, and saw the little girl in her wretched home. Her leg appeared to have been very badly hurt; the doctor, whom a kind neighbor had once brought to see her, said that she would always be lame, and the child's chief regret seemed to be that she would never be able to act at the pantomime any more.

Blanche listened eagerly to all the information Grant had to give, and before she went to sleep that night was plotting and planning how she could accomplish a visit to the fairy's home.

Next day, when Miss Prosser announced that she would dine out in the evening, and had made arrangements for Grant to sit in the schoolroom with her pupil, Blanche looked upon the circumstance as the most delightful optunity for carrying out her plan. Her governess very rarely made engagements for the evening, or left her pupil to her own devices; so it seemed to Blanche the rarest piece of good luck that she should be going out to-night. She knew very well that Miss Prosser would not give her sanction to a visit to the wretched little girl; and though Blanche felt doubtful whether she was doing right in thus taking advantage of her governess' absence, she was so bent upon seeing the fairy again, that she tried only to look at her own side of the question.

She, did not divulge her plan to Grant till Miss Prosser was fairly gone, and then she brought all her coaxing artillery to bear on the maid, who at last reluctantly yielded to her self-willed little mistress.

It was quite a new experience for Blanche

to find herself out walking after dark. As she linked her arm into her maid's, and they began to thread their way along the lamp-lit streets, Blanche felt somewhat of the feeling of adventure which she had on that autumn morning at Glen Eagle, when she found herself alone in the fir-forest. And there was a strange resemblance between the occasions in another way, though Blanche did not know it. On that morning she went, unconscious of it though she was, to bring life and love and hope into the heart of the lonely little maiden who leant against one of the old fir-trees. And, to-night, she was going on a similar mission—not along the pleasant roads of Strath eagle in a sunshiny morning, but through a dreary November drizzle to a wretched haunt of misery, where a poor little desolate heart sorely needed some ministry of love.

Strange to say, the wretched cellar in the narrow court was not so far distant from Mr. Clifford's stately mansion as might have been expected, so Blanche and her guide were not long in reaching the fairy's home.

After going down a flight of steps, Grant led the way to a dreary room. Opening the door quietly, Blanche peeped cautiously in. The poor child lay on a heap of straw. When the

Morag.

door opened, she raised her head and eagerly scanned the visitors. Evidently recognizing Blanche, she fixed her sharp, unchildlike eyes on her, saying, in her shrill voice, "Have you been to it again? Aren't it a pretty pantomime? You seemed much 'appier than that t'other 'un. *We* noticed you. I wish I was there,—I do. It's wery dull a-lyin' here. Tim's never looked near, neither." Then, turning to the maid, she said, in her sharp, querulous tone, "Well, s'pose you've brought me a bit of somethink to eat. You said you would, mind!"

Blanche felt rather repulsed, but she hastened to uncover a dish of fruit which Grant had placed upon a stool near her, and handed some to the little girl, who seized it eagerly, saying, "I haven't tasted nothink since last night—seen nobody—she's been at it again, drinkin' dreadful. And what made a pretty, fine lady like you come to see me?" she asked, turning to survey Blanche more closely when her hunger was somewhat appeased. "'Ave you got anythink else for 'un?"

"O poor fairy! I'm so sorry for you. I came to see you because I was. I have thought so much about you since that evening at the pantomime, and I was so very glad when

Grant told me she had found your home,"
said Blanche, kneeling down beside the child
and taking the little thin fingers into her
hand. The little girl glanced rather suspiciously at Blanche, who, while Grant went to
unfold a warm blanket she had brought, came
closer and whispered in a low, nervous tone,
" And I came to see you besides, fairy, because I wanted so very much to tell you
about a good Lord Jesus, who, I'm sure, loves
you, and will be very kind to you. Indeed
it's only quite lately I've come really to know
Him, myself. But I'm sure He loves you very
much even now, and would be such a kind
Friend for you to have."

" Don't b'lieve it," replied the fairy, as
she drew her hand away, which Blanche had
been stroking. "We see lots on 'em—Tim
and me—at the pantomime. Most likely seed
this 'un. They never give us a fardin, though
we sometimes beg for somethink when they're
a-comin' out of the play. But we're forbid
to, you know," she added, nodding and winking as she glanced at Blanche's earnest face.

" Oh! but indeed, fairy, you are quite
mistaken. You couldn't possibly see him at the
pantomime. He is not to be seen anywhere
at all in the world now. But though we can't

see Him, He lives still, and hears us when we speak to Him and loves us so much,—indeed He does."

"Don't b'lieve it. Tim says them kind hates poor folks, and that he'd choke 'em if he could—and 'opes he'll have the chance some day."

"Oh! but, indeed, fairy, the Lord Jesus Christ does not hate anybody," gasped Blanche. "I know He loves everybody, and just died on the cross a very cruel, dreadful death because He loved people so much. And, indeed, I think He cares especially for poor, sick, sad people, who want a friend."

A look of interest seemed to come into the little pinched face, and Blanche felt encouraged, and continued, in a pleading tone— "And do you know, fairy, if you were to ask Him for anything, He will really hear you, though you cannot see him standing there listening. I know an old woman, and a little girl not much older than you, and they both love the Lord Jesus Christ so much, and speak to Him a great deal. And I do, too; but I've only begun a little while ago. But I'm quite sure He does hear us and help us too," said Blanche earnestly. Her faith in the Saviour seeming to grow stronger every moment as she gazed on this lost child whom He had come to seek and to save.

"He'd give a body somethink, you say," said the fairy presently, looking sharply at Blanche with her cunning eyes, after she had thought over her words for a little.

"Well now, lady, I say it's a shabby trick of the likes of you, as has lots of nice things, to be goin' beggin'. Look 'ere, if He be as good as you say, just you tell Him I 'm a-lyin' here wery bad—and all about it, you know. And ask somethink—a trifle, you know, to begin with," added the child, winking knowingly, as she stuck her tongue into the corner of her mouth, and looked into Blanche's face to see what impression this practical proposal made. "Look 'ere, now; you see how wery bad I want a dress—and there's my boots won't stick to my feet no ways."

Blanche felt sorely discouraged. She saw that she had evidently not been able to impart to this dark soul a glimmering of what the Lord Jesus Christ came to do. She did want so very much to make the little girl understand what a real helper and friend He was; but she felt as if she had only brought confusion into the poor child's mind, and failed to represent the Saviour as anything more than a bountiful alms-giver.

It must be her fault that she could not make it plainer, Blanche thought; and in her perplexity, she lifted up her heart to Him who turneth men's hearts as rivers of waters, whither He will, and asked that His life and light and love might penetrate the poor fairy's darkened soul.

Blanche Clifford rose from her knees from beside the straw pallet with a very despondent feeling; but though she did not know it, her prayer of faith was of better service to the little girl than her clearest teaching or most eloquently spoken words.

"We must really go now, Miss Blanche," whispered the maid. "I'm afraid of your standing in this damp place any longer. And it's getting very late, besides. Do come now, Miss Clifford."

Blanche made a gesture of impatience; but she quickly remembered that she had promised Grant she would leave whenever she was asked, and so she prepared to go without further remonstrance.

"Good-bye, fairy. I'm so sorry I have to go now. But I'll try to come to see you again, one day very soon. And I shall not forget to ask the Lord Jesus Christ to come to you, and to love you and teach you Himself, and give you everything that you need."

"Will you, though?" replied the child, looking keenly at Blanche's earnest, guileless face. "Don't want no teachin' much—dreadful bad for the dress and boots, though;" and then she added, with a softer expression on her face than Blanche observed before, "You're a nice, pretty little thing. I likes you." Then after a pause she continued, in a reckless tone, "Don't b'lieve you'll come again, nor send Him neither, though. Nobody never keeps no promises. Tim hasn't; he's never looked near."

"Well, fairy, I know one Person who does keep promises, at any rate," said Blanche, smiling.

"I don't," nodded the child, decisively. "P'rhaps you keeps your promises. You do look a nice little thing," she added, putting out her thin fingers, and taking hold of Blanche's dress in a caressing way.

"No, fairy; I'm sure I don't always keep my promises. It's the Lord Jesus Christ I mean. I've just been trying to remember one of His promises to tell you, and I've found one —it's this, 'I will give you a new heart.' Will you try to remember to ask Him for that?— do, dear fairy."

"A new 'art. Well, did I ever—as if I

wasn't needin' a new dress a great sight more;" and the child threw herself back among the straw, and laughed shrilly.

Grant had gone to the door to try and open it in the absence of a handle, which had been wrenched off, and Blanche took the opportunity to whisper, "I know you need a new dress very much, poor fairy; and perhaps He'll give you that, too. But will you ask Him—quite low, if you like—just when you are lying here all by yourself—to give you a new heart? That means to make you good and happy always, you know. He does really hear, though you cannot see Him. Will you not try, fairy?"

"Don't mind though I do. Nothink else to do lyin' here. I'm to ask a new 'art, you say,—just as if I was a-beggin' from a gintleman on the street, I s'pose? I know," said the child, with a nod. "Look, she's waitin' for you—got the door open. Now, see you ax Him for the dress and boots."

XV

A RIDE IN THE PARK.

NE result of Blanche Clifford's visit to the pantomime-fairy's home was a bad cold, which showed itself next morning. The maid immediately explained its probable cause to Miss Prosser, taking the sole blame on herself for having allowed the visit. But Blanche presently gave her account of the matter, which represented herself as the sole culprit; so the governess felt doubtful who she should blame, and finally ended by scolding nobody. She listened with interest to the sequel of the pantomime scene, as Blanche gave some passages from her visit to the poor child, pleading that Grant might be sent with some needful comforts to the wretched home. Miss Prosser readily consented; she also set about making arrangements to have the child taken to the Sick Children's Hospital, and commissioned Grant to try to find the mother, and gain her consent to having her removed.

Blanche felt rather reproached when she

remembered how quickly she had concluded that her governess would not sympathize with her interest in the lame fairy, after she found how heartily she entered into all her plans for helping her.

Throughout the day she was kept a prisoner in her room because of her cold—a state of matters which she generally resented greatly; but to-day she felt quite happy and busy, as she helped to fill a box which was to be taken by Grant to the fairy's home. Blanche did not forget the special request which the fairy begged to have made for her, though neither dress nor boots were sent in the box that morning. And before she went to bed that night, Blanche smiled as she drew out her own private purse to see how much pocket-money was left, for she thought she knew what she would like to do with it.

"How much does it cost to buy cloth for a dress, Grant—not a silk dress, you know, or anything of that kind, but some nice warm cloth?" asked Blanche, nervously handling the two gold pieces which were left in her purse.

"Well, that depends, Miss Clifford. Of course it takes more for a grown-up person than for a child," replied the maid, who stood brushing Blanche's long curls.

"I wish I hadn't bought those love-birds, Grant. I shall get no more money till Christmas, you see; and I do so want to buy a nice warm dress for the poor fairy."

"But I daresay Miss Prosser will allow you to give her one of your own old dresses, Miss Blanche. I am sure there are plenty of them folded away up-stairs that you will never wear again."

"Oh yes, I daresay; and perhaps, afterwards, she may get some of them. But this once I should like to get her quite a new dress —bought and made all for herself, you know. You would shape it, would you not, Grant? And, do you know, I want to sew it all myself —every bit of it," added Blanche, in a confidential tone. "I daresay I might have it finished before the poor fairy is able to be out again, if I were only to work very hard. Don't you think so, Grant?"

Next day Miss Prosser was consulted and gave her consent, though she thought it seemed rather an odd idea; and laughingly remarked to the maid that she might quite count upon having to finish the garment, as Miss Clifford had never been known to hem half a pocket-handkerchief in her life. But it might amuse her while her cold lasted; so

Grant was commissioned to get a selection of suitable patterns of cloth, from which Blanche selected a warm blue woollen serge. Then she was all impatience till the initiatory stages of shaping should be gone through, and she should begin to sew.

Such a diligent little woman she looked, as she sat stitching away, her fingers all stained with the blue dye, and, all the while, planning a similar garment for Morag, as a Christmas present. She was still confined to her room because of her cold; and there she sat, hour after hour, with her head bent over her work, sewing so unweariedly that Miss Prosser felt obliged at length to remonstrate, suggesting that she should betake herself to some amusement now, while commending her for her diligence. Knowing well Blanche's dislike to sewing of any kind, her governess was surprised to see such devotion to a piece of needle-work which did not seem very necessary, and looked most unattractive; for Blanche had not explained why she was so anxious that the fairy should receive quite a new dress, made all for herself.

But as Miss Prosser looked at the flushed, eager little face, bending over the rough piece of work with such diligence and interest, it gave her a key to her pupil which had been missing before; and she recognized a motive power which might prove a better thing than a love for fancy work, and could transform the impulsive, pleasure-loving Blanche into a brave, ministering woman.

The next day Blanche received the delightful and unexpected tidings that her father would return home on the following evening. She had not seen him since that eventful morning on which she left Glen Eagle, and he had stood waving a cheerful farewell in the old court-yard of the castle when she was so very sorrowful.

Mr. Clifford intended to have followed his daughter shortly afterwards, but changing his plans, he went on a tour abroad with some friends. He had not meant to return to London till spring, so his coming was a delightful surprise for Blanche.

Her father so rarely lived for any length of time at home, that she had become so far accustomed to his absence; but to have him for a little while was an intense pleasure—to be made the most of while the visit lasted; and Blanche built many castles in the air about the pleasant Christmas time there could not fail to be when her papa was to be with her. But instead of flitting about in a state of absolute idleness, which Miss Prosser, described as her usual practice, when there was any pleasant event in prospect, Blanche stitched her happy thoughts into the fairy's half finished garment, which grew rapidly under her diligent fingers; only laying it aside in time to prepare to welcome her father.

"Why, pussy, how brilliant you look; not even the breezes of Stratheagle gave you peonies like these," said Mr. Clifford, as he looked fondly at his little daughter, who clung to his arm with a radiant face, as they mounted the broad staircase to the drawing-room together, after he had divested himself of his travelling wraps.

"How do you do, Miss Prosser? I must really congratulate you on your pupil's appearance," said the master of the house, as he walked into the drawing-room, and shook hands with the governess.

Blanche presently darted off to inform Grant that her papa was really come, and was at this moment talking to Miss Prosser in the drawing-room, where it might be possible to have a peep at him through the open door. She looked upon it as a great privation for Grant never to have seen her papa, and took for

granted that her maid would be full of im
patience to do so.

"Why, Blanche, how you've grown, my
child!" exclaimed Mr. Clifford, surveying her
as she re-entered the room, while he stood
warming himself by the fire. "I declare you
will soon arrive at the blissful long-dress period
that has been your ambition for so long. Now
come and tell me what mischief you have
been about since I saw you last, pussy! Let
me see, where was that? Ah yes, I remember—not since that morning you and Miss
Prosser left Glen Eagle. And have you quite
forgotten that little wild woman of the woods
—what's her name, eh, Blanchie?"

Mr. Clifford noticed that the peony cheek
flushed even a deeper red as Blanche replied,
"No, papa; I shall never forget Morag as long
as I live. I don't see how I ever could. We
shall go back again to Glen Eagle next autumn,
shan't we, papa?"

"Oh yes; of course. I have taken the
shooting for three years. It's a first-rate place.
And so you would actually like to go back to
Glen Eagle, Blanchie? Did you not find it
very dull sometimes away among the hills—
confess now?"

"Oh no, papa; indeed I didn't find it dull

—not near so dull as here. I don't see how I could ever feel dull at Glen Eagle," said Blanche, decidedly; and then she added, " Well, perhaps if Kirsty and Morag were both away from the Glen, and Shag could not be found to ride about on, then it might be rather sad; because, you see, the fir-wood and all the other places would remind me of them. It would be too sad to see the hut without Morag living there," said Blanche, dreamily, as she thought of the empty room which she saw on the morning she left the Glen, and of how eagerly she had searched for her missing friend. " And how Kirsty's cottage would look without her, I cannot imagine. But do you know, papa, I actually dreamt last night that I went to see her, and she was not to be found, and her old arm-chair was empty,—and the nice, cheery fire cold and black. It was so nice to wake and find it was only a dream, after all!" added Blanche, with a sigh of relief.

" Well, I don't think either of your friends have migratory habits; so you are likely to find them among their native heather next year. By the way, Blanchie, you must send a Christmas box of presents to your friends there. You may fill it with whatever you like best; but only do keep a corner for me. I want to send some present to the boy who fished you out of the loch—Kenneth—isn't that his name? Do you remember that adventure, and how you frightened us all, you troublesome young person? By the way, I arranged before I left Glen Eagle that Dingwall is to train the boy for a gamekeeper,—seeing that appears to be what he has set his heart on."

Before many minutes had elapsed, Blanche's lively imagination had filled a box of such probable dimensions that her father laughingly assured her it would be much too heavy to be carried up the hill to the little shieling among the crags.

Presently the little girl fell into one of her meditative moods, saying at last, with a sigh, "Well, papa, I daresay Morag and Kirsty will be very pleased to get the box of things, and think it very kind—and all that; but though Kirsty and Morag are so poor, I really do not think they ever seem to be anxious for anything they have not got. I was just remembering how Kirsty one day said to me, in that nice, queer accent of hers, 'Bairn,'—she often called me that—'a man's life consisteth not in the abundance of the things he has.' I can't remember exactly what we were talking about at the time."

"Upon my word she must be quite a philosopher, this wonderful Kirsty!" said Mr. Clifford, laughingly, as he stroked Blanche's curls.

"No, papa; I don't fancy she is learned enough for that; but I am sure she is a Christian,—and is that not better, papa?"

"Ah, I'm afraid we are getting beyond our depth now, pussy. Come, little kittens should not look grave," he added, for Blanche had a dreamy look in her eyes which he did not care to see.

She was thinking of the poor fairy who was so greedy as well as so needy; and presently she began to tell her papa a little about her, and how she had gone to see her in her wretched home. She told him, too, that she was making a dress for her—really of her own sewing; and, taking for granted that her papa would be much interested in the garment, she brought it for his inspection. But she did not tell him why she was so very anxious to make it for her, nor that it was meant to be, perhaps. the first token recognized by the poor fairy's dark soul of that Love which "passeth knowledge."

The father and daughter spent some very happy hours together on this first evening of their reunion. And as Mr. Clifford walked up and down the drawing-room, after Blanche ha l

left for the night, his thoughts dwelt with a
new joy and hope on the only child of his house,
whose birth had left his home so desolate.   He
remembered with what a sad heart he took for
the first time the motherless babe into his arms,
and what a sorrowful welcome he could only
give to her.   And now he thought with pride
of what a sweet child-woman she had grown,
how much she seemed to have deepened lately,
and what a beautiful woman she promised to
be!   Mr. Clifford smiled to think of the time
when her school-room days would be at an end,
and she would make her entrance into society
to be his companion; and he felt as if life were
opening pleasanter vistas before his eyes than it
had done for many a day.

The next morning was bright and pleasant
for December; and, to Blanche's great delight,
Mr. Clifford proposed that she should have a
holiday in honor of his return, and go somewhere with him.   After some deliberation,
Blanche decided that the most pleasant way to
spend the morning would be to go for a ride
in the Park with her papa.

The stately bay stood at the door at the
hour appointed, but instead of the little brown
Shag, the pretty white pony Neige awaited his
mistress.   Blanche had not felt so happy since

she left the Highland strath as she did when she found herself riding by her father's side. The yellow fogs had quite withdrawn themselves; the air was keen and bracing now, and the sun shone brightly on the winter landscape. The "Row" was gay with riders and the drive with carriages, taking advantage of this rare December day, and the horses' hoofs rattled pleasantly along the crisp, frosty ground.

More than one passer-by glanced at the pleasant-looking pair of riders as they cantered along in the sunshine—Blanche prattling to her papa with gay, upturned face, her long fair curls floating about, and her pretty blue habit forming a contrast to Neige's snowy back, while her father glanced down at her with fondness and pride reflected on his handsome face.

On they rode, fast and far; for the day was bright and their spirits were high. At last Mr. Clifford reined his horse, and suggested that they should turn homewards.

"Now, pussy, you do purr so delightfully, and we have had such a pleasant ride, that I think we shall beg Miss Prosser for a holiday every bright day. Wouldn't that be a delightful arrangement, Blanchie?"

"It would be very nice, papa. But, perhaps, there may be no more bright days as long as winter lasts," said Blanche, taking a more desponding view of things than she generally was apt to do.

They had now reached home. Mr. Clifford dismounted, and lifted his little daughter from her saddle.

"You are looking tired, Blanche, darling. I am afraid we have rather overdone it to-day. I quite forgot that it was so long since you had ridden before. How pale you are, child! what is the matter?" said Mr. Clifford in a startled tone, as he looked at Blanche.

"I do feel rather queer, papa," replied Blanche, faintly, as she staggered and leaned against her father for support.

Lifting her in his arms, Mr. Clifford carried her up the broad stone steps to the hall door, and hurying into the library, laid her gently down on one of the couches.

Hardly had he laid her there when she became deathly pale, and presently a sudden crimson flow came from her white lips, staining her blanched cheek and fair clustering curls, and Blanche Clifford fainted away!

XVI

THE BORDERS OF THE FAR-OFF LAND.

MR. CLIFFORD again walked up and down his empty drawing-room where only the evening before he had been weaving such a bright future for himself in the companionship of his child; and now the doctors had just left him with the terrible decision ringing in his ears—that she was dying! It might be weeks, and even months; but the fragile frame could not long resist the disease that had been stealthily doing its deadly work for many weeks.

Blanche, the pride of his heart, the heir to his fortune, was passing away from him! Covering his face with his hands, the poor father seated himself on the couch where only a few hours before the bright face had been gazing into his, and the merry laugh re-echoing through the now silent, deserted room.

Blanche lay pale and feeble in her darkened chamber, while servants flitted about, whispering and ministering, and Miss Prosser sat tearfully by the bedside.

At length the closed drawing-room door opened, and the poor, grief-stricken father stood beside his child. They might leave him—he would stay and watch to-night, he said huskily, as he seated himself beside the bed. Blanche had hardly spoken since she had been taken ill; but the sound of her father's voice seemed to rouse her, and, opening her eyes, she welcomed him with her old sunny smile.

"O papa, dear, is that you? It seems such an age since I saw you. I must have been sleeping all day long. I was so tired. I think we did go too far, to-day; but it was so nice, and I did not feel at all tired at the time. But I shall be all right to-morrow, I'm sure."

"I hope so, my darling!" said her father, as he kissed the uplifted face, and stroked the curls sadly.

"This is good-night, I suppose, papa? I have been sleeping so much that I have actually no idea what o'clock it is," said Blanche, smiling.

Mr. Clifford told her it was quite bed-time now; and when she turned to sleep again, he took his seat quietly beside the chintz-curtained little bed, promising to relinquish it towards morning to Miss Prosser, who, tearful and anxious, begged to have a share of the watching.

When all was silent in the room except the flickering fire, and Mr. Clifford sat sad and anxious at his unwonted duty, Blanche seemed to get wakeful again, and presently low tones reached his ear, meant only for the unseen Friend whom his little girl had in these last days been learning to know and love.

Feebly and tremulously she whispered, as she sat up in bed, reverently covering her face with her hands—"O Lord Jesus Christ, I am so tired to-night, I can't remember all I want to say. But, long ago, upon earth you used to know what people needed before they ever asked, and I am sure you do still. Do teach the poor sick fairy all about Thyself. I didn't seem to be able to make her understand about you; and she needs a Friend so very much. Bless my own dear papa. Make him so happy here in London that he will never think of going away again. I am sure you must love him, and he must love Thee; but, O Lord Jesus Christ, I would like him to speak about Thee, sometimes, as Kirsty used to do.

"Help me to be good, to do everything that pleases Thee, so that Thou may never turn away sorrowfully from me, as you used to

do long ago when people would not follow
Thee;" and as she prayed, Blanche fell asleep
again, and all was silent.

Mr. Clifford had been listening to his
child's words with bowed head and shamed
heart. He felt that he was one of those from
whom the Saviour must have turned away
sorrowfully many a time. Through many
lands and in many ways he had sought rest
and solace, forgetting that the heart which
God has made for Himself can only find rest in
Him. And his little daughter seemed to have
sought and found this satisfying portion which
he had been seeking vainly. When her earthly
father and mother had forsaken her, then the
Lord had taken her up; and now He was,
perhaps, going to take her to Himself, though
she did not know it.

Kneeling beside her bed, Mr. Clifford
prayed that God would pardon the wasted,
sinful past, and would give him back his child,
so that, together, they might tread the heaven-
ward path!

When Miss Prosser appeared to claim her
share of the vigil, Blanche was sleeping so
soundly that any watching seemed almost
unnecessary. And in the morning she looked
so bright, though pale and fragile, that the

anxious faces round her caught the infectious brightness, and the gloomy forebodings of the previous day seemed already to belong to the past.

As the days went by, Blanche appeared really to gain strength; and although there was still much cause for anxiety regarding her health, there seemed some reason to hope that the fatal issue might yet be warded off.

Mr. Clifford spent much of his time in his daughter's sick-room. And during these December days, as he sat by his daughter's couch, he listened with mingled feelings to many a childish tale of joy and grief that had marked the years in which he had borne no part.

And so it happened that these days of illness became days of intense enjoyment to Blanche. Ellis had returned to her post, and Blanche confided to her that it was really quite worth while being ill, and having to take all those nasty medicines, to have her papa all to herself for so many days.

The poor fairy was now comfortably housed in the Hospital for Sick Children, and Blanche looked forward to being able to pay her a visit there, one day before long. The half-finished dress was again taken from the drawer, where it had been sorrowfully laid by Grant on the day Blanche was taken ill; and now the little fingers were busy at work again, though they looked pale and feeble enough, Mr. Clifford thought, as he watched them, all stained with blue dye, putting the finishing stitches into the fairy's promised garment.

Blanche pleaded very hard that morning to be allowed to sew; and notwithstanding Miss Prosser's remonstrances, and her papa's joke about the ponderous piece of work which she had undertaken, she worked on, till at last, with a wearied smile, she held out the finished dress for her papa's inspection.

"Look now, papa—it is finished! I have really put in the last stitch. I am so very glad I have been able. I felt as if I could do it to-day, somehow, and that was what made me so anxious to try, though Miss Prosser was so unwilling I should; but I don't think it has hurt me at all."

"Why, Blanchie, it is the most wonderful work of art imaginable. I must really put in my claim for a greatcoat next. The doctor says you may have a drive to-morrow, if it is fine, and we will go to the Hospital; and you shall introduce me to the fairy, and present the dress."

"I hope I shall be able to go, papa. But

it will be sent whether I am or not, won't it? I think the fairy will understand why I wanted so much to send it. I am so glad it is finished," she added, with a wearied sigh, as she laid the dress on a chair, and went to lie on the sofa, which she rarely did of her own accord.

Mr. Clifford made no remark, but, as he glanced at her anxiously from under his newspaper, he could not help noticing, as she lay quietly there, that the little face looked worn and the outline of the cheek sharper than hitherto. She lay with her eyes shut for some time, and presently she said, in a low, firm tone, as she looked up—

"Papa, dear, come to me. I want to speak to you."

Mr. Clifford was not a nervous man, but his hand shook as he laid down his newspaper and went to his daughter's side, for there was a foreboding of trouble in his heart.

Her arm was round his neck, but she did not see his face as she said, softly—

"Do you know, papa, it makes me very sad, as well as glad, to look at that finished piece of work. Shall I tell you why? It seems to me it is the very first useful thing I have ever done in my life; and papa, dear, do you know it will be the last?" and the blue-stained fingers played nervously with her father's hand as she spoke.

Mr Clifford was going to interrupt her, but Blanche went on—

"Yes, papa; I know. I have known it for two days now. I'll tell you how I came to know. I overheard Ellis telling somebody that the doctor said I was—dying. Dear, kind Ellis; I'm sure she would be sorry if she knew I heard that; but she must not be told. I am so glad that I do know just a little before, though it did make me feel very sad at first. Indeed, I cried the whole night in the dark, papa; but now I feel as if it were all right. And I don't think I'm afraid to die now, as I should have been when I fell into the loch," she added, in a faltering tone.

"My darling, you must not talk so. And, besides, Ellis was not correct. You have been very ill, but the doctor thinks you are much better now; and when spring days come, my little Blanche will blossom again with the flowers."

"No, papa dear; I don't really think I am better. I shall never get well again, I know. But, as I lay here, I was thinking how sad it seemed to go away from the world without having been of any use to anybody. And just lately, too, I have seemed to understand better what life was meant for, and to be interested in things I used not to care about. Do you know why I was so anxious to make the dress for the poor lame fairy, papa? I think I should like to tell you," and some of her old brightness returned as she told the story of her visit to the poor child in the comfortless abode. "She was so sad and poor that I felt sure she would be glad to hear about the Lord Jesus Christ. Wouldn't you have thought so, papa? But she did not seem to care, nor to believe that He loved her at all. At last she said that if He were to send her a new dress and boots, she might believe He was good and kind. But I am afraid I was not able to make her understand about the Lord Jesus Christ. I wonder how I can best tell her about Him, papa? if I am able to go to see her again before "—and Blanche's voice faltered.

"My own darling! you must not speak so! You must try to get well, for my sake, Blanchie. What should papa do without his little girl? And I am afraid I do not know the Lord Jesus Christ really any more than the poor pantomime fairy! You must stay with me, my child, and we will seek Him together!"

"Dearest papa, He does teach people so wonderfully; I am sure He will teach you to know and love Him. But I thought you must surely have loved the Lord Jesus Christ ever so long ago," said Blanche, musingly, and then she lay silent for several minutes.

Presently she turned to her father, with a face full of love and pity, and laying her thin fluttering fingers on his arms, she said, " Papa, dear, you will take Him for your friend now, will you not ?—and He will come and be very near you when I am far away. Kirsty says He was such a friend to her when she was left sad and lonely in her cottage"—and with the mention of Kirsty's name there came a rush of memories that made Blanche's eyes fill with tears.

Her father noticed it, and a pang of jealousy shot through his heart. She had spoken such sad words, calm and tearless; and it seemed hard that the thought of those peasant friends, whom she might see no more on earth, should be a sharper sorrow to the child's heart than the parting from himself.

And so far he judged truly. Blanche loved her father dearly, but she did not guess how great was his love for her, nor how shadowed his life would be if she were gone.

As she gazed at the bowed head beside her, Blanche realized for the first time how great and terrible the coming sorrow was to her father, and she began to understand how true it is that in the partings of life "theirs is the bitterness who stay behind."

The exertion of talking seemed to have been too much for the fragile frame. Presently a violent fit of coughing came on, and again that terrible crimson flow streamed from the white lips and on the deathly face!

* * * * *

The winter storm had now set in, and the weather was cold and dark and cheerless; but the interior of Blanche's room looked warm and bright as Mr. Clifford walked into it, on his return from his lonely ride.

On the floor there lay strewed the Christmas gifts for Glen Eagle, and from her sofa Blanche was having an inspection of them before they were sent away. Ellis was doing duty as show-woman; and Blanche's old gleeful laugh, which had become a rare sound now, was heard occasionally as she listened to her maid's remarks concerning the various beautiful presents, as she held them up for inspection.

Welcoming her papa with the old bright

smile, Blanche beckoned him to come and see the nice fur footstool which Miss Prosser had that morning bought for Kirsty's cottage.

Mr. Clifford looked very sad as he came forward and took his place by his daughter's couch. He could not help contrasting the pale fragile form lying there, with the ringing childish laugh, which caused him almost to forget, for the moment, the sad reality which these weeks had brought.

Blanche's quick eye always detected her father's sadness, and she used to try to chase it away by all the loving wiles which she could devise. To the others round her she often talked of dying; but, since the time that she saw her father's distress when the subject was approached, she never had the courage to introduce it again, though there were many things she wanted to say to him.

She kept watching Ellis with wistful eyes as she gathered and carried away from her room the scattered gifts for the peasant friends she loved so well.

After they were all cleared away, she lay quietly back on the sofa, and there was a far-away look in her eyes that made her father unwilling to ask where her thoughts were. Presently she turned to him, and said in a low, nervous tone, " Papa, I want to ask you something. May I do exactly as I like with all my own things ? "

" Certainly, darling. What treasure do you wish to send to the little Morag ? But I thought Ellis was doubtful if she could stow all the things you have already sent,—eh, Blanchie ? "

" Oh, I did not mean in the box, papa ! But you know it cannot be very long now before I have to leave you—and everything," and Blanche's fluttering fingers, so wan and wasted now, played nervously with her father's hand as she spoke.

" Of course you will keep everything you want—and Miss Prosser and Ellis will, too. But I should like Morag to have some of my things when I am gone. She has so few pretty things in the hut; and besides, I really do think she would like to have them, just because they are mine, and they will remind her of me when I'm far away ; " and Blanche glanced round the room at the pretty statuettes and pictures, and the rows of nicely-bound books, of which she used to tell Morag, as they rambled among the woods and braes of Glen Eagle.

" Yes, my darling ; Morag shall have whatever you like," replied Mr. Clifford with an

effort, as soon as he was able to speak; and
presently he continued: " My child, perhaps
I should tell you that you have a great deal
more to give away than your books and pictures.
You are what people call an heiress, Blanchie.
Your mother left you a large fortune, and, besides, you will have all that belongs to me.
Ah, my child ! will you not live ?—I cannot
let you go !   There is such a bright future
in store for you—so many hopes bound up in
this dear life ! "

"Yes, papa, dear; the future *is* bright," replied Blanche, smiling. " I was reading about
it only this morning—'an inheritance, incor-
ruptible, undefiled, and that fadeth not away.'
I learnt the words. It was strange I never
remember hearing them till to-day. But I
suppose God just speaks His own words to us
when we need them and will listen to them.
It's all right, papa, dear," she continued as she
put her arm round her father's neck, as he sat
with his head resting on his hand, absorbed in
his own sad thoughts. "I know the Lord
Jesus Christ will comfort you when I am gone.
And then, you know, papa dear, you will not
be so very long in coming, and I shall be waiting for you, oh! so eagerly, and we shall be so
happy together in the home of God ! "

" Is it not rather difficult for rich people to be good, papa?" asked Blanche, after she had laid pondering a short time. "If I had lived, perhaps I might have grown into a grand lady —like some of Ellis's mistresses that she tells me about—and got selfish and bad when I grew old. But now, papa, dear, I shall always be your own foolish little Blanchie," and she nestled in her father's arm, as he stroked the long fair curls—the last symbol of health that remained.

After she had again laid musing for some time, Blanche sat up, and with some of her old eagerness she said—

"Papa, I've just been thinking that Morag is so gentle, and so clever, and so fond of books, that I'm sure she would grow up very learned if she were educated. I know she would like lessons a great deal more than I used to do, and be much more diligent. Have I enough money to educate Morag, papa?"

"Yes, darling, quite enough; and if you wish it, it shall be done," replied Mr. Clifford huskily, for this conversation was almost too painful for him to continue.

" But after all, papa, very clever people, who know everything, are not always very happy or good—are they? And, besides, I really do not

see how her father and Kirsty could get on
without Morag. And then she is so faithful
and loving—perhaps she could never be persuaded to leave them, to be made a lady of in
the world beyond her mountains," said Blanche,
smiling, as the image of her shy little mountain
friend rose before her.

"No, papa, dear," she said presently, after
thinking quietly for a little; "I really think we
must give up that idea after all. I do believe
the Lord Jesus Christ would like best that Morag should stay in the Glen and make her
father and Kirsty comfortable and happy as
they get older. But I'll tell you what we
might do, papa, dear. Would there be enough
money to build a nice new house for Morag
and her father? That hut among the crags
must tumble to pieces one day before long, I
should think, though certainly Morag does make
it look as nice as possible," added Blanche, pathetically, for she remembered well the morning
on which she saw it last.

Her father listened with a sad interest as
Blanche told the story of that day's troubles,
and how sorry she had been to leave Glen
Eagle without taking farewell of her mountain
friend. And as she told how she had hurried
up the hill to the little shieling among the

crags, only to find it empty, and glowingly described the pleasant interior into which her friend had transformed the once wretched hut, the scene seemed to come vividly to her memory, and to bring with it an intense desire for life, as she lay on the borders of the far-off land!

Some hot tears stole down her cheeks, and with quivering lip and clasped hands she gazed wistfully into her father's face as she said—

"O papa! if I could only walk one afternoon with Morag in the fir-wood, I almost think I should feel well again!"

MORAG'S JOURNEY INTO THE WORLD BE-YOND THE MOUNTAINS.

IT was a wild night at Stratheagle. An eddying wind had been blowing the deep snow into wreaths, and fresh fall-ing flakes were whirling about in all directions through the darkness.

All trace of the road through the mountain pass had disappeared; and it would have fared ill with the Honorable Mr. Clifford's slim English footman, with his elegant calves, as he made his way towards the keeper's shieling among the crags, if he had not taken the pre-caution of securing a guide from the village below.

The steep ascent to the hut was almost impassable, and more than once the man seemed disposed to give it up and beat a retreat to his quarters at the village without fulfilling his mission. But his more stalwart companion cheered him on, assuring him at intervals that

it was only a "mile and a bittock," and pointed to the light in the window of the hut long
before it shed any encouraging ray on the
exhausted flunkey, who went stumbling and
grumbling up the hill through the blinding
drift, feeling himself the most ill-used of persons to have been sent to such regions in such
weather.

The light from the window of the hut was
at last really visible, shimmering through the
darkness, and soon the benighted travellers
stood under the snowy crags which towered
above the little shieling.

Our old friend Morag was, meanwhile,
comfortably seated in the ingle-neuk, reading
laboriously from one of her ancient yellow-
leaved volumes, little dreaming what was in
store for her to-night. Her father sat near her
smoking his evening pipe, but he was not
staring into the fire in idleness and grim silence as of old. He seemed at the present moment quite absorbed in a newspaper, the date
of which was uncertain, seeing it had been
torn off when it was used for lining a packing-
case of game during autumn. But though it
was not a "day's paper," it seemed to satisfy
the keeper's literary cravings, and he had carefully perused it from beginning to end by the

---

light of the fire of peat and pine, which blazed brightly on the hearth.

The snow made a warm covering round the wall, and a secure white thatch on the porous roof, so it happened that to-night the hut was really a more comfortable abode than it had often proved during autumn-days.

Morag jumped to her feet when she heard the sound of voices and the loud knocking; and now she stood gazing at her father with a look of startled surprise.

Laying down his pipe, the keeper prepared to open the door, but before he had time to do so, the injured footman stood in the middle of the floor, stamping the snow from his feet, and inspecting his precious person generally, as he muttered expressions of indignation concerning this unpleasant piece of service which had fallen to his lot.   ·

Morag recognized the visitor at once, and forgetting her shyness, she sprang forward, saying, in low, eager tones, "Will ye no be frae the wee leddy o' the castle? I'm thinkin' there maun be something wrang. Is she no weel?"

"Miss Clifford, I presume you mean, little girl. Well, you are right, so far. I come from her father—my master, the Honorable

Mr. Clifford. I think I've got a letter for you; but 'pon my word it's been at the risk of my life bringin' it here. S'pose I'd better read it myself?" said he, looking round patronizingly at the keeper.

And without waiting for a reply, he tore open the closed envelope, amid the smouldering indignation of the keeper, to whom it was evidently addressed, and began to read as follows :—

" Will Morag come to London immediately to see her little friend Blanche, who is very ill and wants to see her? The Keeper may safely trust his daughter to the servant, who has got all directions how to proceed.

" ARTHUR CLIFFORD."

"Quite safe with me, depend upon it; the master is quite right there!" said the servant, smiling blandly at the confidence reposed in him.

"Well, little girl, what do you say to it? You will come, I suppose? The master has set his 'art on it, sure enough—or he would not have been sendin' me to the hends of the earth on such a night as this. I have a trap hired at the village, all ready to start in the morning. What do you say to it, keeper?—rather sudden, for such quiet folks as you, ain't it?" continued the man, smilingly glancing at the silent, offended keeper.

Morag sat thinking in dumb silence for a little, but presently she sprang up, and taking hold of her father's arm, she said in her low, eager tone, "O father! ye mustna hinner me; the bonnie wee leddy is ill, and wantin' me— and I maun gang!"

Then turning to the messenger, Morag asked imploringly, "She's no jist sae verra ill, is she?"

"Bad enough, I guess. 'Tis a pity—such a pretty little miss she was getting to be. Master so bound up in her, too!"

"Well, keeper, how is it to be?—for I've got to go down that shockin' precipice again —and it's getting late. I'll take good care of the young 'un, you may be sure. And, depend upon it, you won't be the loser, noways, by fallin' in with master's views," added the servant, with a nod of meaning which made the proud keeper resolve instantly that his daughter should not obey the summons.

But never before had Morag been so wildly wilful on any matter. Her father felt quite taken by storm as he listened to her pleadings, though he could not yet be persuaded to give his consent.

The servant stood waiting with evident impatience, and at last a compromise was arranged, to the effect that if Morag was to accompany him, she would be brought to the village inn by her father next morning, before the hour of starting.

It was almost midnight when Dingwall might be seen toiling across the moorland, through the snow, in the direction of Kirsty's cottage. The old woman and he were fast friends now, and he wanted to ask her advice on the startling proposal concerning the little girl who was so precious to them both.

He found Kirsty sitting quietly reading her Bible beside the dying peat embers. Taking off her spectacles, she listened placidly to the story, and presently she replied in low, emphatic tones, "Dinna hinner the bairn, keeper. Lat her gang, by a' means. 'Deed, I'm near awears o' gaen mysel'. The bonnie lambie— an' sae He's til tak' her hame til Himsel? Weel, weel, I thocht as muckle, whiles, when she was comin' aboot us wi' a' her winsome ways. May she hae been early seekin' the face she will maybe see gin lang!"

So Morag gained her point. Her travelling preparations were not long in being made; and, though she had not many hours of sleep that night, she was all ready to go down the hill with her father in the morning.

Just before she started, Kenneth came running up to the shieling in breathless haste. He carried with him the old tartan plaid which had done such sad duty in the fir-wood. Wrapping it carefully round Morag, he stood watching her wistfully, as she started in the grey dawn of a December morning on this first journey into the world beyond the mountains!

*   *   *   *   *

It was Christmas Eve. A fresh fall of snow lay spotless and shining on the ground. The moon was giving a clear, plentiful light, and as it shimmered on the snow-covered streets and squares, it seemed suddenly to transform them into groups of stately marble palaces.

A pleasant crimson glow came from the close-curtained windows of Mr. Clifford's London mansion, shedding a warm, rosy light on the white crisp pavement in front, where stood a group of German lads singing a fine rolling Christmas carol.

Little did they guess how dreary and tenantless those rooms were to-night, which seemed to them to enclose such a paradise of delights as they kept gazing up to the windows, in the hope of an appreciative audience from within the crimson glow.

They did not know that the sorrowful interest of the household was centred in one darkened room, where the only child of the house lay, with life ebbing slowly away; nor that the largess which seemed so munificent came from a little hand that was soon to take farewell of all earthly treasures.

They were still singing, by way of gracious acknowledgment of so handsome a gift, when a cab drove up to the door of the house, and out of it stepped our little friend, Morag. The tall footman, her escort, ran up the broad steps, while the little mountaineer stood on the pavement gazing round, bewildered in the midst of a scene so new and strange.

And this was her bonnie wee leddy's home. Did people always stand there and sing beautifully, she wondered, as she glanced at the German band—and then at the many bright-curtained windows of Blanche Clifford's London home.

At length the great hall door was opened, and a blaze of light fell on the snowy steps. Within were vistas of gilded pillars and cor-ridors, and glimpses of bright soft hangings. To Morag's dazzled eyes, it seemed like the entrance to an enchanted palace. She tremblingly followed her guide, and the door was closed behind her, as the singing boys were watching with interest the little girl who looked so eagerly at everything; and somehow seemed to remind them of their sisters and their homes in the Black Forest.

Another tall footman, the fac-simile of Morag's guide, had opened the door, and now he stood gazing, more curiously than kindly, at the stranger.

"Law, Thomas! what 'ave we got here? Well, I never. Where did you catch that 'un," he said, with a rude laugh as he stood staring at the little girl.

Poor Morag certainly presented a grotesque enough appearance as she stood there in the brightly-lighted hall, wrapped in the great tartan plaid, which was fastened behind, while the ends fell on the ground. And on her head she wore a little scarlet hood, a relic of her infancy, which she had taken from the depths of the old *kist*—feeling certain that Ellis would look on her more favorably if she wore a bonnet. But, unfortunately, the hood was of such small dimensions that it had a constant tendency towards the back of her neck, leaving her black elf-like locks streaming around.

"Come now, Sparks, none of your cheek. She's the nicest little shaver possible—an uncommon decent little thing; wasn't no trouble on the way, neither; always turned up all right when a fellow wanted to go and smoke a pipe, or get a drop of somethink. My word, I'd go back with her to-morrow, I would."

"Where's Ellis ?—ring for her, will you ? I must get this little girl off my hands now. How is missie, by the way ?"

" Better again, to-day, they say. Master is looking brisker, too. Dreadful dull Christmas-time for a fellow, though. There's Ellis wouldn't laugh for a sovereign."

Meanwhile, Morag stood looking eagerly round. She felt sure that she would see her bonnie wee leddy emerge from some of those vistas of brightness; but when she did not come, the little girl began to feel very forlorn as she stood there in the hall. She could not understand what the servants were saying, and she began to wonder what was going to happen next, and longed for a sight of her gracious little friend, who never had failed her before.

Morag had no idea how seriously ill Blanche was, and she had been hoping during her journey that perhaps her bonnie wee leddy might be quite well again by the time she arrived. She had got so quickly well after the loch adventure; and Morag could not conceive of her looking more fragile that she did on that evening when she saw her last, in the old castle of Glen Eagle, lying on the sofa, wrapped in her blue flannel dressing-gown.

At length Ellis came bustling along; and even she was a welcome sight to poor Morag in her forlornness.

"Well, little girl; how d'ye do. Very glad to see you—never thought I should feel so glad to see you. I thought you would come to see missie. Miss Prosser told me the master had sent for you. Miss Clifford does know not yet. She's so weak, you see; any hagitation is bad, but I daresay you will see her in the morning. It's a good step from the 'ighlands—ain't it? I expect you are tired—poor thing," said Ellis, glancing rather pityingly at Morag's wistful face.

"I'm no that tired. But she's no jist verra ill, is she? I thocht maybe she would hae been weel gin noo," said Morag, ruefully returning to the subject that lay nearest her heart, as Ellis led her along what seemed to her a maze of brightly-lighted passages.

"It wasna fallin' intil the loch that hurtit her, think ye?" she asked presently.

"Well, now, I shouldn't wonder though that chill had something to do with it," replied

Ellis, as if she had received a new idea. "Poor dear missie, she is so sweet—almost too good to live, as the sayin' is. She's much better to-day. I daresay she'll be able to have a look at you to-morrow."

Morag's heart sank. The thought of seeing her bonnie wee leddy at the end of her journey had kept her brave through its fears and discomforts; but now she heard that another night must elapse before they could meet, and she would be left alone among all those strangers. It seemed so cruel and hard; and Morag felt sure that if her wee leddy knew she was here, she would not ask her to wait till to-morrow.

Meanwhile, Ellis led the way to the housekeeper's room, leaving Morag to be warmed and fed and generally comforted by Mrs. Worthy. The old housekeeper welcomed the forlorn little maiden kindly, and after divesting her of the tartan plaid, and providing a comfortable supper, she made her sit down in a big arm-chair by the fire,—and, taking a similar one for herself, she began to recall reminiscences of Glen Eagle, and to make inquiries about the dwellers in the Glen whose aquaintance she had made during these autumn months.

Presently, Blanche's illness became the topic

of conversation, and Morag listened eagerly to all Mrs. Worthy had to say about it. Her heart sank when she heard how very ill her bonnie wee leddy had been. After looking meditatively into the fire for some time, she looked up and said eagerly, " I'm thinkin', Mistress Worthy, gin they wad jist bring her til the auld castle o' Glen Eagle to bide, and lat her rin aboot wi' Shag and Chance and me, when the snaw gaes awa, and the bit flooers begin to creep up, she wad get braw and strong again."

" Well, there's no sayin', little girl. I likes to see young folks take a cheerin' view of things. 'While there's life, there's 'ope,' I always say. There's my Sarah Jane was once a-spittin' up—and there ain't a stronger woman to be found nowhere, now; and there's"—

Here Mrs. Worthy's family chronicle of illnesses was interrupted by a bell ringing violently within the room. It sounded so startling, that Morag jumped to her feet, and even Mrs. Worthy looked somewhat alarmed as she rose to answer it.

" Bless me, it ain't often that bell is a ringin'—so shockin' loud, too! What's the hurry, I wonder?" and the old woman bustled away, leaving her companion alone.

Morag thought she could guess why the

bell had just rung; and hoped that it might prove a summons for her to go to the bonnie wee leddy. She sat listening eagerly for the sound of returning footsteps, but no messenger appeared; so Morag's hope died away at last, and she began to feel very forlorn indeed.

As she sat, looking dreamily into the flickering fire, she remembered another evening when she found herself seated in Mrs. Worthy's arm-chair, in the midst of unwonted comforts, and how very frightened and uncomfortable she was till the wee leddy had suddenly appeared and made her feel so safe and happy.

And as she gazed among the glowing coals, she realized, as she never had before, what an eventful evening that had been, and how much had happened during these never-to-be-forgotten autumn days. All at once, her lonely child-life seemed to be filled with love and brightness, and the very hills and glens of her mountain home to be glorified, as she strayed among them with her bonnie wee leddy. And then the friendship with Kirsty Macpherson had grown out of these days too, and what happy changes it had brought to the little shieling among the crags! Her father's brow was cleared of its perpetual gloom; he never said bitter things about his neighbors in the

Glen now, and when Morag and he went together to the kirk, so many people seemed glad to see him there.

And as Morag Dingwall's thoughts went slipping back to these golden autumn days, that had been so full of blessing for her, she lifted up her heart in thankfulness to God for the best thing among all the many good things which they had brought to her—the knowledge of the Lord Jesus Christ, her Saviour. Had the wee leddy learnt to love Him too, she wondered, as she remembered the last talk in Glen Eagle; and then she thought, joyfully, how much there would be to hear and tell to-morrow, when Ellis had promised she should see her friend.

As she sat gazing into the fire, Morag fell asleep in the big arm-chair; and in her dreams she thought she was again with Blanche, struggling through the rippling water, like the Pilgrims in the picture. But neither of them appeared to feel frightened, as they had when they were almost drowned in the loch. At first the water seemed smooth and shining, and Morag could hear the bonnie wee leddy's silvery voice calling to her to come away, for she saw the Golden City quite clearly now—and that the gates were really wide open still, though it was so late at night. Then Morag, all at once, began to feel afraid, for she could see no city lying in the sun; but only a great leaden-looking wave, which came creeping towards her, throwing its gray shadow on the shining water; then she lost sight of her bonnie wee leddy, and could only hear her voice calling her to come. But Morag thought she could not cross the dark wave, and the silvery voice began to sound very far away; and at last she awoke, trembling,—feeling so glad to think that after all it was only a dream.

The fire, which had been so bright and warm when she fell asleep, was now cold and black. The candles, too, were almost burnt to their sockets; and Morag saw that she must have slept for a long time. She began to wonder where Mrs. Worthy was, and whether they meant to leave her there, till they came to take her to see the bonnie wee leddy in the morning.

She would not have treated her so, thought Morag, with quivering lip, as she looked blankly round the solitary room, where everything seemed so gray and cheerless, and she shivered as she remembered the leaden wave of her dream, and began to feel very frightened and homesick, besides being cold and wearied.

Presently she heard the sound of footsteps re-echoing along the silent corridor, and Mrs. Worthy walked slowly into the room with her nightcap on. In her hand she carried a candle, which she almost dropped in her astonishment at seeing Morag seated there.

"Bless my soul, child! are you here still? I was just on my way to bed. I declare I had quite forgotten all about you. Dear, dear, my 'ead's quite confused—and no wonder! Poor dear, you must be sadly tired. Too bad of Ellis not to have taken you to bed. She promised to see after you when she was sent along to you. I've just only now come from missie's room—dear angel: she does look so sweet. You'll see her to-morrow, my poor dear!"

And then, noticing Morag's wistful look as she murmured, "No the nicht," the old woman pondered for a while, and taking the candle again, she said, "Well, well, there can't be no 'arm: they are all cleared away now! Come, I'll take you, poor dear. You haven't been well treated noways among us all, and I heard the master tell Ellis that she was to look to you, and he would see you himself to-morrow."

Morag's heart leapt for joy. If she could only see her bonnie wee leddy even for a minnte, and feel her protecting touch again, she would forget all her past troubles and be quite safe and happy in this strange land.

She followed Mrs. Worthy with joyful steps as she led her along the passages, which were cold and dark now. She smiled as she thought how astonished the wee leddy would be to see her mountain friend, for she remembered Ellis had said that she was not to be told of her arrival till next morning; but it was so good and kind of Mrs. Worthy to take her now. And then she tried to picture to herself how Blanche would be looking. Would she find her lying on a sofa, dressed in her pretty blue dressing-gown, which she wore on the evening she saw her last at the old castle of Glen Eagle? And would she seem much paler than she did then? Morag feared she might, when she remembered what a long time she had laid in bed; but summer days would soon come again, and the sunshine, which the bonnie leddy loved so well, would be sure to make her strong again.

Indeed, in her secret heart, Morag cherished the hope that her own presence might act as a talisman, and she smiled to think of the pleasant voice that would soon bid her welcome; for, since the dark hour in the fir-wood, when she thought Blanche had left the Glen without remembering to say farewell, Morag had never doubted the love and friendship of her gracious little friend.

At last Mrs. Worthy stopped at a closed door, and as she lowered the candle which she held in her hand, Morag caught sight of a familiar friend lying on the mat.

Chance was waiting there in a listening posture, with his nose against the door. Morag stooped down and patted him, but, instead of jumping up at her in outrageous welcome, as he used to do, he merely gave a faint wag of his tail, and looking wistfully into her face, raised a low, whining cry, and put his nose close to the door again.

"I'm thinkin' Chance will be wantin' in—to get a sicht o' her too," said Morag, smiling.

" Yes, poor brute ; hanimals has a deal of feelin'. He's been in a dreadful way ; indeed I thought they locked him up for the night, but he seems to have got loose again," replied Mrs. Worthy, as she opened the door and stepped softly in, followed by Morag and Chance.

The little girl looked eagerly round among the mirrors and pictures and pretty statuettes for the face which had never failed before to smile a sunny welcome upon her, but her bonnie wee leddy was nowhere to be seen, and a terrible stillness seemed to pervade the room.

Drawing aside the rose-colored curtains of a little bed, which Morag had not noticed in her eager glance round the room, Mrs. Worthy beckoned for the little girl to come near, and Morag looked at last on the face of her bonnie wee leddy. She seemed sleeping peacefully; the golden curls lay in rich masses on the pillow, and the fluttering fingers were at rest on the white coverlet. The room was dimly lighted, and a shadow fell from the curtain on her face; so Morag drew closer that she might see her more clearly—feeling a pang of disappointment that she was asleep. But had not Ellis said that to-morrow morning she would speak to her? and she could wait.

"She's sleepin' richt soun' the noo, I'm thinkin'," she whispered softly to Mrs. Worthy, who was holding back the curtain.

"Sleeping! yes, my little dear, you are right. Children does put things nice at times. Dear angel—not dead, but sleeping: a long, long sleep, till the resurrection morn!"

With a long, low cry of anguish, Morag knelt beside the dead body of her bonnie wee leddy, and kissed her cold, dead hand!

She understood it all now. Blanche Clifford had passed away on this Christmas Eve from our lower world—with all its lights and shadows, all its wealth and all its woe—to that other, where the pure in heart are perfectly blessed, for they see God!

Perhaps here we should take farewell of our mountain maiden; for, with the passing away from earth of her bonnie wee leddy, ended the childhood of Morag Dingwall, never again to visit her, save in dreams of the night and memories of the past!

We shall but cast a glance across the vista of years, when these autumn days lay far away in the calm, clear distance, and seem like a tale that is told;—when Kirsty has laid down her frail body to sleep in the little graveyard on the hillside, to await the coming of the Lord she loved so well;—when the keen eyes of the keeper Dingwall no longer scan the hills and moors of Glen Eagle, nor his steady hand takes unerring aim; for his stalwart form lies mouldering in the shadow of the hills he has so often trod!

The keeper's earthly life had closed in the midst of less vivid hopes, perhaps, and shadowed by more bitter memories, than Kirsty's blameless years had wrought. But he, too, had learnt to live in the faith and hope of the words which welcomed him to the table of the Lord below, and to know it to be a "faithful saying, that 'Jesus Christ came into the world to save sinners.'"

The shieling among the crags, which had been his home so long, was a roofless ruin now. And long dank grass and nettles grew on the earthen floor, which had proved, of old, such a sea of trouble to the little Morag.

Kenneth Macpherson, Kirsty's grandson, reigned over the realms of deer and moor-fowl in the Glen now; and the keeper's daughter had become the keeper's wife.

Their home was the loveliest spot in all the strath—a pleasant, light, airy, well-built cottage, placed at a sunny angle of the pine forest, which protected it from the cold north winds when they swept along the Glen.

Firwood Neuk, for so it had been called by its owners, possessed every pretty and useful accessory, within and without, which peasant life could require. It was quite a model homestead, with its wealthy barn-yard and farmstead, and its pretty productive garden—the last earthly gift of a little vanished hand, which had dropped its earthly treasures as she used to do her wild flowers in these woods long ago, when anything more precious came in sight.

Mr. Clifford never came to shoot in Glen Eagle again; but, nevertheless, he was more than faithful to the wishes of his child, and Blanche's friends lacked for nothing which money could supply—humbly and gratefully accepted by these proud Highland spirits as the benefaction of the gracious child who had loved them all so well.

Often, indeed, Mr. Clifford had been tempted, during the earlier years, to go beyond his daughter's wishes when he noticed Morag's insatiable thirst for knowledge: to take her from her quiet haunts, and bring art and culture to aid in her training. But he called to mind Blanche's wise decision, and left the child of the mountains to her "lowlier, more unlettered fate."

Still, Morag's intellectual cravings were not unprovided for. In one of the rooms of her pleasant home there stood a pretty book-case filled with rows of shining books—another memorial of Blanche's love. And, among the handsome bindings, there were interspersed certain old, worn books, which were very dear to Morag's heart, for had they not been taken from the depths of the old *kist?*—and stood there, among the newer volumes, like ancient historical monuments surrounded by pretty modern villas.

It was the twelfth of August, and the keeper's wife stood waiting in the gloaming for her husband, who had not yet returned from the moors.

The work of the day was done, and the children safely folded for the night,—for there were young voices again re-echoing through the forest, and little feet toddling among the brown fir-needles.

Her husband was not yet in sight, so presently Morag wandered into the fir-wood, where the great aisles of pine reared themselves calm and stately as of old.

Leaning against one of the old red firs, which seemed written over with many memories to her, she called to mind one August day long ago. And as she stood gazing dreamily there, she seemed to see again the lovely, singing child, coming like a happy fate towards the desolate little maiden who leant there on that bright morning, to hear again the " glad tidings of great joy" borne unconsciously by the silvery voice to a listening ear and waiting soul, and to feel the soft, sisterly touch of the little fluttering hand that sent glow and warmth to a heart which, but for that touch of human sympathy, might have turned to stone.

Morag had seen many gentle ladies, old and young, since these autumn days long ago. The solitary Glen had got into guide-books now, and every year brought many strangers to roam among its woods and hills; but never could any other dwell in her memory as Blanche Clifford did—never, she thought, could she see "her like again!"

Many a year had come and gone since that memorable twelfth of August, when the southern guests came to seek their pleasure among the moors of Glen Eagle. Silver lines were visible on Morag's once raven black locks, and her step was slower than it used to be, as she sauntered through the old red fir-trees, which were all aglow in the sunset.

With a sigh of weariness she at last seated herself on a gray, lichen-spotted dyke which skirted the forest.

"Ay! and she'll aye be young, though I'm growin' auld," she murmured, for she still retained her ancient habit of speaking her thoughts aloud, acquired n her solitary child-hood.

Leaning her head upon her hand, she sat

watching the sun as it sank behind the old castle of Glen Eagle.

The amber clouds were hovering round the dying sun, like ponderous gates ready to close on the inner vistas of gold and crimson. Morag sat gazing with glistening eyes at the cloud-land scene; she well knew that "richest tenderest glow" which lingers round the autumnal sun, and always loved to watch it.

> "But there sight fails; no heart may know
> *The bliss when life is done.*"

"It's growin' cauld and mirk, and I maun be goin' home," murmured Morag, as she rose to go down the hill, when all had faded into grey twilight. Then she added, softly: "She liket weel to see the sun gae doun amang oor hills; an' it aye min's me upo' her. Bonnie wee leddy! 'Thy sun shall no more go down, neither shall thy moon withdraw its shining, for the Lord is thine everlasting light, and thy God thy glory.'"

THE END.

Stereotyped by McCREA & Co., Newburgh, N. Y.

530 BROADWAY, NEW YORK
March, 1875.

ROBERT CARTER & BROTHERS

NEW BOOKS.

AUTOBIOGRAPHY AND MEMOIR OF THOMAS GUTHRIE, D.D. 2 vols. 12mo. $4.00.

"It is told in the chattiest, simplest, most unaffected way imaginable, and the pages are full of quaint, racy anecdotes, recounted in the most characteristic manner." — *London Daily News.*

THE WORKS OF THOMAS GUTHRIE, D.D.

9 vols. In a box. $13.50. (The vols. are sold separately.)

CHRISTIAN THEOLOGY FOR THE PEOPLE.

By WILLIS LORD, D.D., LL.D. 8vo. $4.00.

CHRISTIANITY AND SCIENCE. A Series of

Lectures, by Rev. A. P. PEABODY, D.D., of Harvard College. $1.75

THE SCOTTISH PHILOSOPHY. Biographical,

Expository, Critical, from Hutcheson to Hamilton. By JAMES McCOSH, LL.D., President of Princeton College. 8vo. $4.00.

By the same Author.

THE METHOD OF DIVINE GOVERNMENT $2.50	DEFENCE OF FUNDAMENTAL TRUTH $3.00
TYPICAL FORMS 2.50	LOGIC 1.50
THE INTUITIONS OF THE MIND. 3.00	CHRISTIANITY AND POSITIVISM 1.75

IDEAS IN NATURE, OVERLOOKED BY DR.
TYNDALL. Being an Examination of Dr. Tyndall's Belfast Address. By JAMES McCOSH, D.D , LL.D. 12mo. Paper, 25 cents ; cloth, 50 cents.

THE WORKS OF JAMES HAMILTON, D.D.
Comprising :—

ROYAL PREACHER.
MOUNT OF OLIVES.
PEARL OF PARABLES.
LAMP AND LANTERN.

GREAT BIOGRAPHY.
HARP ON THE WILLOWS.
LAKE OF GALILEE.
EMBLEMS FROM EDEN.

LIFE IN EARNEST.

In 4 handsome uniform 16mo volumes. $5.00.

NATURE AND THE BIBLE. By J. W. DAWSON,
LL.D., Principal of McGill University, Montreal, Canada. With 10 full-page illustrations. $1.75.

ALL ABOUT JESUS. By the Rev. ALEXANDER
DICKSON. 12mo. $2.00.

THE SHADOWED HOME, and the Light Beyond.
By the Rev. E. H. BICKERSTETH, author of "Yesterday, To-day, and Forever." $1.50.

EARTH'S MORNING; or, Thoughts on Genesis.
By the Rev. HORATIUS BONAR, D.D. $2.00.

THE RENT VEIL. By Dr. BONAR. $1.25.

FOLLOW THE LAMB; or, Counsels to Converts.
By Dr. BONAR. 40 cents.

AN EDEN IN ENGLAND. A Tale. By A.L.O.E.
8 full-page Engravings. 16mo, $1.25 ; 18mo, 75 cents.

FAIRY FRISKET; or, A Peep at Insect Life. By
A.L.O.E. 75 cents.

THE LITTLE MAID AND LIVING JEWELS.
By A.L.O.E. 75 cents.

THE SPANISH CAVALIER. A Tale of Seville.
By A.L.O.E.

---

*CARTERS' 50–VOLUME S. S. LIBRARY. **No. 2.** Net, $20.00.

These fifty choice volumes for the Sabbath School Library, or the home circle, are printed on good paper, and very neatly bound in fine light-brown cloth. They contain an aggregate of 12,350 pages, and are put up in a wooden case. The volumes are all different from those in Carters' Cheap Library, No. 1; so that those who have No. 1, and like it, can scarcely do better than send for No. 2. *The volumes are not sold separately.* There is no discount from the price to Sabbath School Libraries.

Also, still in stock,

*CARTERS' CHEAP SABBATH–SCHOOL LI-BRARY. **No. 1.** 50 vols. in neat cloth. In a wooden case. Net, $20.00.

TIM'S LITTLE MOTHER. By PUNOT. Illustrated.
$1.25.

FROGGY'S LITTLE BROTHER. By BRENDA.
Illustrated. 16mo. $1.25.

FLOSS SILVERTHORN. By AGNES GIBERNE.
16mo. $1.25.

ELEANOR'S VISIT. By JOANNA H. MATHEWS.
16mo. $1.25.

MABEL WALTON'S EXPERIMENT. By JOANNA
H. MATHEWS. 16mo. $1.25.

ALICE NEVILLE, AND RIVERSDALE. By C. E.
Bowen, author of "Peter's Pound and Paul's Penny." $1.25.

THE WONDER CASE. By the Rev. R. NEWTON, D.D. Containing :—

BIBLE WONDERS $1.25	LEAVES FROM TREE OF LIFE . $1.25
NATURE'S WONDERS 1.25	RILLS FROM FOUNTAIN . . 1.25
JEWISH TABERNACLE 1.25	GIANTS AND WONDERS . . . 1.25

6 vols. *In a box.* $7.50.

THE JEWEL CASE. By the Same. 6 vols. In a box. $7.50.

GOLDEN APPLES ; or, Fit Words for the Young. By the Rev. EDGAR WOODS. 16mo. $1.00.

By the Author of

"THE WIDE WIDE WORLD."

THE LITTLE CAMP ON EAGLE HILL. $1.25.

WILLOW BROOK. $1.25.

SCEPTRES AND CROWNS. $1.25.

THE FLAG OF TRUCE. $1.25.

By the same Author.

THE STORY OF SMALL BEGIN-NINGS. 4 vols. In a box . . $5.00	HOUSE OF ISRAEL $1.50
	THE OLD HELMET 2.25
WALKS FROM EDEN 1.50	MELBOURNE HOUSE 2.00

By her Sister.

THE STAR OUT OF JACOB . . $1.50	HYMNS OF THE CHURCH MILI-TANT $1.50
LITTLE JACK'S FOUR LESSONS. 0.60	
STORIES OF VINEGAR HILL. 6 vols. 3.00	ELLEN MONTGOMERY'S BOOK-SHELF. 5 vols. 5.00

A LAWYER ABROAD. By HENRY DAY, Esq. 12 full-page Illustrations. $2.00.

DOORS OUTWARD. A Tale. By the author of

"Win and Wear." $1.25.

By the same Author.

MABEL HAZARD'S THOROUGH- FARE $1.25	GREEN MOUNTAIN SERIES. 5 vols. $6.00
WHO WON 1.25	LEDGESIDE SERIES. 6 vols. . . 7.50
WIN AND WEAR SERIES. 6 vols. 7.50	BUTTERFLY'S FLIGHTS. 3 vols. 2.25

ROSALIE'S PET. By JOANNA H. MATHEWS, author

of the "Bessie Books." $1.25.

By the same Author.

FANNY'S BIRTHDAY GIFT . . . $1.25	THE FLOWERETS. 6 vols. . . . $3.60
THE NEW SCHOLARS 1.25	LITTLE SUNBEAMS. 6 vols. . . 6.00
THE BESSIE BOOKS. 6 vols. . . 7.50	KITTY AND LULU BOOKS. 6 vols. 6.00

By Julia A. Mathews.

GOLDEN LADDER SERIES. 6 vols. $3.00	DARE TO DO RIGHT SERIES. 5
DRAYTON HALL SERIES. 6 vols. 4.50	vols. $5.50

VERENA. A Story of To-day. By EMILY SARAH

HOLT. $1.50.

By the same Author.

ASHCLIFFE HALL. $1.25	ISOULT BARRY. $1.50
THE WELL IN THE DESERT . 1.25	ROBIN TREMAYNE 1.50

THE PERIOD OF THE REFORMATION — 151

to 1648. By Prof. LUDWIG HÄUSSER. Crown 8vo. $2.50.

*SONGS OF THE SOUL. Gathered out of many

Lands and Ages. By S. I. PRIME, D.D. Elegantly printed on superfine paper, and sumptuously bound in Turkey morocco, $9.00, cloth, gilt, $5.00.

THE ARGUMENT OF THE BOOK OF JOB

UNFOLDED. By Prof. WILLIAM HENRY GREEN, D.D. 12mo. $1 75.

THE A.L.O.E. LIBRARY. 37 vols.   In a neat
Wooden Case, walnut trimmings. $28.00.

DR. HANNA'S LIFE OF CHRIST. 3 vols.
$4.50.

CLEFTS OF THE ROCK. By J. R. MACDUFF,
D.D. $1.50.

THE REEF, AND OTHER PARABLES. By the
Rev. E. H. BICKERSTETH. 16 Illustrations. $1.25.

RYLE ON THE GOSPELS. 7 vols. 12mo. $10.50.
Consisting of:—

MATTHEW $1.50	LUKE. 2 vols. $3.00
MARK 1.50	JOHN. 3 vols. 4.50

The volumes are sold separately.

HOME TRUTHS. By the Rev. J. C. RYLE. Containing:—

LIVING OR DEAD.	RICH AND POOR.
WHEAT OR CHAFF.	PRIEST AND PURITAN.

STARTLING QUESTIONS.

5 vols. 16mo. In a box. $5.00.

THE NEAR AND HEAVENLY HORIZONS. By
MADAME DE GASPARIN. New Edition. $1.50.

VOICES OF THE SOUL ANSWERED IN GOD.
By the Rev. JOHN REID. New Edition. $1.75.

FOOTPRINTS OF SORROW. By the Rev. JOHN
REID. New Edition. $2.00.

*** MATTHEW HENRY'S COMMENTARY. In 9** vols. 8vo, cloth, $27.00.   In 5 vols. quarto, sheep, $25.00.

*** HORNE'S INTRODUCTION TO THE STUDY** OF THE BIBLE. 2 vols. in one. 8vo, sheep. $5.00.

DR. HODGE'S COMMENTARIES, &c.
ON CORINTHIANS. 2 vols. $3.50.   ON EPHESIANS. $1.75.
ESSAYS AND REVIEWS. $3.00.

D'AUBIGNE'S HISTORY OF THE REFORMA- TION. 5 vols. in one, 8vo, $3.00.   In 5 vols. 12mo, $6.00.

D'AUBIGNE'S HISTORY OF THE REFORMA- TION IN THE TIME OF CALVIN. 5 vols. $10.00.

TALES OF CHRISTIAN LIFE.   By the author of the "Schönberg Cotta Family."   Containing : —

CRIPPLE OF ANTIOCH.	TWO VOCATIONS.
MARTYRS OF SPAIN.	TALES AND SKETCHES.

WANDERINGS IN BIBLE LANDS.
5 vols. In a box $5.00

PISGAH VIEWS; or, The Negative Aspects of Heaven. By OCTAVIUS WINSLOW, D.D. 16mo. $1.25.

By the same Author.

MIDNIGHT HARMONIES. 16mo . $1.00	HELP HEAVENWARD. 18mo . . $0.75
DECLENSION AND REVIVAL. 16mo 1.00	MAN OF GOD. 18mo 0.75
PRECIOUS THINGS. 16mo . . . 1.25	FOOT OF THE CROSS. 18mo . . 0.75
SYMPATHY OF CHRIST WITH MAN.	HEAVEN OPENED. 16mo . . . 2.00
16mo 1.25	INSTANT GLORY. 32mo . . . 0.30
HISTORY OF JOSEPH. 16mo . . 1.25	THE GLORY OF THE REDEEMER.
LIFE OF MARY WINSLOW. 12mo 1.50	12mo 1.50

KITTO'S BIBLE ILLUSTRATIONS. 4 vols. $7.00
An invaluable set to the Bible student, whether clergymen or laymen.

DYKES ON THE SERMON ON THE MOUNT. 3 vols. . $3.75
*FAIRBAIRN'S REVELATION OF LAW 2.50
FOSTER'S ESSAYS ON DECISION OF CHARACTER . 1.25
FOXE'S MARTYRS. Complete edition. 8vo 5.00
FRASER'S SYNOPTICAL LECT. ON THE BIBLE. 2 vols. 4.00
FRASER'S BLENDING LIGHTS 2.00
FRESH LEAVES FROM BOOK AND ITS STORY . . 2.00
FROM THE PLOW TO THE PULPIT 0.60
GASPARIN'S NEAR AND HEAVENLY HORIZONS . . 1.50
GIBERNE'S AIMEE. A Tale 1.50
GIBERNE'S THE DAY-STAR 1.25
GIBERNE'S THE CURATE'S HOME 1.25
GRAY'S ELEGY, AND OTHER POEMS. (Illustrated) . . 1.50
HALDANE ON ROMANS 3.00
HELENA'S HOUSEHOLD 2.00
HERVEY'S MEDITATIONS 1.50
HETHERINGTON'S HIST. CHURCH OF SCOTLAND . 2.50
HODGES'S OUTLINES OF THEOLOGY 2.00
HORNE ON THE PSALMS 2.50
HOWIE'S SCOTS WORTHIES. (Illustrated) 3.50
AMES'S YOUNG WOMAN'S FRIEND 1.25
JAMES'S YOUNG MAN'S FRIEND 1.25
JAY'S MORNING AND EVENING EXERCISES. 2 vols. 2.00
JOHNSON'S RASSELAS. 16mo 0.75
KER'S THE DAY-DAWN AND THE RAIN 2.00
KINGS OF ISRAEL AND JUDAH 1.50
*KRUMMACHER'S AUTOBIOGRAPHY 2.00
KRUMMACHER'S RISEN REDEEMER 1.25
LAYS OF THE HOLY LAND. Illustrated 4.50
*LEE ON INSPIRATION 2.50
LITTLE EFFIE'S HOME 1.25
LOGAN'S WORDS OF COMFORT TO PARENTS . . . 1.25
MAGGIE'S MISTAKE. 18 Illustrations 1.25
MARSH'S (Miss) LIFE OF CAPTAIN VICARS . . . 0.60
MARSH'S (Miss) ENGLISH HEARTS AND HANDS . . 1.25
MARSH'S (Miss) RIFT IN THE CLOUDS 0.35
MARSH'S (Miss) CROSSING THE RIVER 0.60
MARSHALL'S (Emma) STELLAEONT ABBEY 1.00
MARSHALL'S (Emma) MATTHEW FROST 1.00